The Other Ones

The Other Ones

Dave Housley

Alan Squire Publishing
Bethesda, Maryland

Alan Squire Publishing

The Other Ones is published by Alan Squire Publishing, Bethesda, MD, an imprint of the Santa Fe Writers Project.

Printed in the United States of America.
ISBN (print): 978-1-942892-30-4
ISBN (epub): 978-1-942892-31-1
Library of Congress Control Number: 2021917709

Jacket design and cover art by Randy Stanard, Dewitt Designs
Author photo by Lori Wieder
Interior design by Nita Congress
Printing consultant: Steven Waxman
Printed by Cushing-Malloy

First Edition
Ordo Vagorum

The Other Ones

Yoder

Lawson

CHASTAIN

CRAVER

Robertson

russell

Gibbons

Yoder

YODER FIGHTS THE TINGLE IN his fingers and toes. He looks over the edge. The landscaping people are moving lawnmowers and edgers over from the parking lot and the sound of their Spanish drifts up from five stories below. He never did learn Spanish. He considers this, decides to put it in the okay column. There are a lot of things he has never done and learning Spanish is somewhere between one hundred and two hundred on the list.

He gauges the trajectory, the figures working in his brain whether he wants them to or not—five stories up, a man of two hundred forty-five pounds, sixty-three years old, not in good health but not in poor health either. He tries to find an equation, this plus that minus a percentage of the other—but of course he has no equation for this. If he had had more time. He looks over the edge. Does he have more time?

The landscapers shout preparations back and forth. The wind whistles. He can hear the bells on campus. Can he hear the lottery people in the conference room? The sounds of shouting and laughing and back-slapping. They were listening to some rap song from the eighties or nineties, maybe more recent, something about money and problems.

Typical. None of them will ever have to work again and they choose
to celebrate here, in the office, with total disregard for the rest of them,
the two hundred or so who did not put in their dollars, sign their names
on the sheet, the two hundred who will have to continue to slog in to
Keystone Special Marketing Solutions at nine every day, limp out at five,
who will fill out time cards and fill up coffee mugs and go to holiday
parties and make small talk and try not to think about the unthinkable
fact that... but no, he has made his choice and the others will make
theirs, will make it every day, every morning, every time the alarm clock
rings, every time a meeting reminder dings into their company-owned
computer screens, every time they punch that elevator button. Whether
they want to, have to, whether they even realize they are doing it or not,
each and every one of them is making their own decision. He has felt
this for a long time, knew it was coming, or that something was building, growing, metastasizing, and now this, this ridiculous intervention of
fate, of god, karma, luck, whatever, is only the last straw.

He looks out over the ledge. From here he would land in the grass
not far from where they'll soon be mowing. He thinks about moving
over to one of the other sides—the parking lot, the sidewalk that leads
to either set of side stairs that he often walks up to avoid seeing anybody on the way in. Will the landscapers have to clean him up? Will the
burden of seeing him fall, of hearing his body collide with the ground
at fifty miles an hour, of feeling for a stopped pulse, seeing his legs and
arms contorted and broken, hearing a last rasp, will it all be too much
for one of them? They are men and boys. They are getting paid slightly
more than minimum wage. Everybody has made their decisions. Yoder
has made his.

He holds a foot over the edge and butterflies swarm in his stomach.
He has never liked heights, has stayed away from roller-coasters and
balconies for the past forty-some years. Ironic that it will end this way.
Is it ironic? He remembers that song, hearing it for the first time and
thinking that the singer didn't really understand what irony was. Irony
is a sixty-three-year-old accountant who is afraid of heights standing on
the ledge of his office building at eight forty-five in the morning. Isn't it
ironic? The tune comes back into his head. Don't you think?

He flashes on Ruth and the apartment in DC, the white noise of the city traffic and the feeling of walking to work with his briefcase, his Dockers and tie, and thirty-dollar haircut. He remembers walking around the mall, considering this shirt or that one, which would convey the signals he was looking to transmit—this one is an up-and-comer, this one is on the fast track, this one is more than Altoona Pennsylvania and the Penn State Hazelton branch campus. This one belongs.

He looks at his shirt. He doesn't really even remember getting dressed, eating his breakfast, driving to work. It all seems like a quaint scene from a movie he saw some time in the past. That was before. Now, after walking out of the elevator and hearing the strange noises of happiness, of celebration first thing on a Monday morning, now he knows that everything since he heard the word "lottery" shouted out of that conference room will, whether he takes a step forward or not, be After.

Reasons not to: the coffee sitting warm off to his side, the bagel sandwich in his briefcase, the remaining thirty-two episodes on his yearly rewatch of *The X-Files*, the happy hour he has scheduled with Singer and Avery and Russell two weeks and three days from now. But all Avery will talk about is the place in Florida, the plans they have for the move. Singer will just complain about university politics, not even real politics but whatever slight he imagines the Board of Trustees or the provost or the president has levied on the specter of the Old Days. Russell is a shell of even what Russell used to be, and that was never much to begin with. Fuck that, he thinks. Happy hour goes in the other column, the long one.

He looks at his belly, protruding like half a basketball is tucked into his shirt. His Achilles tendons ache and a hangover stirs in his head. Yoder at fifteen, at twenty, twenty-five, thirty, thirty-five would be disgusted with this old man standing out on a ledge. A thin trickle of music reaches him and he imagines the sound of laughter, of celebration, working its way out of that conference room, down the hall, through the stairway doors and up onto the roof like a ghost, a ghoul, a nightmare in plain Monday morning light. It has come to this. He looks straight ahead. He takes the step.

Lawson

LAWSON PULLS IN AT EIGHT fifty and parks in the back of the lot as usual. He will still be on time for the nine. He checks his phone, pulls up the calendar. Meeting meeting meeting. It is okay, he tells himself. It is good. This is what he has signed on to when he took the position working for Sarah. Assistant Director is not a bad title for this point in his career. And besides, the two o'clock will be interesting. Analytics never lie and there are some fascinating truths worming their way to the surface if you really dig in past the initial key performance indicators.

As he walks, he feels his belly pushing up against his belt. He needs to go on a diet. He needs to start working out, get back on the dating apps, start journaling again, check out the creative writing classes he's heard about at the library. There are a lot of things he needs to do but right now he has only enough time to go to the bathroom, maybe fill up his water bottle before the nine. He should walk up the stairs, start walking up the stairs all the time like what's his name, the kid in the Server Department but Lawson suspects that, like most of the stairs people, that kid is just doing it to avoid talking to people in the elevator. Not a terrible position, but one that Sarah would never advocate and he needs to stay in her good graces.

He hits the elevator button and feels his phone buzzing. A text from Karl: "You're not going to fucking believe this."

Great, he thinks. Monday morning and already shit is blowing up. He wonders if it is the server again, or if the update they'd installed last week had caused issues further down the line. They really need to put a better quality assurance process into place. It is always interesting, though, watching Sarah in these situations. She is best when things are the worst and he knows that if he is going to be sitting in her chair someday, he needs to be able to be the same.

He waits out the elevator, enjoying the peace and hoping nobody else gets on. He rubs his eyes. He should start working out in the morning, then he would have all the time in the world to write at night and still check the trades, the blogs, the email, and the articles that Sarah forwards around to the Core Team.

He rounds the corner and registers that something is off. There are sounds, happy sounds, coming from the conference room closest to the elevator. Laughing and shouting. Music playing. He wonders if it is a birthday, if the building has started renting out conference rooms to other tenants. Karl is standing there with a familiar look on his face, the one that says there is bad news and he can't wait to share it.

"Figured I'd just wait until…" Lawson starts, holding up the phone and pointing back to the elevator.

"You didn't play, did you?" Karl says.

"What are…" Lawson says. "What's going on in there?"

Karl's eyes are bright and he is trying to fight a smile. This must be really bad, Lawson thinks. Nobody loves things going wrong as much as Karl. Somebody must have died. Maybe there's been another 9/11. But then why are they blaring Biggie Smalls and hooting and drinking beer in the conference room?

"You didn't put in last week, did you?" Karl says again.

Lawson pauses. Put in? "Look, we're gonna be late for the nine," he says. "I can't worry about whatever is happening in there."

"Those assholes," Karl says. He points to the conference room. "Won the goddamn lottery."

CHASTAIN

"THOSE JACKASSES WON THE FUCKING lottery?" Chastain says. She says it out loud and then looks around but there is nobody in the hallway, nobody in the office yet. They are all either celebrating in the conference room or gossiping in the kitchen, the hallways, in the entrances to their cubicles. She checks the clock. Craver will almost certainly be late. She realizes she is looking forward to telling him, to commiserating, sneaking down the back steps and smoking a Parliament Light and talking about what assholes they all are, how ridiculous everything is, whether they should start drinking at lunch or wait until happy hour.

Good god those assholes won the lottery. She is not sure whether she is going to burst out laughing or throw up right here on her keyboard. She stares at the computer. She checks her phone again.

She owes twenty-nine thousand five hundred and sixty dollars on her student loans. Two thousand six hundred and twenty-three on the Visa. Three thousand four hundred on the Mastercard. She is not sure if the Exxon or the Kohl's or the Macy's cards still exist but she imagines there to be at least five hundred or so on each of them. She remembers seeing the Macy's logo and the number eight hundred something or other. The lottery. Those assholes.

She stands up and sits down. Garner waddles by, talking into his cell phone. He has a folder in his hands and a little bounce in his step. She always thought it was so typical, these idiots tithing themselves to the state in the most stupid possible way—two dollars here, a dollar there, a hundred bucks a year that could go somewhere else.

Would she have missed a hundred dollars a year? She puts the thought out of her head. Those assholes. The lottery. Jesus they really are the worst of the entire company, almost every old or middle-aged man who skeeves her out, checks her ass as she walks by, stares in meetings, watches as she bends down to pick up a Post-it off the floor, almost all of them are in the lottery group.

She plays through them in her head: Mowery, Cowens, Pappas, Czuba, Fitzgerald. A thought hits her and she actually sits up straight and puts a hand on her chest. Craver. Did Craver play?

CRAVER

CRAVER PAUSES AT THE DOOR and checks the time on his phone. He's not too late, hopefully can slip through without Lawson, or worse, Sarah noticing anything. His checks his phone. Twitter notification, two Facebook messages, a few emails. He pushes the door open slowly and nods to Chastain.

"You hear yet?" she says.

"What?" He is still breathing heavy from the stairs. A line of sweat runs down his side. Chastain has her hair curly today. She'll tell him later that she didn't have time to dry it, that she looks like a crazy person. She'll tap at her cigarette and shake her head and tell him she is going to stop smoking, apply to graduate school, look into CrossFit or Orangetheory or the Y. He will nod and swallow the compliment welling up in every part of him—you look great, you always look great—and offer her another cigarette, anything to spend another ten minutes listening to her complain about her friends and the office and the ridiculous things the Bachelor or the Bachelorette has done now.

She stands and gestures to the hall. "You're not going to fucking believe this," she says, a pang of real emotion—sadness,

8

jealousy?—creeping into her voice. It is unfamiliar and he wonders if somebody died. "Wait," she says. "Did you play last week? With those dumbasses?"

"Play?" He notices for the first time a strange sound in the office. Laughter, shouting, music, party sounds coming from another part of the floor.

"The lottery. The fucking lottery…"

"I think?" he says. The lottery. Did he play the lottery? He is a part-timer with the lottery. Sometimes he plays and sometimes he doesn't and it depends mostly on whether he happens to have a dollar, or two dollars, in his wallet at the exact time when Garner sends the email. Or if he has a meeting in that part of the building. Or if…

"You think? You think? Those assholes won. Eight point eight million dollars. Per asshole. So you better figure out if you played. Jesus Christ you might be a fucking millionaire, you asshole. I need a cigarette."

Craver watches her walking back to the desk, opening the drawer, tapping the pack. Did he play the lottery? He remembers the email, wondering whether he had any actual money on him (Garner setting a standard of only paper money, no coins, no IOUs, no PayPal or Venmo… Garner being super organized around this one thing). He is sure he got the original email. Garner always includes him even though he doesn't always play. Did he get the confirmation email? Did he get Garner's scan of the tickets and the standard rundown about how "when we win, we will take the cash payout and not release our names?" Jesus, did he play the fucking lottery last week or not?

"There he is!"

Craver jumps. "Fuck, another one," Chastain says.

Mowery is standing right there, wearing jeans and a Toby Keith tee shirt. He is holding a beer and an envelope. "There he is!" he says again. He holds his envelope up to Craver. "Better go get one of these," he says, then holds the beer up, "and one of these, too." He comes closer, holds a palm up for a high five.

Chastain taps a cigarette out of the pack and puts it in her mouth. "I might have to smoke this right here in this goddamn office today."

Mowery laughs. "Don't think anybody would care too much today," he says. He turns to Craver, pushes the hand further up toward his face. "Don't leave me hangin' buddy," he says. Craver taps his hand, his mind still turning. Mowery pushes his hand to the sky and makes an explosion sound. Craver almost pauses to explain to him that this isn't how high fives work but decides against anything that might prolong the interaction. "Well come on, man," Mowery says. "We're all over in the conference room."

"I have to…" Craver says. Did he get the confirmation email?

"You don't have to do jack shit, man. Not anymore," Mowery says. "None of us do. Well, sorry Jenny."

Chastain gives him the finger and takes out her lighter.

Mowery laughs. Craver doesn't really like the way he is looking at Chastain, like he is considering something, like he is actively pondering what might be hiding beneath her gray sweater and black skirt.

"Fuck this," Chastain says. She lights the cigarette and exhales.

Craver reaches out and she hands it to him. He takes a deep draw, feels the cool scrape in his lungs. "Okay let's go," he says.

"I'm going," Chastain nods toward the stairs.

"See you in the usual," Craver says. "After I…"

"Yeah, yeah," she says, and he worries briefly that she is annoyed and then Mowery punches him in the shoulder and starts out toward the hallway.

His feet feel funny, his head is fuzzy. Did he play? Did he get the confirmation email?

The music and the shouting get louder as he gets closer to the conference room. He feels like he is floating, like he is a balloon attached to Mowery, following him through the door, holding up his hand for high fives, feeling the slaps on his back. Somebody hands him a beer and he puts it back down. He checks his phone. It is 9:18 on Monday morning and he is a thirty-year-old Marketing Associate and maybe his life has just completely changed.

Garner is in the corner, handing an envelope to Miller, who Craver didn't even think worked here anymore. He looks at Craver and nods, then takes another look at the papers in front of him and turns quickly. Too quickly. Garner stands. He is walking toward Craver.

"Hey man, I'm sorry," Garner says. He places a hand on Craver's shoulder. Craver notices the spots on his glasses, the mole on the side of his neck. He holds up a piece of paper and all Craver sees is a list of names, handwritten in Garner's teenagery bubble handwriting. "You didn't play last week," he says.

Robertson

ROBERTSON TAKES ANOTHER SIP FROM his beer and watches the room. They are all so old and he wonders if this is how he will end up. He wonders if it would be worth it, put in thirty years at some ridiculous job and then hit the lottery with a bunch of people you can barely tolerate? Could he just save his money and wind up in the same place anyway?

Jessie would not even believe the scene laid out in front of him, a bunch of beer-bellied middle-aged people listening to Biggie Smalls and drinking Bud Light Orange first thing in the morning. Jessie lives in a different world. Robertson lives in this one.

Robertson is twenty-four and has been working at Keystone Special Marketing Solutions for fourteen months. Robertson cannot imagine a situation in which he would start playing the lottery. It all just seems so sad. Even knowing that they won, that they are all millionaires, eight point eight each, to be specific, even with all of that, it still just seems so corny.

It just all feels impossible. Pappas, who steals tape from the supply room, entire rolls of toilet paper from the bathroom closet, pens and microwave popcorn and Microsoft Word, standing here in his Dockers and Gap sweater, a millionaire? Cowens, who Robertson had to personally tell to stop saving porn to their cloud-based file storage? Mowery, with his weird Central Pennsylvania accent and his eBay store where he sells the motherboards they are supposed to be recycling, is worth eight point eight million dollars?

Mowery weaves toward him. Jesus, the guy is wearing a tee shirt with some country asshole on it, jeans that look like they have never been worn, with cowboy boots and that red MAGA baseball hat. A terrible grin is plastered on his face. It looks all wrong, more a grimace than a smile, more out of place than the cowboy boots or that ridiculous hat. He is sipping from one red cup and spitting into another, his lip swollen with what Robertson assumes is tobacco.

"High five!" Mowery says. He puts his cups down on the table, holds his hand up, the angle just wrong enough to indicate that he may never have had occasion to high five somebody. Robertson would ordinarily catalogue this under the man's ever-growing list of sad failings but today he feels like he needs to start another list. He holds his hand up and Mowery slaps it with his hand, popping his arm upward like a cheerleader.

"Have you ever high fived anybody?" Robertson says.

"I didn't know you played," Mowery says.

"Played?" Robertson is thinking about basketball, about the many times he's had the occasion to high five a teammate, how he needs to get out and start playing again before he winds up like the rest of these people with their beer guts and second chins, their decades-old Dockers trapped in place with a twenty-year-old belt.

"Don't know who they're going to get to finish those virtual machines or the PHP upgrade," Mowery says.

"You mean played the lottery? All this?" Robertson says.

"Of course," Mowery says. "Or maybe you'll be one of those *I'm going to work anyway* people, huh? Like Garner. Dumb motherfucker thinks he's going to keep on working here."

"I didn't," Robertson says.

"I didn't quit yet, either," Mowery says. He sips from his cup. "They're all down in HR right now, trying to figure out what the fuck to do when all of us quit. They have charts and red Sharpies. I heard some of these poor motherfuckers might actually get raises today but a raise isn't eight point eight million fucking big ones, is it?"

Jesus, this guy. Robertson may not be a millionaire but at least he won't have Mowery bossing him around, whispering under his breath, thinking his probably racist thoughts, playing his country music too loud on his machine and fucking up the servers every time he gets his hands on them anymore. "I didn't play," Robertson says. He finishes his beer and fishes another out of the cooler. "I never play the lottery because playing the lottery is..."

Mowery picks up his red cups, takes a gulp from one and then spits into the other. He turns to Rachel from Marketing and gives her the same awkward high five. He is getting no better at it. "Because playing the lottery is stupid," Robertson says, under his breath.

russell

RUSSELL SEES THE FLASHERS AND the first thing he thinks is that this is going to make being late even harder to hide. He can walk up the back stairs but now everybody will be talking about whatever this is all about, gathered into the coffee room or over by Chastain's office, already grouped together and gossiping, speculating, starting rumors. He can hear Chastain, "Where's Russell? Late again?" That hint of sarcasm, of condescension she can't keep out of her voice. The goddamn receptionist. Administrative Assistant? He realizes he has no idea what Chastain's title is, but probably it's something like Junior Organizational Associate.

Receptionist.

One, two, three, four ambulances. He wonders what happened. It is too many for a fire alarm. If he turns into the parking lot, he will have to sit there while whatever is going to happen plays out. Or he could take the stairs, but his plantar fasciitis has been flaring lately and he really hates how walking up even these four stories makes him breathe heavy, sweat through his button-up. He needs to go to the doctor. The dentist. The dermatologist. He is a year late for another colonoscopy and every time he thinks about it, he blushes, pushes the thought out of his mind. If they told him he had cancer, at least he wouldn't have to make the rest of these appointments.

He drives past the parking lot. EMTs and cops and firemen are standing off to the side, behind the dumpsters, the place where people who don't want everybody to know they smoke go to smoke. He checks his phone. No messages. He could still call in sick. Email in sick, perhaps the only improvement that technology has brought to this world.

The building is in his rearview, the flashers flashing ever smaller and then they are not there at all. He pulls over on the side of the road. He could go to Target and walk around. He could go to the diner. Starbucks. He wonders what was happening back at the office. Probably some kind of drill—fire or earthquake or active shooter. There is a poster up on the break room refrigerator for a new program called "Run, Hide, Fight." When somebody comes in the door shooting an AK-47, they are to run, then hide, then fight. Russell knows he will never attend this training. If they want him to do it bad enough they will make it a webinar and then he will read the transcripts of the videos, fill out their ridiculous questions. Run, Hide, Fight. He will go to Starbucks.

CRAVER

CRAVER FINISHES HIS BEER AND motions to the bartender.

"I just can't believe it," Chastain says. She lays her head between her arms on the bar.

"Shots?" The bartender asks.

Craver nods.

"God yes," Chastain says. Her head is still on the bar. Craver notices the gap in her shirt. He notes that she is wearing a black bra. He forces himself to look up.

The bartender places two more beers in front of them, two empty shot glasses. "One of those days, I guess," he says. Craver has the feeling that he has said this before, that it is a thing he says to people like them, day drinkers in business casual.

"You wouldn't even believe," Chastain says. She looks up. "What's your name?"

Craver regards the bartender. He is young, tall, and Asian and good-looking. A panic rushes through him. Not today.

"Never mind…Eric," Chastain says. She points at his name tag and

17

he nods and laughs like she has said something funny. Are they flirting? "So, these assholes," Chastain says. "These assholes we work with just won the fucking lottery."

Eric pauses his pour, puts the bottle of Jim Beam on the bar. "That was you? I mean, you know those people?"

"All. Too. Well," she says.

Eric puts the Jim Beam away and pours them each a Basil Hayden's. "Holy shit," he says. "I heard about this on the news. Ticket was bought at the Snappy's right around the corner."

"Right around the corner," she says.

Craver doesn't know why but he repeats. "Right around the corner."

"Holy shit," Eric says. "Can you imagine?"

"Indeed," Chastain says. "Indeed, I can imagine." A waitress comes up to the bar and waits for Eric. "This asshole right here," Chastain continues despite the fact that Eric is now talking quietly to the waitress, "plays the fucking lottery most of the time."

"Most of the time," Craver says. Rent is due in two weeks. The car payment in three.

"But not this time," Chastain says. "Not this time."

Craver finishes his shot and drinks half the beer. "What are we going to do?" he says.

"I guess keep drinking?" she says. "Maybe get some wings. Some nachos. Nachos."

Craver pictures his apartment, the dishes he left on the sink, the laundry basket. He has a deadline next week for the draft content for next year's conference emails. He owes something like fifty thousand dollars on his student loans. "I mean what are we doing?" he says. "Like really doing."

"I'm really going to be eating nachos," Chastain says. "Nachos nachos nachos."

Craver finishes his beer and motions to Eric. He pauses. He has had five beers and two shots and he is sitting at the bar at Applebee's at three in the afternoon. With Chastain. "I mean, are you going back to work, you think?"

"No I'm not going back to work. It's...what time is it?" She picks up her phone. "It's three oh five."

Eric delivers two new beers. He pours them a new round of shots. Jim Beam. Craver waits for him to move back to the other end of the bar. "I mean," he says. He leans in and his voice goes low. He feels like he might cry. He looks at the mole on Chastain's cheek, the green of her eyes, the way her chin tucks into a perfect little bulb. "I mean are you going to go back tomorrow?"

"Am I going to go back?" she says. "I guess? I mean, I don't have another job. I didn't win the motherfucking lottery. Oh my god I can't believe those motherfuckers won the motherfucking lottery." She takes a drink and puts her head back on the bar.

Craver pictures himself walking in the doors, hitting the elevator button, waiting. He pictures his desk, the computer, the pencils and pens and paper clips. He feels like he is swimming against a current. He peeks at the top of Chastain's bra, a slice of black satin.

"Let's go. Let's leave this place and…I don't know, let's drive across the country." The minute he says it he knows this is what he wants to do, has wanted all along. This is where it has all been leading, the cigarettes and the private jokes and the flirting, the fact that he didn't play the lottery and the rest of them won. It has all been leading to this: him and Chastain slipping out of town like a Springsteen song.

"Now?" Chastain says. She giggles.

"I'm serious," Craver says. "Hey! I'm serious." He puts a hand on hers and she looks at him. "Let's just go. Tomorrow."

"Just go?"

"Like we're in a Springsteen song."

"Tramps like us," she says.

"Baby we were born to run," Craver says.

"Eric!" she shouts. "Two more shots. I believe we have a plan."

Lawson

THEY HAVE STARTED WITH THE data: who quit, who didn't, who is likely to quit, who is likely to stay. They assume that all of them are likely to quit, of course, even the ones who say they are staying. Why would any of them stay?

"We did not cover this in school," he says, writing the last name MOWERY on the board.

"Do we have to worry about the others? People who didn't win?" Sarah says. She is unruffled, business as usual. She taps a manicured nail on the table, takes a sip of her coffee. She has already contacted HR, has printed out the copy they used for jobs similar to the ones being vacated, has talked to Budget about the funds for advertising, and sent an email out to all of the internal and external clients.

"You mean are they going to jump off the top of the building, too?" The minute he says it, he knows it is not funny. "Sorry," he says. Sarah shoots him a look and then writes something down on the sheet in front of her.

Lawson has googled "what happens when a company group wins the lottery" and spent an hour just staring at his computer, imagining what it would have been like had he played. Had he just fucking played the stupid lottery last week. No, he needs to focus. This is a good job. Sarah is a good boss. He needs to step up here. Lead. Still, eight point eight million dollars would have been nice. Eight point eight million dollars would have cleared the way for him to do whatever he wanted, finally go back to school, maybe start writing again, start painting. With eight point eight million dollars he could have done anything.

"Let's list out all the current projects," Sarah says. "And deadlines. And put anything that has a real-life deadline in red. Those are the ones we're going to have trouble with right now."

Lawson moves up to the whiteboard. He writes "Fall Brochure: photos, copy, design, print buy."

"That one should be red," she says.

Lawson wipes the board with his hand, looks at the dark marker smeared there like a bruise.

Sarah looks at her computer. "Syens was supposed to do the design for that. Shoot, Fitzgerald was on the copy."

He picks up the red marker and draws a line over his hand. Like blood. Like a fat vein. How are they going to just keep on working, keep on making plans and projections and ad copy and Google display ads and annual reports when somebody like Mowery is running around doing whatever you would do if you won eight point eight million dollars? How are they supposed to be producing brochures and websites and ad buys and copy when somebody like Pappas is suddenly a millionaire? A millionaire. Pappas. The copywriter who they assign all the non-copywriting work, the stuff even Pappas couldn't mess up because it wasn't so much copywriting as putting words together in an order that makes sense. They give Pappas the shit work, the stuff that doesn't make a difference, the content work, and now he is a millionaire with all debts paid who will never have to work again.

"Are you…" Sarah says. "Is something…"

"I'm fine. Sorry." He looks at the words he has written on the whiteboard. Letters and spaces. It is so odd that they blend together to make meaning. "It's weird, though. Right?" he says.

"It's not going to help us meet our first quarter numbers," Sarah says. She directs her attention to the laptop, clicks, starts typing. Lawson draws another thick line down the underside of his left arm. A vein. A gash. An ending. A beginning. Pappas is a millionaire several times over. Cowens will never have to make a car payment again. Fitzgerald and Mowery and Squillante, Mancus and Brady and Perez, all have already quit their jobs. All are now millionaires, retired, people of leisure. Lawson draws a line down his left hand. He had wanted to be a painter once. He should wipe it off before Sarah completes her email. He should excuse himself to the bathroom, wash his hands, his arm, get his shit together.

"What are you doing?" Sarah says. "You have a thing, from the marker, there on your arm." She points to the board.

"I do?" he says. He wipes at his hand.

"Getting bigger," Sarah says.

It is going to take so much work to replace them all. Even just updating the projections, writing the report, communicating to stakeholders. He is about to spend the next year of his life chasing these ghosts, filling these holes, and all the while Pappas and Mowery and the rest of them are going to be traveling the world, buying boats and Jet Skis and beach houses and who knows what. They could be doing anything, anything in the world.

"I think you better go clean that off," Sarah says. "We have a lot of work to do here."

"I don't think I can…" Lawson says. He pauses. This is a good job. Sarah is a good boss. Now is the time for leadership. "I mean, yeah. Okay. So, the Fall Chamber of Commerce campaign?"

Yoder

YODER WAKES UP ON HIS feet. Was it a dream? Oh thank god, it was a dream. Just a stupid dream. He doubles over with relief. He breathes slowly. In. Out. In and out. Oh, what a fucked-up dream. He stands and looks around. Something is off. This is not his house. He is in a kitchen. A sink overflows with dishes. Beer cans are everywhere, a few random vodka bottles scattered among them. Five pizza boxes sit on the counter. On the refrigerator, a brochure for something called "The KISS Kruise."

Yoder looks down and sees nothing. In the space where his legs should be, nothing. His arms, nothing. Hands. Feet. He can feel his body, knows it is there, but he cannot see a thing. He leans over. He can still feel the ache in his right Achilles, but nothing is there at all.

Okay, he thinks. You are still in the dream. You just need to wake yourself up, get some coffee, get down to the office.

The office. He remembers how real it all felt, the strange gravel of the roof, the workmen standing below, that final decision to make the step, the wind whipping through his hair and then the ground getting closer, closer, too close.

From outside he hears voices. Laughing. Music. "Eight! Point! Eight! Fucking! Million!" somebody shouts.

"Shut up!" somebody shouts from across the street. "Respect your neighbors, man. I have kids sleeping over here."

"Ain't gonna be my neighbor much longer! Eight point eight fucking million, motherfuckers!"

Yoder sits down on a pizza box, feels it wiggle beneath his weight. It cuts into his legs. It is Cowens's. He is at Cowens's house? It was real? He holds his hands in front of his face and sees nothing. He wiggles on the pizza box and it remains unmoved. He picks a pen up and throws it across the room. It hits the wall, bounces back to his feet. He picks it up again and watches the object float toward the table. He can feel it in his hand but there is no hand to see.

A door opens and he can hear somebody urinating in the bathroom, things being taken out of pockets, a drawer rummaged through. Some kind of terrible heavy metal music rumbles from the backyard. People talking. A light turns on and Cowens is there in the doorway, looking straight at him. Yoder is frozen, trying to think up some excuse. Cowens pauses, looks at the refrigerator. "What was I…" he says. He wanders to the fridge and pulls out four beers. Bud Light Orange. Being in Cowens's house even for just a few minutes has confirmed everything he ever thought about Cowens.

"Eight point fucking eight million." Cowens sings it like a jingle and Yoder imagines that he's been doing this all night, all day, has had a fairly long time to perfect this tune and this is as far as he's gotten.

Cowens opens a drawer and pulls out a pack of cigarettes. He stops at the counter, where several limes have been sectioned. He cuts three more pieces with a long knife and folds them in a paper towel.

Jesus, Yoder hates this guy. This is the guy who wins eight point eight million dollars? Yoder picks up the pen and throws it into the living room. Cowens jumps. "The fuck?" he says. He stumbles into the room and looks around. "Chelsea?" he says. "The fuck are you throwing around in here?" He pauses, waits. He opens a beer and takes a drink.

Yoder feels something harden inside him. So this is it? This is the fucking afterlife? Cowens's house? He hadn't really thought about it very much and when he did, he imagined it as nothing, black, sleep. But this? This is an outrage. Cowens's house? He feels his chest, his shoulders. He runs a hand over his face like a blind person. It is all still there: his mustache, his belly, his penis. Nothing has changed. Except…everything has changed.

Cowens bobbles back down the hall and out the back door. A chorus of voices greet him, their sounds happy and sloppy and what is the word? Pure? Untroubled? Yoder cannot see his feet, his hands, his belly. They are so young and stupid. They are careless. The word he is looking for is "undeserving."

Yoder stands. He picks up the knife Cowens had been using for the limes. He holds it with both hands, plunges it into his chest, right where he imagines his heart to be. He can feel something—a pressure and then a lightening when he pulls the knife out. He looks down. Nothing. He looks at the knife. No blood.

From the backyard, "Eight point eight fucking million fucking dollars!" He sits back down, lets the knife drop onto the floor, fights the urge to move his ghost feet as it clatters. This is worse than he ever could have imagined.

CHASTAIN

CHASTAIN HEARS THE PHONE VIBRATE again. How many texts has that been? She wonders what might be happening. Probably her mother and sister arranging some kind of vacation she could never afford. She opens her eyes and looks at the ceiling. The fan has started to wobble and it makes a small crick with each rotation. Crick crick crick. She should really stand up and make it even, but she can't imagine doing that right now with the pounding in her head. Could she even trust herself to stand on the bed? If the ceiling fan hit her in the forehead, would she have to go to the urgent care for stitches? Would she have to fill out forms, sit there and wait in some dingy urgent care facility, trying to remember the password to her health spending account?

Another text. Jesus Christ, Mom. Or Sally. Whoever. It is nine thirty on Tuesday morning. She hasn't even bothered to email in sick yet but she can't imagine anybody even came in. Could the building even be standing after that ridiculous news? Who would be there? Sarah, Lawson, Garner. She pictures them sitting there, each of them working away like an automaton, like yesterday never happened, like those assholes weren't all eight point eight million dollars richer today.

26

Eight point eight million fucking dollars. She pulls the covers over her head. The ceiling fan crick crick cricks. The phone vibrates again, longer this time. A phone call? She wonders if it is Allison calling from the office. She should have just texted in sick. Can she imagine ever going into work again, though? To that place?

The phone rings again. Craver. It all comes back to her: the bartender—what was his name?—finally cutting them off after their fifth or sixth shot, after so many beers, a brief run through fruity drinks, and then a coffee before they walked out into the shocking remaining sunshine of six fifteen Monday evening.

The phone vibrates again. A message. She checks the texts. Five from Craver, one from her mother.

Oh Jesus Christ, Craver. She had kissed him. Again. Same as the last time—drunk, flirty, finishing cigarettes on the sidewalk. Same as after the holiday party and the retirement happy hour for Kirkpatrick and the Super Bowl party when they had started drinking every time somebody said "Tom Brady." Each time, some making out, some talking, and then silence, awkwardness, and finally a return to their usual flirty office thing. She had never taken it any further because she didn't need to take it further. Was it up to him to try to take it further?

The phone vibrates again. Well at least now he is taking the initiative. Still, he couldn't have been really serious about it, the two of them driving across the country with no real goal in mind other than San Francisco eventually.

"Destination: San Francisco eventually," he had said before stumbling toward his car, turning to wag a finger at her as if they had just committed some light act of rebellion.

Did she mean it? At the time, maybe. After however many beers and shots and a Mai Tai and a half a pack of cigarettes. She hopes he didn't actually quit. He wouldn't actually quit, would he? That would be idiotic, unnecessary. Nobody will be in there today except Sarah. They won't even realize who is or isn't there, who quit or didn't quit or just stopped coming, for another full month. If there was ever a time to coast, to stay home and bank on general incompetence and confusion, it was now.

She reads the texts:

Craver: I just quit! Destination San Francisco Eventually here we come!

Craver: Pick you up at 9? Grande skim latte two splendas?

Craver: Hey are you up?

Craver: ????

Craver: Hey I know we were drunk last night but let's do this Destination San Fran Eventually! I'm not going back. I can't. I would love to do this with you to see what we have going on here, finally maybe. Eventually.

Craver: Ugh is this how it's going to go?

Craver: Okay sorry. Sorry sorry sorry.

Craver: Are you up?

Craver: I'm going to leave at 10. I hope you'll come but if you don't want to, if you can't, I get it.

Craver: I know this is pretty stupid and that's part of the appeal tbh.

Craver: I've never done anything quite this stupid so, you know, seems like time to do something real stupid before I turn 33.

Craver: ;-)

Craver: Hey if you want to come just text me back once, something, and I'll come and get you.

Craver: The screen door slams, Mary's dress waves, like a vision she dances across the porch as the radio plays…

Craver: oh oh oh oh Thunder Road oh Thunder Road oh Thunder Rooooaaaaad

Craver: ;-)

Craver: It's ten

Craver: heading out.

Craver: San Francisco Eventually here i come!

She looks at the clock. It is ten fifteen. He really left. He quit, packed his stuff into his Honda Civic, and drove west. The ceiling fan turns. Crick crick crick. She puts the phone back on the nightstand and pulls the covers over her head.

Gibbons

GIBBONS DROPS HIS COFFEE ON the desk, turns on the computer, puts his bag in the corner, and goes to the bathroom. The halls are empty and for a moment he wonders if it is a Saturday, or one of the off-brand holidays, President's Day or MLK. But he would have remembered, would have heard something, there would have been an email reminder if they were off. No, it is eight forty-five on Tuesday, as usual. He shakes his head. People will do anything to avoid working. He retrieves a yogurt from the kitchen refrigerator and goes back to his cubicle.

Twenty-three emails have come in overnight. He deletes seventeen and parses the rest. One from Lawson about the fall campaigns that will have to be dealt with right away. He understands what they are doing, appreciates the professional approach. This is certainly worst for Sarah and Lawson and the others who need to try to keep everything moving. Three meeting invitations, all along the same lines. He quickly accepts and files away the times in his head. He will need to prepare. There is one email about his compliance training. Two test marketing emails for the upcoming "Try It" campaign.

He opens the fall campaign spreadsheet. So they won the lottery. They really won. Something like eighty percent of lottery winners wind up bankrupt.

The fall campaigns usually almost run themselves but he understands what Lawson and Sarah are doing. Everything will need to be triaged now, deadlines broken, pushed back, changed. They may even have to farm some of it out in order to keep all the contracts, reassure their clients that all will proceed as planned, that there's nothing but business as usual despite the strange recent news.

Which of them will go bankrupt? Not Garner. Not Mancus. Cowens for sure. Probably Pappas.

Two campaigns are slated to kick off within the month and those are already in the pipeline, the creative done, marketing plans approved, buys completed. Six more are in the pipeline, some version of creative started but not approved, marketing plans drafted or initiated, buys in some early stage of development and pending results of the campaigns that are set to launch soon. The others, will it work to just say it's too early to tell? They need numbers. Sixteen planned, no work done other than the campaigns they're simply rerunning, which leaves twelve with no work initiated or in the pipeline. He does some quick math. An average campaign takes sixty hours of Creative, thirty Marketing, eight Analytics, about the same from the search engine marketing people. Roughly one hundred twenty-eight hours per campaign. Times twelve? Sixteen? They will need to bring people on quickly or farm work out.

If he won the lottery, Gibbons thinks, he would buy a campground, that nice little place he and Nancy went last summer for Labor Day. Happy Acres. He pictures the two of them, working the front desk, checking families in while the children shout from the playground, sharing a beer on the stoop of the big cabin at the end of the day, fireworks and sing-alongs at night by the big fire. The lottery. It really is something. They will all be working eighty hours a week to try to keep things in line.

He opens a browser. He checks the campaigns channel on Slack. Nothing.

The lottery. He would buy Happy Acres.

Robertson

HE MOVES LUIGI RIGHT, RIGHT, always right. Jump. Jump. Over the Venus flytrap things, over the bullet thing, and then falling. He tries to jump. The music plays and Luigi disappears.

"Come on, man," Jessie says. She is still moving Mario right, right, jumping, sliding under things, picking them up.

Robertson finishes his beer and reaches into the cooler for another. "Open one for me," Jessie says. Her eyes stay on the screen and she continues moving right, right, jumping, throwing fireballs that decimate the Goombas and Koopas and shells and turtles and whatever else is in her path. She has five lives left. He has zero. It is a fitting score. She is better than him at all things in every way and he lives in more or less constant fear that one day she will notice.

He takes a long drink from the can and looks around. He had dressed for work and he still wears a light blue button-down, now unbuttoned and lightly dappled on the left side with drops of BarrelHouse IPA, and the tan Dockers that have become his uniform at Keystone. He thinks about them all in that conference room, high fiving and dancing, singing those terrible eighties songs.

Mowery in his MAGA hat and Toby Keith shirt and those brand-new jeans.

He can't get the way Mowery high fives out of his mind: his hand held at breast level, an upward push, awkward contact, and then a continued thrust until his hand was held high. He replays it again in his head. It is as if an alien had been taught to high five by having it explained to him by a five-year-old. What is so hard about a high five? You wave your hand and slap. Maybe you have a certain rhythm to it, depending on the scenario. Maybe you have a certain flair, a personal style. Robertson used to favor a no-nonsense high five that indicated he was, yes, congratulating you or receiving congratulations, but also mostly getting back on defense.

Robertson remembers a line from an old song he used to hear in his mother's car: "…because how you play is who you are." He had been a businesslike player, smart and disciplined. He played The Right Way. He stretches his right leg, aware of the semiconscious motion every time he thinks about it. He feels the friction of the new knee, not a pain so much as a presence, a reminder.

"Are you pouting again?" Jessie asks. She is still moving right, right, jumping jumping, sliding, picking things up. Somehow she has garnered a new life and she now has six remaining to his zero.

"Not pouting." He finishes his beer, reaches for another, but the cooler is empty.

Jessie moves right right and then the familiar sound of Mario crashing into some dragon or ocean or blank space. "Kind of a relief," she says. She takes a drink from her can. "Do you want to talk about this? Whatever this is?" She waves her beer at him like a magician summoning a rabbit.

"I just didn't feel like going in today," he says. "They didn't even call. Or email. Or anything. I mean, those guys…"

The Mario game is playing its ridiculous circus music. Jessie scoots up in her seat. He has fifty thousand four hundred dollars in student debt, three thousand eight hundred on the Visa, two thousand something on the other Visa. "All those people, they're just so…I don't know. So, like, corny."

"Corny? You're moping around here because they're corny?"

If she left him now, she would be fine. She is beautiful and smart and can code PHP and JavaScript and C++ and Perl and Visual Basic and whatever is coming next with her eyes closed. She has one point four million followers on YouTube who watch her play video games in this very room.

"Corny? Really? That's the problem?" She puts down the controller and looks at him.

As always, he wants her full attention and then is embarrassed when it finally lands on him. He looks at the television, where the familiar pitfalls await Mario's return. He will die again and again and again, even with Jessie at the helm. There will always be more lives. What is the point?

"Can't you change that music?" he says.

She doesn't move a muscle but something changes in her eyes, a not-so-secret judgment. He is not sure he wants to know what she is thinking. "That's the Mario music," she says. "That's the music that plays when you play Mario. You know this."

"It's just that most of these people, they're like the worst people. Like most of the people there are pretty bad, right? Except Sarah and some of the SEO people and the poor old motherfucker who jumped off the fucking building. But then say everybody else is like a five out of ten…"

She hits pause on the game. "So a five out of ten, like, as people?"

"As people." He is aware that he is being ridiculous, but he is already down this path somehow. How does he always find himself in this situation?

"So who is a ten?" she says. "What's our baseline here?"

"Who is a ten? I don't know, LeBron James is a ten. Beyoncé."

"Steve Jobs."

He pauses. Now is not the time to get into that again. "Okay, so that's a ten, right? These people. The lottery people are, you know what, not fives. So say the average Keystone marketing person is like, a four."

"What am I?"

She is looking at him again. How did he get himself into this? She clicks the controller and Mario is again resurrected. "You're a ten," he says.

"I'm like an eight, person-wise," she says. She moves Mario right right right, jumps, shoots fire out of his fist.

"So these lottery people, though? They're like twos, like some of them are sub-two."

"Sub-two is not a good human being."

"Right. So a bunch of sub-twos win the fucking lottery. It's fucking depressing. Discouraging. Spirit-wise."

She moves Mario right right right. "His spirit is discouraged."

"That's a good summary."

Mario is hopping up up up a moving concourse of stages. He leaps toward a rotating structure but she has timed it wrong and he bounces off, slides down. The death music plays. "Goddammit," she says.

Robertson looks out the window. A steady stream of cars moves past the yard, each of them containing another person who did not win the lottery, another plus-two rated human being, most likely, consigned to a life of work and toil and frustration and all for what? If he does go back to work, he will need to make thirteen virtual machines, three different configurations, two data point integrations, all configured to work with the ridiculously outdated sign-on functionality fucking Mowery acquired before he won the goddamn lottery. He thinks about that ridiculous MAGA hat, his brand-new jeans and Toby Keith shirt. He realizes the whole thing was just a big fuck you to him and everybody else. "Goddammit," he says in a low whisper.

"His spirit is discouraged," Jessie says, and she moves Mario right right right.

russell

"HE JUST...JUMPED?" GINNY SAYS.

Russell nods. He takes another sip of his wine. "He just walked right off, they say."

"I am so sorry." Ginny puts her hand over his.

He notices the crumbs on the table, the scratches. The mail sits unopened in a pile in the corner. Ginny has been biting her cuticles again and there is an angry red patch below the nail on her ring finger. He places a finger on it and rubs. "You have to stop doing that," he says.

"Oh I know," she says, too quickly.

"I know," he says. He is sixty. She is fifty-seven. At this age, his father, a bus driver on Long Island, was retired on a government pension. They have done the math—the bills, the mortgage, what they have in retirement, how long they could possibly continue working, all of it—and it does not paint a pretty picture.

"We were going to do this thing. Remember that movie *Office Space*?"

Ginny pulls her hand back. She stands and refills her wine. "Have you been having trouble with your TPS reports?" she says, and laughs. "Sorry."

"No, yeah, that's the one. So, Yoder had this computer he just hated. One of these big heavy Dells, got super hot, battery conked out whenever he had it unplugged for an hour, couldn't even bring it to a meeting, you know, because halfway through the thing would start making this whirring sound, whirrrrrr, and then it would just die."

Ginny takes a sip of her wine. "So you were going to teach it a lesson?"

Russell laughs and finishes his own wine. "We were! When he got the new machine, which I think he was on the list for next fiscal, we were going to take the old Dell out into the parking lot and give it the old *Office Space*. Baseball bats and everything."

"Baseball bats and everything?"

"Very specifically, yes. We had a plan." He wants to laugh, makes his mouth make the sound, but what comes out is more of a honk. "It was so weird in there today," he says. "You know almost nobody came to work?"

"Because of Arthur?"

He thinks. Was it because of Arthur? Does he want to cement what he is almost sure of by actually saying it out loud? "I don't think so," he says.

"What?" she says, with real shock in her voice.

Immediately, he wishes he had taken the other path, told her what they both wished to be true. "I think it was more because of the lottery. The ones who won and the ones who didn't."

"Well that's just ridiculous," Ginny says. The oven timer goes off. "They didn't come to work just because…that's terrible." She turns off the timer and opens the oven. It is Wednesday and sure enough the smell of lasagna fills the kitchen. "Every day of most of our lives we don't win the lottery and we just keep going back to work anyway."

He is relieved she didn't pick up on the other thing, the thing with Yoder. The truth is most of them are probably hungover in their houses or apartments or condos and not even remembering that Keystone's longest tenured employee chose to take his own life rather than live through another day. They are nursing beers or checking ZipRecruiter or updating their LinkedIn profiles and Yoder has nothing to do with any of it. Ginny stands there, holding the lasagna, waiting for a reply. "It's true," Russell says. "I know most days I don't win the lottery and I keep on going back."

"Millennials," Ginny says. "The trophies, that's what this is."

Russell considers telling her the way he drove past the building, kept on driving until he got to Starbucks and then sat in there reading *Lonesome Dove* all day. It was a truly lovely day, a lovely few hours, at least, until he got the double whammy news about the lottery and then Yoder. He considers telling her that somewhere in the cocktail of feelings about all of this, there is a fair amount of jealousy of Yoder, too. All of the things Yoder will not have to deal with, the spreadsheets and worry and constant watching the 401k, the colonoscopies and appointments and teeth cleanings, not even to mention the slow and steady process of being pushed out of the center of things, being whispered about, left out of conversations, slowly aging into irrelevance, onto the sidelines of nearly every situation. Yoder will not have to go through any of it. Not anymore.

"You okay?" Ginny says. She puts her hand over his again. They have been married for thirty-six years.

"Sure," he says. "Sure, of course. I'm fine. That lasagna looks great."

CRAVER

CRAVER LOOKS AT THE SIGN: Columbus, ten miles. Sure, he thinks. Columbus. It's a college town and he could use a drink. He's been on the road for six hours and already the car is strewn with wrappers, Arby's and Burger King and Tastykakes and David Sunflower Seeds. He will need to get some discipline but for today, fuck it. He checks the phone again. Nothing.

"Proceed to the route." He thought it would be funny or interesting or tragic or...something to plug his route into Google maps. Valley Station to San Francisco, California. Forty hours, two thousand six hundred and eighty-four miles. Around Pittsburgh he decided to move in a Jack Kerouac direction and got off the freeway, just started following small roads west and north. "Proceed to the route," the Google Lady says.

"Right?" he says. He passes a gas station, a laundromat, a car wash. He stops at a light. The area is starting to get more developed. He guesses he's getting closer to Columbus. "Proceed to the route. Proceed to the route. You are correct, Google Lady. What's your name?"

He actually looks at his phone, wondering if she will answer. He checks the texts again. Nothing.

The radio is tuned to some country station and a thin, lonesome voice is singing about going downtown. He passes a Dick's Sporting Goods and a Target. He pictures Jack Kerouac walking into Target. "The great American road trip," he says. If he were to write a book about this it would be called "Proceed to the Route."

"Google Lady, what is your name?" he says. He passes a McDonald's and thinks about stopping. He is hungry, but for the past few hours he has been picturing the evening in his head, a night out at some local place, an IPA and a burger, a big plate of fries, a friendly beautiful local waitress or a table full of interesting strangers. He did not picture a soggy Big Mac, a car full of wrappers and stray french fries, a greasy stink already emanating from the interior of his Civic. He was picturing Chastain sitting in the passenger seat, making sarcastic remarks, lighting his cigarettes, handing them to him with that conspiratorial look in her eye. He was picturing them pulling into a little hotel or an Airbnb. He was picturing a lot of things.

He checks the phone again. A text from his mother. He will have to explain to her what is happening but that is going to be a Whole Thing and his inclination is to wait until he is in the middle of the country, when he is so far into this that she can't talk him back home.

"Proceed to the route."

"My thoughts exactly," he says. Proceed to the route where you play the goddamn lottery the one time in a million, two million, a billion that those idiots actually win. Proceed to the route where you don't quit your job to drive across the country with a woman who will only pay attention to you when she's legally drunk. Proceed to the route where you basically make all new decisions starting with where to go to college, what to do there, where to move after, what kind of work you will find, just about every single way you could possibly proceed differently. Proceed to that fucking route, Google Lady.

"Proceed to the route."

"You always know just what to say." He needs the bathroom, a shower, to lay down on an anonymous hotel bed and check his Facebook. He needs to stop talking to his phone. He wonders if he is going crazy already. An analysis of his actions today might actually indicate that. If he looks at the analytics, what is the picture they paint for him?

A half tank of gas. No job. Five hundred seventy-five dollars in his checking account. How much in the savings? A thousand fifty? The credit card debt is not too bad right now. He can run up a few thousand on the Visa and he's never even used the other two Visas or the Discover card that he signed up for drunk at a festival to get a bucket hat that sits in the trunk now, in a box with a raincoat and an umbrella and some mostly empty cans of sunscreen. Twelve texts to Chastain and nothing back. Two calls. What else? He has masturbated in the car once already but that was more to keep him awake, take up a few minutes of time with something other than staring. The analytics do not lie but he knows from experience that they can be interpreted, spun, moved in certain directions.

Chastain. It all seemed so good last night. They had a plan, a do-over, a goddamn theme song and a catchphrase. He wonders what she is doing now, if she went to work, what she is wearing and whether he should be texting her locations, airports she can fly into, something or anything that would say hey, we can still do this, it's not too late, tramps like us, baby we were…

"Proceed to the route," the Google Lady says.

He picks up his half-finished Diet Coke bottle and considers the heft. If it was glass he could really do a number. It would feel so good to smash something. He wonders if Chastain ever got out of bed, what she was wearing yesterday under her black pants and gray button-up. He wonders if he will ever hear from her again. He holds the bottle at the top and considers the dashboard. But no, it would just bounce, or explode all over him. He pictures the news report: Man Who Did Not Win Lottery Dies in One-Car Accident. It would be silly, funny, an entry in the Darwin Awards.

"Proceed to the route," the Google Lady says.

He lets the bottle drop. He will text Chastain something whimsical and funny, something on just the right line between entreaty and suggestion, the kind of thing a grown-ass man would send to a woman he is interested in. "Hey that's me and I want you only. Don't turn me home again. I just can't face myself alone again."

On second thought, that second part is maybe a little too spot on.

On the right he sees a glowing sign: Holiday Inn Columbus. There is a TGI Fridays next door. Good enough. He pulls in.

Yoder

YODER WAKES UP ON HIS feet again. He pauses, looks around for the dirty dishes, for Cowens's stupid cigarettes and Bud Light Oranges and pizza boxes and squalid little kitchen. But no. This is a different place. Yoder breathes. He wonders about the physics of his situation. He can pick things up. He can feel his body but he can't hurt it. He can breathe. People can't see him. Fuck. There's just no way around it: he is a ghost.

He thinks about Catholic school. Is this purgatory? He looks around again. He is in a house. It is night. It is not Cowens's house, thank god. But whose house is this? The kitchen is clean, a few washed dishes sit in a rack. Three bottles of wine sit on the counter. Car keys on a kitchen table, some mail.

Yoder sits down. He riffles through the mail. He is in Pappas's house. First Cowens and now Pappas.

He looks through the mail. Bill bill junkmail junkmail card card card card. Of course they would be getting cards. Congratulations cards. Congratulations on your stroke of blind fucking luck. Congratulations on being stupid enough to be harassed into tithing two dollars a week to the state of Pennsylvania Lottery System. Congratulations on being strong-armed by a forty-five-year-old Assistant Manager of Data Analytics into throwing away two dollars a week. He can't remember who said that the lottery was like a tax on stupid people but he never forgot the line.

He remembers taking that step, the ground far away and then getting closer so fast, the feeling of air whipping past him and almost holding him up, like if he could just find the right angle he might whoosh past the hedges and the landscaping guys, the first-floor meeting rooms just starting to fill up with sleepwalkers busying themselves for another day. And then black.

He looks through the cabinets, wondering at his invisible hands on the cinnamon or the salt shaker, the way he can feel it, can pull a drawer and it opens, push and it closes. He picks up a packet of sugar and throws it onto the table. He takes out a box of Honey Bunches of Oats and empties it onto the floor. He finds a bottle of aspirin and pours the contents into his mouth and watches as they clatter on the tile. A cat, a big orange tabby, appears in the corner and at first Yoder isn't sure if it is a ghost, or whatever he is, or if it is indeed Pappas's cat.

The cat sniffs the tablets, the cereal, and then hops up on the table. It pushes at an envelope until it falls onto the floor, then does the same with every other piece of mail on the table. Yoder likes this cat. He bends over to pet it and as soon as he makes contact the cat yelps and explodes up into the air. The cat is airborne and then it lands and it is gone.

He remembers the ground getting closer, closer, too close.

But this, whatever this is, it is not the black sleep that he imagined. It is definitely not heaven. Is it hell? He has awakened into Cowens's home and now Pappas's. He will need to consider the idea that this might be hell.

He follows the cat into a living room. Outside, two Mercedes SUVs sit in the driveway. Of course Pappas would buy a fucking Mercedes SUV. Like those two words should ever be next to one another in the same sentence. In the living room there are boxes, Best Buy and Macy's and Eddie Bauer. Of course Pappas would go buy a bunch of Eddie

Bauer bullshit faux outdoorsman gear to wear in his Mercedes sport utility vehicle.

He fishes in the Best Buy bag and pulls out a box. HTC Virtual Reality System. That answers the question of what is the dumbest possible thing you could buy at Best Buy. He throws the box against the wall and a light goes on down the hall.

"Snickers, Jesus Christ what are you doing out here?" Pappas's voice sounds thick and slow. He stumbles into the hallway. Yoder is standing right there. "Snickers, what the fuck?" Pappas says. He takes a few steps and pauses. The cat slips down the hall and disappears.

"What's going on out there?" A woman's voice.

"Nothing. Snickers just…" Pappas's mumbling drifts away and the door shuts. Yoder walks down the hall. Already there is snoring from the bedroom. He turns the doorknob and pushes the door as quietly as he can. He does not know why he is being so quiet but it seems that he should. Are there rules? He leans over the bed. Pappas's wife or girlfriend is pretty, blond, thin, maybe mid-thirties. The sheets are pulled up and all he can see is her face. Pappas is balled into the corner of the bed, the blankets pulled over his head. Of course Pappas would sleep like a hamster.

He walks out, lets the door close shut behind him. "Snickers!" Pappas shouts. "Jesus."

Yoder goes back into the kitchen. He finds the largest knife, plunges it into his heart. A feeling like a squish and then nothing. No blood, no pain. He sits down at the kitchen table and waits.

CHASTAIN

CHASTAIN HITS THE ELEVATOR BUTTON
and hopes nobody else will be able to get on before the doors shut. A
hand in the door. They open. Of course it would be Garner.

"You're still here," she says.

"Oh yeah. I always said even if we hit it big I'd keep on keepin'
on here and, well, here I am." He is wearing jeans and a bright yellow
sweater. Nothing about him seems changed at all.

"That's..." she thinks of all the words she would like to say: stupid,
ridiculous, crazy, sad, pitiful, super fucking annoying. "Amazing," she
says.

"Well, if I was just hanging around the house all day, I think Mary
would wind up killing me." He says it as if he is telling a joke, a joke she
guesses he has told a hundred times already, and she laughs dutifully.

They stand. She brings out her phone, acts like she is checking a
message, clicks into Facebook: dog, dog, baby, politics, child, not sure,
not sure. She closes the phone. She smiles at Garner.

"Wednesday," he says.

Jesus Christ, is it possible it is only Wednesday?

44

The elevator dings and they arrive at the fourth floor, just like always. Just like always she nods, smiles, and goes to her desk. She watches Garner hurry down the hall, toward the Data Analytics area. "Motherfucker," she says, under her breath.

Her phone buzzes. Craver again. She pauses. It is so quiet in the office. Too quiet. Nobody in the kitchen, nobody else getting off the elevators. She is two hours late and somewhere between hungover and still drunk and there is nobody to even worry about catching on to her. She hadn't even considered the idea that the rest of them might feel the same way, had just pictured them sleepwalking through the day like nothing ever happened, like a bunch of idiots too beaten down already to even question the idea of coming in to work after a bunch of other idiots won the goddamn lottery.

The text is a picture of Craver standing in front of a large ball. "Largest Ball of Twine" is written on a sign behind him. He has gotten no better at taking selfies despite the fact that this is the fifth he's sent in the past forty-eight hours. He is funny, self-deprecating, ironic, a little dark. But she knew that already. What she didn't realize is that he would actually go, would quit his okay job and close out his okay apartment and put his entire okay life into his okay car and drive, and this new piece of information has dislodged something in her understanding of Craver, knocked everything askew, poked some kind of hole in some of the protective wrapping she had mentally bundled the whole thing up with.

Technically she is probably still drunk. She moves down the hallways, still watching the phone for the next text, which she knows will be the closest airport. He has not given up. Another piece of disarming information. Her phone buzzes, and there it is: "Indianapolis International Airport. Tonight, tomorrow."

"Hi Jennifer." She jolts, realizes she is still standing outside the kitchen.

"Hi," she says and then looks up with a quick shock of recognition. "Oh, hi Sarah."

"Thank you for being here today," Sarah says, and nods. A professional nod—a nod that conveys thanks and understanding and a feeling like it is time to move on. Is this what people mean when they say they feel seen? Chastain could work here for five more lifetimes and never be able to give that kind of a nod. She watches the woman move down the hall. If the building fell down right this moment, she is pretty sure that Sarah would simply continue to work in the rubble until a new building was built around her.

It is so weird that this is the same building, she thinks. The lottery. Yoder's suicide. Craver's road trip. And now Sarah bustling toward her office like nothing ever happened. Of course, Sarah is bustling toward her office like nothing ever happened.

She moves toward her desk and actually recoils at the idea of sitting there. She is going to sit at that desk and schedule meetings and pay bills and read emails and answer questions? Can she? Is it even a physically possible act?

She sits down and clicks on the computer. She puts her coffee on the desk, her bag by the chair. At every moment she expects something to crack, for the thing that will indicate that the entire world has changed to reveal itself, like a vampire opening its mouth, a zombie finally lurching toward its victim. She looks at the emails filling her screen. They all seem so stupid now. The notes she has placed around the computer area—reminders to call this person or schedule that appointment. The fluorescent lights. The colorless carpet. The fire alarm signs pointing to the back stairway. The motivational posters that line the hallway. The phones and the computers and the chatter from the kitchen. The whole thing is ridiculous. How are they all still even here?

She takes the Post-its off the computer and drops them in the trash can, one by one. She watches them sitting there like petals discarded from a cheap yellow rose. She takes out her lighter and considers torching the entire thing.

"Thank you for being here today." She fights the hitch in her throat, realizes in a rush that it is perhaps the kindest thing anybody has ever said to her in this office.

The phone buzzes again. Craver's trip is as ridiculous in its way as the computer and the stapler and Garner strolling toward the bathroom, a goddamn millionaire off to take his morning shit before he checks the Adwords campaigns.

She stands up, sits down again. She fishes the Post-its out of the garbage and smooths them out on the desk. She pictures Sarah walking back toward her office. "Thank you for being here." She stands and walks in that direction.

Gibbons

GIBBONS PUTS DOWN HIS COFFEE and checks his email. Six new messages in the past two hours. Who has a two-hour meeting on a Friday morning and doesn't include food? Donut holes are the baseline. You start with donut holes and move up through donuts, bagels, breakfast sandwiches based on degree of difficulty. He imagines walking into a Friday nine o'clock someday and seeing an entire hot breakfast buffet lined up along the wall, with those big carryout things of Starbucks and real orange juice.

Spam, spam, meeting invitation, meeting invitation, meeting invitation, newsletter. Fine. Nothing from Sarah or Lawson. Nothing from Creative. Nothing from Purchasing. No Slack notifications. He checks the production schedule again, but he already knows they are two days behind on the content for the Susquehanna Mall buy, a full week behind on the ad banners and the bus wraps for the Penn State account.

In their Slack there are messages in the random and the social committee channels but no direct messages, nothing in campaigns or general.

He looks behind him, scans the cube aisles, and opens up his Gmail. Nothing. He scans the cube aisles, and opens up Twitter. No interactions. He clicks on new tweets and scans for something interesting but he doesn't even know what he is looking for and anybody walking past the office will see exactly what he is doing. He closes the browser.

Should he call a special meeting about the Creative delays? Should he email Carl in Purchasing? He will update the production schedule channel in Slack, note the delays, play it straight but be all business, no attitude either way. He will stay in his lane.

A notification shows up in the bottom right of the computer. Email from CBS Sports. The subject line flashes and disappears and all he sees are the words "fantasy football."

He checks his work email. A meeting invitation from Sarah. He sits up. Any meeting with Sarah is an opportunity, an indication that he is part of the Core Team, the inner circle, the people who are really making a difference at Keystone. He remembers a poem somebody forwarded to him, written from the perspective of one of the yellow shirts, the worker bees from *Star Trek*. "The heart of the ship, the heart of the ship, you are working in the heart of the ship." It is how he feels every time he has an important meeting: Gibbons is working in the heart of the ship. He opens the invitation, clicks accept, and as the message disappears, he notes the meeting subject: "All Staff Check-In."

russell

RUSSELL CRUISES PAST YODER'S CUBE to
stake out the situation. Somebody, almost certainly Sarah, has placed a
vase of flowers there along with a card and an interoffice envelope that
he knows will have a note that says "for the family," along with enough
fives and tens to make it seem like much of the office has already gen-
erously donated.

With Yoder gone, Russell is pretty sure he is the oldest person left
in the office. He pictures this same situation laid out in his own cubicle:
the note in Sarah's hand, the money from Sarah's pocketbook, his co-
workers carefully avoiding this corner of the office until the funeral is
over, maybe some of the older ones reminiscing over a few beers, some
of the younger ones making fun of his pants or his glasses or the sounds
he made when he had to walk up more than one flight of stairs. This will
be, he knows, the full extent of his legacy at Keystone Special Marketing
Solutions. No gold watch, no retirement ceremony, his name will not be
etched on a golden plaque displayed in some common space. They will
wipe his computer, put his pens and pencils and notebooks and Post-its
back in the supply room. They will recycle his papers, throw away all the

things they find in his desk and drawers—the peanuts and SpaghettiOs and spreadsheets and reports. Somebody will take the couch he took from Old Snyder's office when he retired. Somebody will take the iPad they gave him a few years ago, when it seemed like everything was going to be iPads. Somebody will take his stapler, a red Swingline he bought soon after he first saw the movie *Office Space*. And that will be it.

Yoder's computer is right there on the desk. Like nothing ever happened. Russell stops, puts five dollars into the envelope. Everything is still plugged in, ready for Yoder to come back and start it up and then go make coffee while the machine whirrs and chugs itself slowly to unpredictable life.

Russell backs up, yawns, checks the aisle and the opposite cubicles. Nobody. He leans back, pretends to be reading the card, nodding his head in sympathy while he unscrews the monitor cord, unplugs the ethernet, pops out the headphones and the keyboard and the mouse. All of these ancillary devices, single-function machines. On his first desk, he had a pen, a phone, and an inbox. Now, one of these kids shows up and forgets their laptop at home and they turn around and head back to get it without even talking to anybody. God forbid they would go to the bathroom, even, without their phones. Everybody staring at their devices all the time, texting somebody in California or Germany or the next cubicle over, looking at pictures of babies and dogs and people's feet in the sand in the Bahamas.

He eases the machine out of the workstation, then turns around for one more look. Nobody is around. He notices how empty the office is, wonders how long this will last, but he knows eventually this, too, will pass and the place will be buzzing with young people typing and talking and walking and trying far too hard, caring so much, striving to meet key performance indicators they will all forget by next year. He tucks Yoder's computer under his arm and walks back toward his own cubicle.

Yoder

YODER WAKES UP ON HIS feet. There is a couch, a love seat, a television, a hot tub? Another television. It is dark. Night. He sits down on the couch. Is he in Pappas's house? Cowens's? No, this place is unfamiliar.

He listens, hears voices outside, music playing. The hot tub gurgles in the corner. It is a rubber model, light blue. An orange extension cord snakes into the kitchen and he follows. He picks up a letter. Of course this would be Mowery's house. He pauses, recognizes the country music coming from outside. On the kitchen counter, a row of tequila bottles and a Make America Great Again hat and three bags of Cheetos. Fucking Mowery.

Yoder wanders. Exactly what kind of asshole is Mowery anyway? He feels something under his feet and then realizes the entire kitchen floor is covered in scratch-off lottery tickets. So Mowery is the kind of asshole who wins the lottery and then spends part of his winnings on scratch-off lottery tickets.

He pauses and considers how long it has been since the last time he awakened. Is he awakening? Is he always there but doesn't remember sometimes? Is he sleeping? Is this all a dream?

He kicks at the floor. Fucking scratch-off lottery tickets?

There is shouting coming from outside, the sounds of engines starting up. He sees headlights in the windows, more shouts. Either a motorcycle or a four-wheeler. At least Mowery is consistent.

He walks down a short hallway. Mowery's bed is messy. Bottles of beer and Gatorade littered on the dresser and the bedstand and the floor along with Taco Bell and Arby's bags. What kind of asshole wins the lottery and spends his money on Nachos BellGrande and shitty roast beef sandwiches? The engine roar gets louder outside and he hears a whoop and a rush and then the small bedroom is flooded with light. He puts a hand on the window. Outside, two four-wheelers spin circles in the yard. He worries briefly about the cars parked not ten feet away along the road, then remembers how he got here.

How did he get here? Where does he go when he is not awake? This is definitely not heaven, but it is not hell, either. Perhaps he is being tested. He can't remember how *It's a Wonderful Life* worked. Did Jimmy Stewart have to do something to go back to his life? Was that heaven? In *Scrooged*, Bill Murray can't change the course of events at all, has to sit there and watch his idiot brother complain about his Christmas present. Yoder never did like Christmas, if he is being honest about it. As he grew older and his circles diminished, his parents died and cousins had families of their own, as his college friends moved and married and grew distant themselves. He had come to dread the holidays, and then to resent them, and eventually he had made some kind of peace by trying his best to enjoy the time off and ignore the rest. It's a wonderful life? With scratch-off lottery tickets littering all of Mowery's house? With Mowery and his redneck buddies ripping up his own lawn on brand-new four-wheelers, all of these idiots literally set for life based on one stupid decision and a confounding stroke of luck?

He pounds a fist on the window and it rattles. He could punch through it right now. He wonders what that would look like from outside, whether Mowery and his redneck buddies would even notice. One of the four-wheelers comes to a coughing stop. The other pauses. The man is wearing no helmet and he can make out Mowery's ridiculous mullet, the faint outline of his mustache like a stain across his face.

He taps the window with his fist and then punches and the glass flies. Mowery jumps and so does the four-wheeler and then it is headed right for him. Yoder stands and watches as the machine lurches, Mowery hanging on with both hands and running as the four-wheeler bounces toward the house and crashes into a tree.

Yoder remains standing. "Fuck!" Mowery shouts. "What the fuck was that?"

His friends are laughing, both of them doubled over. "Nice riding, Mike," one says, and they both sit down on the ground giggling.

"You see that?" Mowery says.

Yoder waves. Mowery stands not five feet away, staring into the bedroom. Yoder wonders if he could throw something, hit the man right in his stupid head. Mowery stares. "You see something in there?" he says. "It's weird."

"You hit your head, Mikey?" his friend says. The other one laughs like he is making a joke, like he is making the funniest joke in the world. Was everybody else just high on marijuana the entire time? Yoder wonders. It would have explained a lot. He makes a funny face, gives Mowery the middle finger.

"Okay," Mowery says, shaking his head and turning to his friends. "Let's get that tequila."

Robertson

ROBERTSON COMES IN LATE AND looks for a spot in the back. "All Staff Check-In Meeting?" Other than the holiday party, there is never a time when the entire staff is in one place at one time. He knows this because with their IT staff depleted ever since he's been on board, he has been responsible not just for system administration but also coordinating meeting technology. Did you bring your cord? Did you turn it off and turn it on again? Did you try dialing the number in the meeting invitation? If he hadn't pretty much started out that way, it would have been enough to turn him against every last one of them.

But this meeting has been called by Sarah and organized by her new assistant Chastain, and Robertson knows he is okay coming in late and looking for a spot in the back. That they would have been in here early making sure everything is working.

The back several rows are nearly empty and he slides in a few chairs away from Neary. He opens his laptop and checks both emails, Twitter, the IT Slack channel. He puts his phone on the table and looks up.

"Well, we should probably get started," Sarah says. "First of all, if you haven't noticed already, we have donuts up here and some coffee, some hot chocolate." She points at a table laid out with boxes of donuts and a few Dunkin takeaway coffee urns. Robertson is hungry, but going up there now would attract attention. He gauges the remainder of the donuts. Still plenty left. Garner stands up and walks toward the table. That guy is still here. The older guy who used to hang around with the other older guy, the dead older guy, waddles up behind Garner, stands there waiting like he's at a post office, like standing there waiting for donuts in the middle of whatever an All Staff Check-In Meeting is the most normal thing in the world.

"Yes, by all means. If you haven't had one already, come on up," Sarah says. She is trying to be jovial but as always Robertson can see a layer over top her attempts at regular conversation. She is a poor actress and he wonders if anybody believes she is playfully joshing. He has always considered her something of an impressive robot, manufactured for the purpose of being a model Marketing Director. "Playfully joshing" is the setting she would be set at right now, before moving into…he isn't sure exactly what this meeting is all about.

"So we need to talk about the elephant in the room," she says. Robertson imagines a hand turning a knob, moving from "Playfully Joshing" to "Keeping it Real, Corporate Flavor." There is grumbling, chairs shifting, but mostly silence. "Right," she says. She looks to her left, toward a man and a woman sitting in the front row. They are both fortyish, good-looking, wearing glasses and business casual clothes. There is something familiar about the man and Russell realizes that he is dressed exactly like Steve Jobs, the black mock turtleneck, the jeans, the New Balance sneakers. The man nods almost imperceptibly and Sarah continues. "I don't expect to be doing all the talking here. What I'm hoping…" she turns to the left again and Robertson watches the man and woman nodding. Who are they? "What I'm hoping is that I actually won't be doing most of the talking here. What I'm hoping is that we can all do some talking here and really hear each other as well." Something is different about her. The usual robotic focus is gone. Jesus Christ, Robertson realizes: she is nervous. "We're a family and like all families, we don't always get along. We don't always agree. But we do need to abide. We need to get through this together, and we will."

Garner shoots a hand up and Sarah nods at him. "Is this about…"

"It is," she says. "Something significant happened here and I want to acknowledge it. I want to acknowledge you, each of you who made the commitment to be here today, every day really."

"Do you want me to…" Garner starts.

"Of course," Sarah says. "I appreciate the fact that you're still here."

"I appreciate that," Garner says.

"If I may." The Steve Jobs man is standing. His hands are pressed together as if he is pleading or ending a yoga session. He is tan and lean, with long salt and pepper hair pulled into a short ponytail at the back. He smiles in what he clearly hopes is a kind manner. Robertson imagines this setting to be "Benevolent Corporate Marketing Type."

Sarah moves toward him and smiles, the tension relaxing in her face. "I'm very happy to introduce Chad Stephenson from Stephenson Consulting. He and his colleague, Nicole Stetler-Stephenson"—the woman stands and waves and then sits down again—"are here to help us get through this."

"Thank you so much, Sarah," Chad Stephenson says. He is still making the namaste gesture. "You all are very lucky to have a leader like this. Very impressive."

He turns to the room. "Tell you what I'd like to do here." Robertson shifts in his seat. This has all the makings of an icebreaker. It's one thing for every asshole in the company to hit the lottery, but if they expect the rest of them to be doing icebreakers it is really going to be too much. He considers leaving. With the servers in their fragile state, he could believably be pulled out of any meeting at any time. Chad Stephenson holds his pause and then pushes his arms up over his head. "Let's stretch and breathe. Everybody just stretch…" he pushes his arms up, wiggles his fingers. "…and…breathe…" He breathes deeply, holds it, and exhales. "Go ahead. Let's stand up and stretch. Let's get our breathing on. Together. Let's get this going together." Robertson watches his co-workers slowly surrender their personal dignity and rise to their feet. They stretch. God, it is an ugly group of people. Old, out of shape, Docker-clad. Robertson stands, but he will not stretch. He will not breathe. He needs to remember details. He needs to tell all of this to Jessie.

"Great," Chad Stephenson says. "Just great. When you're ready…" They sit down with a great shuffling.

Chad Stephenson walks across the room. Robertson pictures him watching TED Talks in his sad room in the Valley Inn, his lips moving along to some other more successful corporate idiot, wishing for one of those face microphones. "Okay, first of all—thank you," he says. His hands are back in the namaste position and Robertson knows immediately and with great certainty that for the rest of his life he will hate anybody who makes this gesture. "It is a great privilege to be here. We are humbled to be able to work with you."

Garner raises his hand again. "So what does that mean exactly? Working with us?" Chad Stephenson walks the room. Robertson expects him to pull out one of those headgear microphones any minute now. He is like a TED Talker in a Hallmark made-for-TV movie. "I'm glad you asked that. Thank you," he says, making namaste hands at Garner. This is certainly the first time anybody has made namaste hands in Garner's general direction. "You've been through something. That's it. It's really as simple as that. Any time you go through something, you come out the other side and…you're different. Maybe weaker, maybe stronger, maybe you've changed in ways you can't quite elucidate yet. Almost certainly. But…" he holds the moment, turns to every side of the room. Robertson can feel the man's eyes on him but he won't give him the favor of his attention. "You. Are. Different. So we're just here to help you get through this. As Sarah said, this is a family and it is our great privilege to be welcomed into the family for even just these next three to sixteen months." Robertson is on their website, which mentions no pricing or fee structure but features a picture of the two of them, Chad Stephenson and Nicole Stetler-Stephenson, on some stage doing the namaste hands while a conference room full of people wearing name tags stands and applauds. He wonders how many hundreds of thousands of dollars Keystone will be handing over to these low-rent TED Talkers.

His phone buzzes. A text from the server monitoring system. Server down. Another server down. Another. For just a brief moment, he misses Mowery, who was always calm and assured when things went wrong, who wasn't afraid to be the person out front, explaining when things would be right and how they were going to make sure this didn't happen again.

Robertson closes his laptop and hops up, the alacrity a signal to everybody else in the room. He might as well shout, "server down." He catches the eye of Chad Stephenson on the way out and it takes every ounce of restraint he has to not acknowledge the attention. Nicole Stetler-Stephenson is saying something about continuity. Robertson moves through the rows of chairs, trying to convey a sense of urgency. Chad Stephenson maintains eye contact and Robertson has the terrible feeling that this will earn him individual attention. Chad Stephenson nods as he moves along. Chad Stephenson makes namaste hands and Robertson shoots through the door.

Lawson

LAWSON PAUSES OUTSIDE THE CLASS-
ROOM. He glances in. A few older women chat in groups, a few
older men sit at the tables lined up in a square around the room. He
could leave right now, go to Starbucks or Panera, sit by himself and
enjoy a coffee. He could go find a spot in the library. He could find a
spot in the bar. He could say screw the hundred and twenty-five dollars he's spent for this short story workshop and save some dignity and
admit that he is no kind of artist, that he'll never be anything more than
a pretty good online Marketing Analyst.

"Would you like to sit?" He jumps. An older man with short cropped
gray hair and a Ramones tee shirt gestures at the chair to Lawson's left.

"Sure. Yeah," Lawson says. He sits. He checks his phone. He pulls
out the laptop and a notebook. The guy with the Ramones tee shirt is
wearing headphones, typing away at a laptop. Lawson is embarrassed at
how relieved he is that they do not have to share small talk.

He waits for the laptop to start up and scans the room. Fifteen-
year-old Lawson would have a field day with these people. "Beginning
the short story." It is much too late for most of these people to be learning

about how to begin anything. At the very least, the demographics of the workshop are ironic. Ironic? Ever since Alanis Morissette released that song, he's been a little wary of using that word. He remembers the song and then the parodies of the song and the standup routines and the late-night jokes. Isn't it ironic? Don't you think? If the song's writer didn't know the proper use of the word, who is Lawson to go and try to use it appropriately?

But that was him before, the person who was too scared of failing to even try anything new, the person who somehow went from being an honors English major with a marked-up copy of *A Good Man Is Hard to Find* and a handwritten manuscript in three and a half different note-books to a middle manager who spends most of his time looking at spreadsheets, hoping to tease conclusions and clues and predictions out of data, a person who relaxes by rewatching *Battlestar Galactica*. A person too afraid to even look at those old notebooks, who feels the burn of embarrassment on his cheeks when he thinks about the fact that he has moved them to three increasingly larger apartments without ever opening the box in which they are contained.

And then those assholes won the lottery and it was like all he had been doing just seemed so silly. What would fifteen-year-old, eigh-teen-year-old, twenty-three-year-old Lawson think about his life? The spreadsheets and the online porn and the Lean Cuisines and the fact that he has rewatched *The Wire* in its entirety four times to date?

Almost everybody in this room looks like they are retired. A grand-mother type over there, a schoolteacher type there, three grandmother types chatting by the coffee, two grandfather types talking golf in the corner. A gray-haired man reading the newspaper. Another checking his phone.

All of these people are in their sixties or seventies. Have they all done that much better at saving for retirement?

No, he thinks. More likely they are like his parents, boomers, the Greatest Generation, who just happened to hit the Wall Street tsunami of the nineties tech boom and jump off before it ran into the wall of the recession. His father still can't update his browser but made enough on his 401k to retire early with his Pennsylvania pension.

He opens a new document on his machine. He thinks: Just write. It is six o'clock and there is no sign of the instructor yet. Most people in the room are talking or looking at their phones or typing away on laptops. He wonders what kind of stories they are writing. He remembers those Flannery O'Connor stories. So funny and moving and weird. Flannery O'Connor died when she was thirty-nine. Flannery O'Connor never had to worry about retirement or Google analytics or conversion rates.

He looks around. Lawson lost half his retirement when the housing bust came. He will have to work for ten extra years until he can retire. Seventy, seventy-five, eighty. Is that even possible? And those assholes go and hit the goddamn lottery.

A youngish man comes in the room and walks to the front. He is short and bearded, wearing a black jacket and a Fugazi tee shirt. "Hi everybody, I'm Joe. Let's go ahead and get started," he says.

Lawson folds up his laptop. He thinks about running out. He could go to the coffee shop. He could go to the bar.

"I like to start with a prompt," Joe says. His voice is kind and calm. He looks like a college professor in a soap opera. Lawson relaxes. He opens the laptop and directs his attention to the front of the room.

CRAVER

CRAVER WAKES UP AND KNOWS that something is wrong. What happened last night? Where is he? He rolls over and bumps into a person and then he remembers everything: Indianapolis, Chili's, the waitress.

He rolls carefully out of bed and pauses. What was her name? Aubrey? Carol? Susan? At one point she started comping his drinks and he still has no idea what he did to incur that kindness, but she had straight blond hair and intelligent blue eyes and a slight Midwestern accent and he stopped asking questions fairly early in the process. If he had been chosen, then the best approach was to keep drinking free margaritas and allow whatever hand he had been dealt to play out.

She snores lightly. Her hair is a mass of yellow. Her back is smooth and lovely. He wonders if he will fall in love with her. He imagines them driving across the desert, the neon lights of Las Vegas a hint and then a glow and then they are laughing, looking at each other, shaking their heads at the ridiculous American beauty of it all.

He wonders what Chastain is doing right now. The time difference is, what? An hour. Two hours. It is 9:35. Chastain will be waking up any time now. He should text her. At this point he has taken her silence, the fact that he has sent some two hundred texts and she has not replied once, as a kind of tacit encouragement. She is like a silent partner. A distant father. A coach who breaks you down and then builds you up again. He had considered keeping a journal on this great American road trip, a Kerouacian record of everything he did and saw, but the texts quickly replaced any ambition for actual writing. Texting is writing. Texting is Now's American writing. He can picture it as a multimedia installation: The Great American Road Trip in Texts.

He can see light peeking in from the corners of the Holiday Inn windows, two lumps of clothing on the floor. A bra, jeans, her dark Chili's shirt and apron. A phone buzzes and he wonders if finally Chastain is texting him back, but realizes he is holding his phone. The waitress's phone buzzes again and she pushes further into the covers, pulls the comforter up over her head. He watches the bare skin of her back retreat and wonders if he will have a chance to see it again. It has been a long time since he has been in this situation and he is unsure of the protocols from here. Are there protocols? Are they different in Indianapolis? With the younger people? Are there more rules or less? He is guessing more. Everywhere, there seem to be more.

He checks his phone again and then realizes that he is just standing there, hovering, still staring at the woman's blond hair, the tufts of it that stick out from the comforter. Surely this is creepy behavior. Surely this is not the protocol, whatever the protocol is.

She really is lovely. He could lean over and rub her back, stroke her hair, every color of yellow at once. He could push her into the mattress, quick like a heartbeat, could pull down the covers to reveal whatever she is wearing or not beneath. He could slap her tight backside and pretend he was joking. He could do almost anything.

He moves toward the bathroom. Her phone buzzes again and he leans over to read the display, but with a great sudden effort she pushes out of the comforter's cocoon and sits up. She picks up the phone, reads the screen, hits a button, and puts it back down. "Oh hey," she says. "Where are you headed?"

THE OTHER ONES | **65**

He sits down on the side of the bed, careful to look away from her bare legs on the bedside. He focuses on the television. They are all the same, the Holiday Inn televisions, and he has taken some surprise comfort in the familiarity. "Nowhere," he says. "Bathroom."

"No today, dummy," she says. "Where are you headed today? What great ridiculous tourist attraction are you going to see today?"

Now he remembers. He actually told her the truth about his trip, how it had started one way and quickly devolved into another thing entirely. "Um…" he says.

"You'll text me, though. You'll put me on your list." She stands and walks to the bathroom. She is naked and he feels a quick glimmer of shame for the thrill that runs through his body when he sees her. He sits down on the bed while the water runs. What is the protocol now? Has the introduction of her naked backside changed the equation somehow, reset the situation like a halftime break?

The texting. He told her the whole thing. It seems so stupid now, in the light of day. At the time he had registered himself in some kind of dinner party chat zone, buzzed enough to be uninhibited, sober enough to avoid making an asshole out of himself.

Now he remembers later in the evening, the two of them in a booth at Applebee's, throwing out terms like "new American road trip" and "post-mall America" and "texting is our greatest modern art form." At some point he had realized that throwing "American" in front of almost any word would make her nod and squeeze his hand and laugh and look at him as if he was actually saying something. Now he blushes. His stomach turns. The toilet flushes and he loiters in the corner as she settles back in the bed.

The great American salad bar. The great American all-you-can-eat buffet. The great American hotel snack machine. Jesus, he is an idiot. A faker. A nothing.

She is getting dressed and then she is dressed and Craver sits on the bed, looking out the window into the Great American Holiday Inn Parking Lot.

"So west today still?" she says. He nods. "Okay," she leans over to hug him and he has a rush of her fragrance, something between his mother's expensive perfume and that hippie smell, patchouli. She is taking control of the situation and he is infinitely relieved. He would be writing down his address, making promises, holding out his hand for a businesslike shake. She just pauses at the door and smiles. "Bye!" she says, and then she is gone.

CHASTAIN

CHASTAIN CHECKS HER PHONE. NOTHING.
It has been almost a full day since she's gotten a text from Craver.
Before that, he had been averaging thirty-two a day, photos and song
lyrics and just random thoughts. At first it was cute, then disturbing,
and then she grew to regard it almost as an art project. He had always
talked, after the fourth or fifth beer, about wanting to be a writer, these
dreams he had put away of driving the country like Jack Kerouac, writing and listening to music and having some kind of "pure American
experience."

Sarah appears in the doorway and she slides the phone aside.
"Another one today," she says. "Bilger."

"Bilger?" Chastain says. "Is he the one in ad buys?" She can't picture Bilger.

"Traffic," Sarah says. "Marketing emails."

"And he's…"

"Two weeks' notice."

"So…"

"We run that drill."

Chastain pulls up the human resources site. She is well acquainted with this process by now. "As soon as possible?" she says. But Sarah is already bustling back toward the printer.

She picks up her phone. So strange. He could have gotten in an accident. That is a possibility, especially if he decided to start drinking early. She starts typing a message. But no. She is not sure exactly what they are doing, or what his project is with the texting, but it seems clear that they have established a set of guidelines, at least, and this communication, whatever it is, is intended as one-way.

She opens up the spreadsheet and adds Bilger's name to the list. Their percentage is roughly twenty, but twenty is not bad and the new people are, what is the word Sarah used? Encouraging.

She almost hates to admit it, wonders what Craver would think if he was here, but since moving to work for Sarah she is actually interested in what she's doing. She is happy. Jesus, just thinking it feels absolutely cheesy. Tacky and ridiculous. And still, there it is: she is sitting at work at nine forty-five on a Wednesday and she is happy. Huh.

Gibbons

GIBBONS FINISHES HIS COFFEE AND thinks about going for more. It is eleven, coffee borderlands. He could get another and maybe feel a little too caffeinated for lunch. He could wait it out and have one in the afternoon. He looks at the computer, taps his hand on the desk. He picks up his fidget spinner, a half-in-jest gift from Nancy that he enjoys more than he would ever admit. The little machine feels good in his hand, the pleasant feeling of motion, of solid craftsmanship, the amazing open horizon of possibility in the fact that this machine did not exist a few years ago.

He will get a cup of coffee. That should take up a good fifteen minutes, and then it is just about time to figure out what he will have for lunch. He is relieved to find the kitchen empty. Somehow it seems like Garner is always in there, washing something or other, preparing some kind of elaborately preserved microwave lunch. Gibbons has no idea what to say to him after the lottery. On the one hand, it is admirable that the man came back to work. It says a lot about him, about work, the value of it all and blah blah blah. On the other hand, why not just buy a campground or a sailboat or a ticket on some cruise?

He washes his coffee cup and inserts the K-cup into the Keurig. At first he bemoaned the transition to the little machines but now he enjoys the small ritual, his own version of a Japanese tea ceremony. He runs it through the eight ounce and then adds two Splendas and a creamer and runs the same cup through the four ounce. The machine makes a pleasing hum and then he is sitting back at his desk, hands wrapped around a warm cup of coffee.

He opens his email. Two new messages. Meeting invitation, Slack notification. He opens Slack. He has been tagged in the campaigns channel, a note from Dorsey in Creative. They will not have the ad banners ready for the new deadline. Same old story: capacity issues. There is another note from Jennings in Accounts about the client becoming impatient. They are all being very polite but he can read between the lines. He will need to set up a meeting and let Lawson know what is going on before anything blows up.

He could go to the mall, the food court. The Asian salad place—California something?—has a great Chinese chicken salad. The pizza place is actually good, much better than you would expect from mall pizza. He could drive into town and get a gyro, or pho, or a fancy sandwich at the place by the Taco Bell.

He looks behind him, scans the cube aisles, and opens up Instagram. He doesn't really understand Instagram other than it is not quite Twitter and not quite Facebook and mostly pictures, but the chicken place by the grocery store posts their specials there every day. He leans back, checks the aisle. There seem to be very few people in the office lately.

The heart of the ship, the heart of the ship, you are working in the heart of the ship.

He could go to the sub place, but parking is a mess. He could go to the burrito place but it will be jammed with students. He could go to the Chinese place but he finds it to be kind of desultory during the day. He could go to the hippie coffee shop but if they don't have veggie chili today, he will have to panic order and last time he did that he wound up with some kind of paste and vegetables that were delicious but he was so hungry he had to stop and buy a gas station meatball sub halfway back to the office. He could go to the Korean but it is expensive, the Indian but it seems like a place you should go with other people, the burger place but it is next to the sub place and same issue with parking.

A Slack message appears on the campaigns channel, Creative pushing back on Accounts. One more message and supervisors will be added, the whole thing will blow up into something that gets to Lawson and maybe even Sarah.

He has Instagram up on the desktop. Thursday special: boneless chicken breast medallions in your choice of sauce over brown rice and quinoa with spicy broccoli. The chicken place it is.

He checks his email. Nothing. He checks the calendar again. Two to four in room 5 a/b.

The fastest thing will be to post to Slack, spray some water over this thing before it blooms into an all-out fire. "Hey guys," he posts. "Totally get both sides and we will definitely figure this out. Tough times and I know everybody gets it on up the chain." Good to recognize what was about to happen, but this is really for Lawson when and if this whole thing gets escalated. He is demonstrating belief in his supervisors, in their ability to recognize the difficult situation and work with everybody to come up with solutions. "Will get a meeting scheduled asap so we can talk this through in person."

They have the best sauce at the chicken place, kind of Asian but not straight sriracha, kind of American but not straight buffalo, something different and buttery and sweet and spicy all at once. He clicks submit, picks up his keys, and walks for the side stairs.

Robertson

ROBERTSON ROUNDS THE CORNER AND
stops. He nearly drops his coffee and smiles, thinking about what a
cliché that would be, what a sitcom move. Be cool, he thinks. He probably just wants to talk. He nods and walks to his workstation, notes the
screen has gone to black. He had been half-finished configuring a virtual machine and Garner just wouldn't stop talking in the break room
and now he is timed out. His notes sit off to the side.

"Make yourself at home," Robertson says. He sits in the guest chair,
the one nobody ever sits in.

Chad Stephenson is pecking at his phone. "Sorry," he says. "One
minute."

Robertson reaches across the cube and wiggles the mouse. He types
in his password.

"Sorry," Chad Stephenson says.

Robertson's work is still on the screen. He clicks save and sits back
down in the guest chair.

"How can I help you?" he says.

Chad Stephenson taps at his phone and turns toward Robertson.

"Andre?" he says. "I'm Chad."

"I saw you the other day," Robertson says. "I get it."

Chad Stephenson smiles. Robertson has the feeling that he's about to make the namaste hands and he doesn't know if he'll be able to contain his contempt for the gesture. "Cool," Chad Stephenson says. "Very cool." Up close, he is older than Robertson had taken him for in the All Staff Check-In meeting. His hair is dyed an unnatural dark brown, the hair color of college football coaches and state senators. There are lines around his eyes, his mouth, the skin pulled tight. Today he is dressed, again, in his Steve Jobs cosplay outfit: black pullover and jeans, New Balance sneakers.

"So you're here to…" Robertson says. He has four more virtual machines to set up this morning.

Chad Stephenson leans back and crosses his legs. Robertson figures he is dying for him to comment on the New Balance sneakers and he wishes he didn't know what brand of shoes Steve Jobs wore, but there it is.

"My job is simple," Chad Stephenson says. Robertson has the feeling he is about to give a monologue he has given many times before. If he reaches under Chad Stephenson's shirt, he wonders if he will find a TED Talk lanyard. "All I do is watch." He pauses for effect and Robertson understands that he is to give Chad Stephenson a push here that will get him to the next part.

"Really?" Robertson says, hating himself the minute the words come out of his mouth. He should be throwing Chad Stephenson out of his work space but instead he is lobbing alley-oops, prolonging this whole…whatever this is.

"I just watch," Chad Stephenson says. "And I listen. But mostly I watch."

Again, he pauses. This is the point where he would walk from one side of the TED Talk stage to the other, leave his audience waiting for the turn into unexpected wisdom. Robertson watches the screen behind Chad Stephenson go dark again. "I really need to…" he says.

Chad Stephenson sits up and braids his hands together in one fist. It is better than the namaste hands, Robertson thinks. "And when you watch," Chad Stephenson says, "you see."

"Right," Robertson says. "Cool. Hey I really have to make some virtual…"

"You see who is in, and who is out. You know what I mean?" Chad Stephenson says. "And let me tell you, what happened here? This? There are a whole lot of people who are out. Checked out. Punched out. Left out." He pauses, looks Robertson right in the eye. "Out!" he says, practically shouting.

Robertson nods. It is the most accurate, interesting thing the man has said. "So you noticed that, huh?" he says.

Chad Stephenson sits up. "But not you," he says. "You are still here. Present. And that is…" He gestures to the chair, wiggles the mouse, and the screen comes back on. "That is interesting." He stands and waves at the chair.

Robertson sits down and swivels to watch Chad Stephenson striding out of his work area. He stops and turns around. He makes the namaste hands and Robertson wonders if Chad Stephenson can read his mind, if he is being gaslit, trolled. "We will talk again soon," Chad Stephenson says. He winks, points his hands at the screen behind Robertson. "Better get going on those virtual machines," he says.

Yoder

YODER WAKES UP ON HIS feet again. It is dark. Night. He is in a kitchen. Why always a kitchen? He leans against the counter and takes stock. His Achilles tendons ache. He can feel his arms, his chest, his penis, legs, but he cannot see them. In the movies, ghosts are always able to see themselves at least, even if others can't. Another bullshit expectation they programmed into him at some time or another.

His life. He had tried to be a good person. He worked hard, did his best. Sure, he drank a little too much, but what harm did that do anybody, a forty-five-, fifty-, fifty-nine-year-old bachelor drinking boxed wine in an apartment by himself. In the end it was all bullshit. Every diet, salad, trip to the gym, new car, report, project, performance review. What did it all get him? He is a ghost in some stranger's kitchen, some asshole who probably won the lottery.

Whose kitchen? This one seems modest, normal, orderly, no beer cans or bottles of tequila along the counter, no dishes in the sink, no Best Buy or Amazon boxes lining the walls. Just a normal kitchen owned by apparently normal people. On the refrigerator there are two pictures. He gets up close enough to see. Corgis. Jesus Christ, he is in Garner's house.

It is midnight. All is quiet. No music or shouting or four-wheelers. He walks into the living room. Again, nothing. Just a normal living room. He wonders how many emails Garner sent about the lottery, how many tickets he bought, scanned, emailed out to his little group with the note that started "When we win…"

Yoder sits down on the couch. From somewhere down a hallway, he hears a dog whimper and then bark. Could it be true that animals can sense him, or even see him? The couch looks like leather but it feels like plastic. Fucking Garner. Maybe he can get himself something other than a pleather couch now that he's a goddamn millionaire. Is it better or worse that Garner hasn't apparently gone on some kind of asshole spending spree? Cowens with his KISS Kruise, Pappas with his virtual reality headsets, Mowery with his four-wheelers and sad indoor hot tub. And Garner is sitting on his plastic couch watching a twenty-two-inch television.

It is worse. Much worse. Who the fuck does Garner think he is? He was always quiet, polite, a little weird, nerdy enough that even Yoder felt kind of sorry for him with his flip phone and belt buckles and center-parted hair. He was good enough at his job. Reliable. Yoder always thought there was something else there, though, some kind of condescension buried deep behind those "how you doings" and "looking forward to the weekends."

He remembers exactly when he stopped playing the lottery, the day after his fiftieth birthday, the invitation from AARP sitting on the kitchen table. He had been purposefully neglecting to do the math until then, but with fifty behind him it seemed finally time to see how he was positioned for retirement. Maybe he was a little hungover. Maybe still a little drunk. He had a feeling about what the numbers were going to look like, a buried pulse of hope that they were going to be better than he could have imagined. He plugged his savings to date, plus the retirement, plus his age and location into the calculator. He did it again. Googled and found another retirement calculator and did it again. They all returned the same result.

He broke into a cold sweat and then a deep blush. His glasses fogged. He didn't shout or go lash out at somebody's Internet comment.

He just sat there, wiping his glasses and looking at the numbers on the screen. He would be able to retire in forty years. At the age of ninety. It was the first time he thought about killing himself. He googled it quickly and then closed the page, wiped his history clean, bought a box of wine and had his first glass with lunch.

From there he focused on saving, paying down credit cards, getting rid of unnecessary luxuries. He downgraded his boxed wine, started buying Dockers from the Goodwill, cut out even the two dollars here or there to play the office lottery.

And now Garner doesn't even have the good sense to go and get himself a new goddamn couch? There is a plastic vase on the coffee table, dog magazines stacked neatly. Yoder throws the vase against the wall and it makes a hollow knock and then bounces into the kitchen. From down the hall he can hear the dogs going crazy, their high-pitched bark and whine, and then Garner speaking calmly. The door opens and Yoder freezes. He checks again to make sure he is invisible. A ghost. A whatever.

The dogs are fussy and cute, fuzzy, with little stumpy legs. They move through the room, sniffing, their noses ticking up and down. Garner follows. He is wearing a bathrobe and slippers, rubbing at his eyes. "Okay guys. See? Nothing here," he says. The dogs circle the room. One hurries into the kitchen and the other stops near Yoder. It turns to look right at him. It sniffs, turns its head, and then barks. Yoder backs up. He takes his feet off the floor and sits on top of the plastic top of the plastic couch. "Really, Hermione?" Garner says. "Barking at ghosts again?" He turns to the kitchen. "Come on, Harry. Back to bed."

Of course Garner would name his dogs Harry Potter names. Hermione continues to stare right at him. He waves a hand and her attention stays in the same place. She can't see him but she knows something is there. Interesting.

Garner pats her head. "Come on, girl," he says. "Back to the big bed."

The dog continues staring. She barks. Yoder is just about to reach out and touch her when Garner takes control of her collar and leads her down the hall. They walk past the vase.

CRAVER

THE ROOM IS THE SAME as the room always is. A small comfort but a comfort nonetheless. He puts the bag down, closes the blinds. He lays on the bed. His feet are starting to ache. His butt itches and he will need to check the rash. Too much time in the car. He will need to take a day off here or there. But to do what?

The blinds are green and he knows they will be rough to the touch. In the corner, a small table and chair, the Wi-Fi and the number of the front desk in a hard plastic stand. In the bathroom there will be four large towels, two small, two washcloths. There will be a bar of soap, still in the green wrapper, small bottles of shampoo and conditioner.

He realizes he hasn't spoken to anybody other than to place a food order or say thank you since Indianapolis. "Thank you," he says. The words are flat, his voice scratchy. "How are you doing? Yeah? Me? I'm just…well, it's an interesting story…"

He checks his phone. Baby pictures baby pictures dogs meals vacations. No email. No texts. He wonders what Chastain is doing. He could probably still check his work email, since he technically never quit. He wonders how long they would have paid him, but also doesn't really want to see how much he has remaining in the bank account. The card still works. He has evolved a plan over the past few days to just let everything dry up, the bank account, credit cards, whatever other strings he has left hanging. Let it all dry up and die and start over in San Francisco. Maybe he will get a job as some kind of laborer. Hard, honest work. The ending to *Office Space* always just made a certain kind of sense.

He puts his finger over the Outlook icon on the phone. Surely nothing has even changed. He would only see the same old meeting invitations and notices about the shared refrigerator in the break room. He pictures Garner waddling down the hall, his phone strapped to his belt, his pockets stuffed full of god knows what.

Did I play? Garner is many things, but disorganized is not one of them. And still, he flashes on the email: "Re: Lottery." Jesus Christ he never even really checked, other than a brief glance at Garner's handwritten paper in the conference room while the rest of those assholes danced around and slurped their dumb American macrobrew.

He didn't even question it. If he's being honest, he was more interested in getting drunk with Chastain, sharing that first cigarette, counting beers to see if she would get drunk enough to make out with him.

Did I play? Eight point eight million dollars and I just took the word of a middle-aged man with a cell phone strapped to his belt?

He opens the curtain and looks out at the parking lot. A family is getting out of a van, unloading bags, shouting at their children about one thing or another. At least he is on his own, no responsibilities to anybody for anything.

"Re: Lottery." He can picture the subject line. He should have double-checked. He could still do it now, assuming they haven't disabled his account. He clicks on the Outlook button and realizes that he is holding his breath. "Account inactive: check with your administrator if you believe this is in error."

So they did disable his account. So it's really over, that job. That part of his life. He exhales. He could ask Chastain if she can get into his old emails, or maybe she could talk to that young kid in IT, the one who always seemed embarrassed to be working at Keystone. Outside, the father has stacked all the bags in a neat row. The mother kneels, talking to the youngest child while the other two wait, staring at the luggage like they're standing at a baggage claim.

The woman is good-looking, about his age. The father is boyish, wearing cargo shorts with a cell phone attached at his side. He looks like a youth pastor or Little League baseball coach. The woman stands. She is slim, brunette. She could pass for Chastain's slightly older sister. When he thinks of Chastain, he always thinks of the time at Kirkpatrick's wedding when she wore thigh highs and he got a brief glimpse as she leaned over to pick up a spoon. The dark top of the sheer black stocking, the promise of what was even further up the leg.

He stares at the Outlook app. He never even really checked. Certainly there are ways to find out. Nothing is ever really lost in the cloud, everything is permanent, even as it disappears with each click and tap. Chastain should have made him check. She was always a little better with technology. She could still find the emails, but is there anything to find? Eight point eight million dollars.

The family outside has finally started shouldering their bags. The mother carries one duffel across her back, the strap pressing in between her breasts. She is beautiful and haggard. Her breasts are slightly larger than Chastain's, but he was never attracted for that reason. Still. He watches as she makes slow progress across the parking lot. He looks at the phone. Account deactivated. Eight point eight million dollars. He considers smashing the phone against the cheap desk, throwing it across the room. He can hear the quick smash, feel the release. But he needs the phone, he needs Siri and the Google Lady to tell him how to proceed to the route, proceed to the route, proceed to the route. The texting project is stupid, but it is the only thing telling him this trip is anything but a boondoggle, a terrible mistake or a midlife crisis.

He takes the plastic Wi-Fi stand and pulls the sides apart. They stretch and he finally puts it over his knee, presses until he feels a satisfying snap. The pieces fall to the floor. He crumbles the card. Outside, the family has almost disappeared beneath him. He could walk downstairs, pretend to be asking about the Wi-Fi. He could pass her, see what she looks like up close, see if she wears the same perfume as Chastain. He stands, puts his phone in his pocket. He walks to the door. He pauses, tosses his phone on the bed, and lays back down.

russell

RUSSELL PARKS AND LOOKS AROUND. He
is starting to feel less sure of the whole thing. It is supposed to be a lark,
a celebration, a memorial to Yoder and his friendship, to the way he was
misunderstood by the rest of them, something about the way the man
was able to maintain his dignity, his sense of humor, even a modicum of
confidence as he got older and the office and the rest of the world got
younger all around him. The both of them. Now, sitting in the car, staring at the elementary school, empty and quiet on a Saturday afternoon,
with cars driving by on the road behind him, a woman walking a dog
across the road, he is not so sure.

He imagines Yoder stepping off that roof. What was it like at
the very end, that step and then falling, flying, the ground growing
closer, and then what? Quiet? Nothing? Heaven or hell or some way
station?

He thinks about the pack of cigarettes in the glove compartment.
But that wouldn't do. Ginny would smell them on his breath, on his
clothes. Somehow he has lived through the era where everybody was
smoking all the time and into this new one where even the smell of a

single cigarette will announce the perpetrator as some kind of deviant, a threat to the public health.

He steps out of the car, pulls the duffel bag from the back seat, takes the baseball bat lying on the floor. It has been years, decades since he held a baseball bat in his hands. The last time would have been Billy's Little League, the eighties. Even procuring this bat felt ridiculous. So many things feel ridiculous now. He searched the garage for hours, sure that some of the old sporting goods would still be there. He could picture a bin full of gear, footballs and lacrosse sticks and baseball bats. But it simply was not to be found. Maybe that time they cleaned out the whole garage after Billy graduated from college, preparing to be empty nesters by cleaning the nest, or at least that is how the joke went at the time.

The bats at Dick's Sporting Goods seemed too expensive and were autographed by people he had never heard of, or who he pictured as twenty-year-old phenoms, too young to be doing something like selling autographed bats. At Walmart he found a normal one, just a good old baseball bat. It seemed weird to be buying just the bat, so he added some turkey pepperoni and a glue gun, but the cashier of course didn't even notice and soon he was on his way.

The bat feels good in his hand, solid. He walks up the hill to the playground behind the school. There is nobody here, as he anticipated, but the school doesn't offer as much cover as he imagined, and he can still see cars rolling along the road, the backyards of several houses that abut the playground. He is just a man with a bat and a duffel bag, headed toward the baseball field. Nothing ridiculous about this at all.

His plantar fasciitis is acting up and the dull pain is worse on the uneven ground. Yoder was always complaining about his Achilles tendons, was resigned to some kind of operation sometime in the next few years. Well, that is one thing he won't have to worry about anymore, one of about a thousand, he guesses.

Russell pauses and looks around. He is in between the baseball field and the playground. The backyards are empty. He is far enough from the road that probably nobody will notice. What he is doing isn't illegal anyway, he reminds himself. Just strange.

When he thinks about Yoder, he remembers a particular moment when they had been talking in the office kitchen, Yoder waiting for his Keurig coffee to be ready. "How many years left, do you think?" Yoder had asked with a quick glance to be sure they were alone.

"Years?" Russell said.

"Until?"

Just then Sarah had come in and started chatting with Yoder in her professional way, friendly but not too friendly, always with a bit of distance between her and the employee, a bit of premeditation in her casual banter.

Russell still isn't sure what the question was but he assumes it was retirement. Four years, four months, eighteen days until he is sixty-five. Not that he is counting. Not that there is any way he could ever actually retire at sixty-five. He wonders how far Yoder was and then realizes that this is one more thing Yoder won't have to worry about anymore.

He opens the duffel and holds the laptop. God, it is heavy. Heavy for these times, at least. Russell remembers when they got computers on every desk—small monitors with deep bellies, like squat aliens, floor units with less computing power than the phone in his pocket. He places the laptop on the ground and picks up the baseball bat. In the movie, it is a printer and there is rap music playing, one of the characters going kind of crazy, losing it, shouting at the machine as he assaults it with the baseball bat. He would not like for there to be rap music playing, but maybe some heavy metal. He could queue up some AC/DC or Led Zeppelin on his phone while he takes his whacks.

But no, that would seem even more ridiculous if somebody were to happen on this scene. He picks up the bat. "Well, old friend," he says, and then pauses. Well what? He had imagined that he would be feeling more emotion right now, that this would all feel right. He taps the laptop with the bat. He jabs straight down. Nothing, not even a mark. He rounds up and takes a full swing. The bat rebounds off the machine and pain shoots into his fingers, his arm. He winds up and does it again. The top of the laptop has come askew. He swings again. He is starting to sweat, can hear his breath in his ears, ragged and raw. He really needs to go back to the gym.

He swings and hits the laptop at a wrong angle and recoil shoots through his fingers, up his right arm, into his shoulder and neck. He drops the bat and walks away. Motherfucker. He rubs his neck, his fingers. This is not a good idea. If he wakes up tomorrow with back spasms, he will be out of it for a week. He pauses. The houses behind the playground are nice. He wonders if they were purchased for their proximity to the school, whether the people who live there now are empty nesters like him and Ginny, really trying to fill that gap, never quite doing it, mostly feeling like they are holding off for some ill-defined future event. Retirement? Death? Christmas vacation? A week at a condo in Ocean City, Maryland?

This would be much more fun, he thinks, if Yoder was here. Yoder did have a knack for making even the regular bullshit just a little more fun, didn't he? Did he? He pictures that funeral, the few of them who made it to the church, the fewer more standing in the rain in the cemetery. That was when he decided he would actually do this, send Yoder, Yoder's machine, at least, out the way they had planned.

He winds up and takes another whack at the computer. The laptop jumps, lifts off the ground. It feels good. "Yes," Russell whispers. He stalks a few steps away from the machine. He remembers when his body used to do what he wanted it to do, when he was younger, in his teens and twenties and even thirties. The forties were when things started going stiff, awry, when he popped a muscle in his calf playing basketball, and then the bursitis in the elbow, the back spasms and then all of a sudden it seemed like he couldn't jog anymore, like his legs were going numb.

The laptop is separated into two parts now, opened up like a clam. He is making progress. He swings, and finally there is a satisfying crunch as he smashes the monitor. He swings at the keyboard and small pieces of plastic go flying. He thinks about Yoder standing in the kitchen, waiting for his Keurig, walking down the hallway, sitting on the sidelines of their many, many meetings and waiting for his turn, keeping his mouth shut, getting slightly fatter and grayer and very slowly vanishing into thin air one day, one meeting, one shitty cup of office coffee at a time.

He pauses and leans on the bat, like a major leaguer waiting for his turn in the rotation. The laptop is demolished, bits and pieces, wires and circuits, and what he guesses is a motherboard. Funny how much it looks like something that would be called a motherboard. He had pictured himself saying something, something funny and wise and resolved, something worthy of the way Yoder made his way in the world despite the fact that he was vanishing, that they are all vanishing in very small ways every minute. But he cannot think of anything. He realizes now that he did not bring a garbage bag. He starts to walk away but the idea of schoolchildren finding this, of teachers wondering if it had belonged to the school, an investigation, scuttlebutt, he cannot live with any of those things. He bends down. His back aches. God if he has thrown his back out doing this. He picks up the pieces and puts them back in the bag. He makes his way to the car.

Robertson

"THEY PUT YOU ON A what committee?" Jessie pauses
the game, looks at him. She chortles, a sound he wasn't sure he could
identify until he actually heard it.

"That was a chortle," Robertson says.

"A chortle committee?"

"That would be much better," he says. He lets his backpack drop
on the floor, settles into the beanbag chair. The thing has always been
better in theory than practice but he needs to just be for a while, lay back
and let it all go, and the beanbag chair, with its retro lack of effort in
general, looks about right for once.

Jessie flicks a finger and the game starts up again. Her character is moving down a well-lit corridor, fluorescent lights overhead.
Characters walk by in business clothes. "So, this chortle committee,"
she says.

"Employee Visioning and Vision Board Development Executive
Core Team," he says.

She stops, looks at him. Her eyes are wide open like a cartoon character. On the screen, her character is losing power as more people hurry

past. They are all wearing suits. "What kind of game is this?" he says. "Is this a beta?"

"Employee. Vision. Board. Committee," she says.

"Ing," he says.

"Ing?"

"Vision-ing. And Vision Board Development. Executive Core Team."

"Is there a junior Core Team?"

"Not that I know of."

"What the actual…" she says.

"Right?" he says. He has no call to be embarrassed, but there it is, sweat dripping down his back, his glasses starting to fog up.

"So…" Jessie says. She starts up on the screen again and her character moves forward. It stops and hands something to somebody, and then she keeps on going.

"It's this consultant," Robertson says. "These consultants they brought in. I guess it's like a morale thing?"

"But what does it actually mean? And why you, if you don't mind me asking? I mean, you're a sys admin. You know this."

He looks at the ceiling, notices again how the tiles are not quite right, the tracking slightly off. "We are to…hold on, you're actually not going to believe this." He has placed the mission statement in his pocket for exactly this purpose. He unfolds it and reads. "Mission: The Employee Visioning and Vision Board Executive Core Team will motivate our Keystone partners—oh, we're not employees anymore, we're partners—to reach their potential through the visioning of the positive future of the partner and the organization in a way that emboldens without embalming our own unique skill sets."

"What the…"

"Pretty sure the emboldens without embalming part is copyrighted, by the way. It has one of those little things next to it. They seemed pretty happy with that part."

"So what does this actually mean, though?"

"Today…oh Jesus, you are going to chortle again."

"I'm past chortling," she says.

Onscreen, a character with a mustache and eighties glasses has stopped to address Jessie's character. He points a finger and speaks rapidly. She has the sound turned down. "What game is this?" he says again.

"Office Mail," she says. "It's in beta. Daryll made it. So far I can't quite figure it out, but that's part of the deal."

"Office Mail," he says.

"So what did you do today with your vision board committee?" she says. "Excuse me. Vision-ing."

He had been looking forward to this, telling her about how ridiculous it all is, but this is not turning out to be as much fun as he thought. He is not sure why he is humiliated. He should be everything but. He did not choose this. They chose him. In particular, for some reason, Chad Stephenson chose him. That might even be a good thing, if he cared.

"What did you do? Did you go on a vision quest?" She grabs the controller again. Her character hands something to the angry man—mail, he realizes, letters and folders. The words "Interoffice Mail" pop up on the screen. The registers that track her power and accomplishment ratings go up ten points.

"You will not believe what we actually did." She moves the character down the hall, takes a right turn, and she is in some kind of kitchen or…a break room. Refrigerators and soda machines. "Is that…" he starts.

"Hahaha yeah, a cigarette machine," she says. "I take it we're in the eighties. Or the seventies?"

"Eighties," he says. "I think some *Wall Street* action going on here. The movie."

"What I thought," she says. "Daryll loves that movie for some reason."

He might as well get it over with before she gets further down the weird rabbit hole of this game. Daryll has always been in love with Jessie. Everybody has always been a little in love with Jessie. "They gave us magazines. They told us to cut out pictures. To envision our positive futures."

She pauses again. At least he has her attention now. "Your positive futures? Wait, like hard-copy magazines?"

"We cut out pictures that portrayed our positive futures," he says.

"You made a collage," she says.

He sighs. Onscreen, the angry boss from the hallway has entered the break room. He wants to just be quiet and watch Jessie figure out how to beat Office Mail. Daryll's game is good, he admits to himself. Really good, down to the details of the man's glasses, his boxy frame and Rolex and white collar, the way he follows you into the break room and smiles. "And then we glued them to our personal vision boards," he says.

"Oh. My. God," she says. "Can I see it?"

He congratulates himself on seeing this one coming and also stuffing the vision board into the garbage can at the 7-Eleven. "No," he says. "No, you can definitely not see my vision board."

"But what was on it? I'm honestly curious. What does your positive future look like?"

"Better than yours, I guess," he says, pointing at the screen, where the angry boss is again lecturing the mail carrier. "What's going on there?" he says. The angry boss is holding a small whip. "Daryll is getting his freak on here," he says.

"We're not done," Jessie says. "I'm going to hear what was on that board." She turns to the game and backs slowly out of the break room. The angry boss smiles and cracks the whip on his open hand.

Lawson

LAWSON ORDERS THE USUAL AND checks his phone. No emails. No texts. It took him ten minutes to drive to the diner, so he is not really sure what he is expecting. He opens the laptop, turns it on, returns his attention to the phone. Facebook is the usual mix of kid pictures and outrage. He rarely posts and doesn't understand the algorithm that delivers his college roommate's child's graduation, his high school basketball teammate's political indignation, his neighbor's marathon training to his iPhone, but he is occasionally glad for the distraction. Right now, with the computer glowing and ready, practically panting like an expectant dog, is one of those times.

He scrolls past photos and articles and posts like cries for help, for attention, affirmation, whatever, and then he sees it: "Local Man Organizes Winning Lottery Effort, Then Goes Back to Work a Millionaire." And there is Garner, smiling, standing outside the office with his Dockers and golf shirt, his phone attached to his belt. He is a doofus but a millionaire doofus who Sarah has made very clear is very welcome at the office right now, with all the other lottery winners gone, Craver in the wind, Yoder dead, productivity and morale down across the board. Even Sarah, the most competent person he has ever met, has had to call in for outside help. Another check in the column for her competence, although he must admit he has no faith whatsoever in Stephenson and Associates or this ridiculous Visioning Activity they seem to have sold everybody else on.

He closes Facebook. Checks Twitter. More outrage, less babies. He follows his high school and college friends, some rock accounts, some web analytics accounts. It is funny how analytics is constantly changing, not just what they are doing but the way they are doing it. The only way to maintain any kind of mastery, or even bare competence, is to continually evolve. His father was an accountant and he wonders if he got the same satisfaction from tax codes, income statements, whatever it was that the old man did exactly. He wishes again he had had more time, that he had asked the questions. Their conversations had devolved to complaining about the Phillies and Penn State football and then the heart attack and that was it.

He clicks on an article about secondary key performance indicators, written by a woman he had seen speak at a conference a few years earlier. This is something he's been talking about in a low-key way, looking for an opportunity to introduce the concept. The computer glows and then goes black. He closes the phone, clicks on the laptop. Don't get distracted, he thinks. You are here to write.

"You ready?" It is the waitress, an older woman who has waited on him before but never seems to recognize him. He is not sure whether to be glad of the anonymity or resentful that he has never merited regular status.

He orders and returns to the laptop. Joe has given them a prompt, two lines of a song Lawson is not hip enough to have heard before: "He's got the pages in his pockets that he ripped out of the Bible from the bedstand in the motel." It seems like a poorly constructed sentence, and not much like song lyrics, but he thinks he understands why Joe would have given them this exercise. "Take it anywhere you want," he said. "Get weird. Get normal. Get your yayas out." Joe seems like a kind man. Lawson googled him, of course, before he signed up for the course, and his publication credits seemed impressive, especially for somebody in this town, teaching adults through the library. Some literary

magazines Lawson may have heard of before, a collection of short stories, an association with a small press with a purposefully obscure name.

Lawson settles in front of the machine. He writes, "He's got the
pages in his pockets that he ripped out of the Bible from the bedstand
in the motel." There. It does feel better, having something to start with,
a not-entirely blank page glowing up at him. They are to write something more than five hundred words and less than a thousand. "Flash
fiction" is the phrase Joe used. "Just get started," he said. "Write words.
What you need for short fiction is a person in a situation, so think of
the sentence you have and imagine a person in a situation. Then write."

Lawson puts his hands on the keyboard. It sounds so simple. A
person in a situation. "He's got the pages in his pockets that he ripped
out of the Bible from the bedstand in the motel." He imagines a man,
older, hungover, sitting on the subway.

His food arrives. "Need anything else?" the waitress asks, and she
is gone before he answers, which is well enough. A person in a situation. He takes a bite of his club sandwich. The idea of secondary key
performance indicators is interesting, counterintuitive by name even:
secondary key performance indicators. The woman at the conference
had been impressive, funny and smart and thoughtful. He can still picture her: about his age, long hair, a black suit.

He picks up the phone and then puts it back down. Focus. You are
here to write. A person in a situation. He takes another bite of the sandwich. A person in a situation. "The subway car lurches and stops," he
writes. Subway car. Is that right? He deletes car.

He stares out at the diner. A family, a few old men at the counter,
the old waitress refilling coffees.

That article was kind of interesting, though. What would their
secondary key performance indicators be? Are they talking about remar-
keting? Returning visitors? Performance indicators of the lifespan of the
engagement? They have been too focused on lead generation, he thinks,
and only in a very specific way. There are a thousand ways a person
might become a lead, a thousand different ways to measure the indicators that something is happening on their site, in their database, in the
world. He closes the laptop. He opens the phone.

CHASTAIN

CHASTAIN SCANS THE BAR. NOBODY who meets the description, but she has been fooled by the description before. She checks her phone. A man walks in the door and looks her way. She fixes her attention on the sidewalk behind him, people walking by on their way to one place or another. The man continues on and sits down at a table with a few others. She checks her phone.

In the corner of the restaurant, a shout goes up: "Keep 'em coming, honey!" She recognizes the voice but can't place it. She searches her mind. General displeasure registers. The voice belongs to somebody she does not like. She considers bailing. She can text…what was his name? Something vaguely old-fashioned. Stan. She can text Stan and say she doesn't feel well, had to go home.

"One for the bar! I always wanted to do that," the voice bursts out to a round of laughter. She checks her watch. Five. Who is that voice? She is starting to place it. She leans back and checks. Jesus Christ. It is Pappas and Cowens and two women she recognizes from the print shop they used to do the brochures last year. She pops back up before they can see her. This is untenable. She starts texting.

"Jennifer? Jen?" A man is standing there. He is tall, blond, with kind eyes and acne pocks on his cheeks. "I'm sorry, are you…"

"Stan?" she says.

"Everything okay?" he says. "May I sit down?"

"A gentleman," she says, and smiles. "Of course. It's just…"

"Those guys over there giving you trouble?"

"No. Yes. Well, I mean, I know them."

"Anything I can…"

She finishes her drink, motions to the bartender. "What can I get you?" she asks.

He nods, as if he has considered something and assented. "I like it," he says. "Beer. Whatever."

"Two more," she says, pointing to her amber ale.

"So those guys," Stan says.

"It's actually interesting," she says, thinking of Sarah, the discussions they've had about morale, numbers, the need to move on but recognize that something significant and very unsettling has indeed happened to all of them. Those are the words Sarah has chosen to describe the lottery—significant and very unsettling—and in her mind Chastain has chosen that as the name of the book she will write about the event and its aftermath. "Or maybe it's not interesting. I don't know. I'm kind of in the middle of this whole thing right now."

"Whole thing?" Stan sips his beer. "Nice. Thanks. So, a whole thing with those guys?"

"Kind of." She takes a deep drink of her own beer. "You remember that group that won the lottery?"

"Lucky bastards," he says. "Of course. Jesus. Oh, sorry if that…"

She waves him off. "So those idiots over there are two of those lucky bastards. And I used to work with them."

"Holy shit," he says.

"Right?" she says. "I used to work with all of them. That whole group, it was a work thing. My work."

"And you didn't…"

"I did not."

"Holy shit," he says again. He takes a drink.

"It's actually interesting?"

He smiles. She takes note of his jeans and his shirt. Normal. Grown-up. Normal coolish grown-up. "Interesting? That's not what I thought you were going to say."

"My boss is the person who runs this department. The whole branch of the company, really. She's, well, she's pretty incredible, and I've been able to watch her try to move on from this, dealing with it, with, like, all of it. There's a lot of it to deal with—first of all, they all quit except this one idiot. So that's thirteen jobs to fill right there with the millionaires."

"Eight point eight million a piece, right?"

"Oh god and the guy who killed himself. You heard about that I'm sure."

"Off the building?"

"Off the roof while those idiots were celebrating in a conference room."

"Oh god, I'm sorry," he says. They both drink from their beers. She feels comfortable and registers this as a surprising fact, a check in a column.

"So the part where it's, what did you say? Interesting?"

"So," she says. "Bam, fifteen percent of our capacity is gone. But then there are the ones who didn't win the lottery. They're all kinds of… all kinds of…"

"Fucked up?" he says.

She puts a hand on his arm. "Thank you. They are all kinds of fucked up."

"But not you."

She considers this. It is a question she hasn't asked herself since she started working for Sarah. She flashes on that night with Craver at the bar, in bed hungover the day after, at being so surprised to see other people in the office the day after that. Ever since she started working for Sarah, she's actually been pretty happy to go into work. "No. Actually. No, I'm not fucked up."

"But everybody else is," he says. He finishes his beer, waves at the bartender for another.

"So fucked up," she says, and they both laugh. From the corner, she hears Cowens shout, "Turn it up!"

"So what do you do? Why has it been interesting?"

"Well, that's the thing. We have to fill these jobs, right? But also we have to assess our capacity, figure out what we're going to do, what we can't do, what we can cancel, and what we can postpone. We have to fill those positions with even better people who aren't idiots who play the lottery. And in the meantime we have all these fucked-up people who are just kind of bumming around all day, googling 'chances of winning the lottery' and trying to stay off social media so they don't have to see all the stupid bullshit their work buddies are buying with their eight point eight million dollars."

"And you're helping." She likes the way he says it. Warm, solid. It makes her feel like she is actually doing something. Is she actually doing something? Is she helping?

"I guess so," she says.

Gibbons

GIBBONS PUTS DOWN HIS COFFEE and drops his bag on the chair. He has sixteen new emails. He scans the cubicle entrance and then the aisle. He opens up a browser. The fantasy football draft is in four weeks. He is pretty sure he has added the date and time to the Google calendar but he checks anyway and there it is. He is ready. Well, ready but not ready.

He unplugs the laptop from the charging station and turns his chair around so he is facing the cubicle entrance. He can sit this way, with the computer on his lap and his legs up on the desk, a position that is mostly uncomfortable but will allow him to get a half hour or so with the computer turned away from the doorway, enough time that he can at least do some initial research on quarterbacks. His strategy of choosing a solid but not flashy veteran on a middling team in the later rounds backfired dramatically last year and he is going to need to rethink the whole deal if he is going to beat Carlton or Phillips or at least stay ahead of Myers this year.

He scans the doorway out of habit, googles "fantasy quarterback rankings" and then he hears them, Sarah and Lawson and somebody else—the consultants? He closes the window, swivels as quickly as possible, and is reconnecting to the charging station when they walk by, talking quickly, Sarah laughing at something Chad Stephenson says. Lawson gives him a wave and they are gone. Was the consultant really dressed up like the guy from Apple again? Could that be?

Gibbons waits while the machine connects. That was not wise. What was he even thinking? There are consultants here, consultants who are going to…he has to admit he really isn't quite clear on what the consultants would be doing.

Sixteen emails. No messages in Slack. He still has the Google search open and clicks just to see what kinds of things come up. He makes a note that most of the top results are paid, which seems like a change from years past. Of course they are paid. He remembers when his father was doing rotisserie baseball with his buddies, calculators and the *Sporting News* spread out on the card table on the patio.

He checks his calendar. There is a four to five to talk through the updated dates for the Great Awning campaign. Everything is pushed back.

He goes into the kitchen to get his coffee. In the kitchen there is a milk frother, a typed note that says "Try me! There is milk in the refrigerator." He looks behind him, glances out into the hall. Nobody. What is this? In the refrigerator, there are four cartons of milk: regular, dark chocolate almond milk, vanilla oat milk, chocolate oat milk. He looks into the hall again. What is happening? He selects the oat milk for some reason. It is free, he might as well try something different. He pours it in the coffee and sticks the frother into the mix and clicks. The machine hums with efficiency and soon there is a light frothy top on the coffee. This is delightful.

He moves back to the office and checks the calendar. Meeting in forty-five minutes, the regular stand-up about the Live Oaks campaign. It is amazing how a little bit of froth changes a cup of coffee. He wonders if this was Sarah or the consultants or one of the admin assistants. Those seem like the only viable options. His guess is one of the admins but it could be Sarah, especially since whoever did this did not take any credit. He is not sure what to make of the consultants. They are fine. It is all fine. He works his eight hours, takes an hour for lunch, and it is always fine.

He will need to find some time to do some research. His tight end from last year has retired. He realizes that he has never once altered his drafting strategy and over the past several years, it has performed increasingly poorly. He will have to totally rethink his approach. Should he take two running backs first, and then take a tight end? But running backs are always getting hurt, and there are always a bunch of surprises: this guy gets caught assaulting his girlfriend in a casino and the next guy runs for fifteen hundred yards. Sheilds used to select a quarterback first and then that quarterback's best receiver next. Klopper always chose the best active player from Penn State, a strategy that has started working again lately, which is annoying. Young Snyder takes as many Patriots as possible. It is a quandary, a mystery, and he needs data and research to come up with some kind of strategy.

Half an hour until the stand-up. He finishes the coffee. Is this a permanent thing? Will there always be a frother and a wide assortment of exotic milks in the kitchen? Are they in every kitchen? This could be a small step toward some kind of Google-like free pantry. What would he think about all day if everything he might eat was always ready for him just a hallway away? A blessing and a curse.

He checks his email. Four new messages. Twenty-five minutes until the stand-up. Nothing on Slack. He considers another coffee. The froth really does make a difference.

Yoder

YODER   WAKES   UP   ON   HIS   feet. Goddammit. He sighs, looks around. He is in a kitchen. A familiar one. No mail on the table. He looks at the KISS Kruise brochure on the refrigerator. He is in Cowens's house again. "Goddammit," he says, surprised at the sound of his own voice. He realizes he has never tried to speak, not since...whatever it is that has happened to him.

What has happened to him? He is dead. That is for sure. But what exactly is he? What are the rules? There should really be an orientation, a handbook, an intranet, a quarterly review procedure, a webinar, at least.

He sits down at the table. Data. He needs data. What day is it? He feels for his phone but of course it is gone. A newspaper. But then he remembers that he is in Cowens's house and would be more likely to find a four-wheeler or a Jet Ski than a newspaper. He looks for a laptop, a computer. He wonders if he could activate a screen or a keyboard. He realizes for the first time that he will never again access an Excel document.

It was all such bullshit.

The kitchen is even messier than before. Corona bottles fill the sink. Taco Bell wrappers and Amazon boxes line the counters. Fucking Cowens.

Data. He has woken up four times so far. Is "waking up" the right way to think about it? Where is he when he is asleep? Has it been a day or a year or a decade since the last time he visited this kitchen? He needs a way to track these episodes. A google document would actually be just the thing. He will find a computer either here or at the next one. He should have thought of this when he was at Garner's house. That doofus had a floor unit from the nineties.

He listens. The senses seem to come back one at a time. If he could find a computer, he would make three columns: sight, touch, sound. He has not tried to taste anything. He wonders if he could eat. But he is not hungry and the idea of eating seems…weird. If only he had felt that way more often when he was alive.

He would make columns for date, location, location of awakening, last name, lottery winner or not. He would make a column for time. It seems that he would not need one for city, state, country.

A television babbles down the hallway, a rerun of *Seinfeld*. "Not that there's anything wrong with that," Jerry is saying. He looks out the window. No shouting, music, four-wheelers, hot tubs tonight. He wonders how long it has been. Maybe Cowens is off on his ridiculous KISS Kruise. Goddamn it bothers him when they misspell words that way. It is embarrassing, infantile, another sign of the thing that is wrong with the country, the distance between his father's generation and these Millennials.

His father died of emphysema in a VA facility in Altoona. He coughed to death over the course of a decade. Yoder feels fine with how he went out. He feels a little bad for Russell, still left there. If he could will himself to one of these kitchens he would find himself at Russell's, but that is not how it works, and even without an orientation or an intranet he understands that he cannot choose.

He wanders down the hallway, toward the sound of canned audience laughter. The lights are off and the television glows. This room is also trashed, crammed with bottles and bags and boxes. He thinks about

Pappas and his goddamn virtual reality headsets. He is positive he could find their match among Cowens's loot.

He walks to the center of the room, stands in front of the television. He wonders at how quickly he has gotten used to not being seen. It is not so much different from the way he felt most of the past twenty years—moved aside, carefully shunted away, ignored. Still, as he turns, he half expects Cowens to recoil, but of course he does not, just stares ahead. Yoder waves his hands around. He sticks out his tongue. Cowens is lying on his side, with a comforter pulled around his chest.

Yoder sits down. Something is wrong with Cowens. He looks sad, or drugged. Incapacitated by stupidity, the idiot. Maybe if he buys more boxes from Amazon, more Corona, more four-wheelers or hot tubs.

Cowens checks his phone and Yoder has a pang of jealousy. There was one thing that had actually made life better. If he had his phone, he could open a Google document right now.

He considers grabbing the phone and retreating to the back of the house. He does not know what the rules are here, or even if there are any rules. Can he take things? Bring things with him? Could he smack Cowens on the back of the head and run? He needs to find a computer.

Cowens rolls over. He wipes his eyes. Jesus Christ, he is crying. Eight point eight million fucking dollars and he is sitting in his living room watching *Seinfeld* by himself and crying.

In his entire life Yoder never saw his father cry. He himself has not cried since elementary school. Even that day, the lottery, standing on top of the building, he never once considered crying.

He moves back into the kitchen. Cowens is crying. Eight point eight million. He is, what, thirty-three, thirty-eight? He will never have to step foot in that office again, will never have another performance review, another all-staff meeting. He reaches over and picks up a Corona. A lime swims in a puddle of liquid. Yoder considers the beer, and then before he realizes what he is doing, the bottle is in the air and then it is shattering. "What the fuck?" Cowens says. His words are slurry. "Patches, what the fuck? Fucking cat." Yoder throws another bottle. He wipes his arm along the counter and boxes fall. So maybe there aren't any rules?

Cowens appears in the doorway and his face is a mixture of confusion and sadness. "What the fuck?" he says. Yoder freezes. Cowens wipes tears. Yoder considers taking his phone. He has already crossed some borders he did not intend to cross tonight.

Cowens walks to the refrigerator. He takes out a beer. "Fuck," he says. Yoder sits down at the kitchen table. Jesus Christ, Cowens is too stupid to be properly haunted. He is like a ghost himself, barely there, too wasted and ignorant to notice things flying around the room.

"I don't know," Cowens says. He drinks half his beer. Yoder notices that he is wearing no pants, just white briefs and an Eagles shirt.

This is the afterlife? Yoder is unsure what he can do to influence this situation. Is there a person, a being, some kind of entity watching over him? Is there a board that he can appeal to? He would prefer to not spend the afterlife, or whatever this is, in Cowens's squalid kitchen. If only there was some kind of manual. If only he had some kind of training. Is there really no structure to this situation at all? He looks around. He wanders to the living room and looks out the windows. There is nobody there. He is alone. He will need to find some information. He needs to be able to track these comings and goings, the time when he is awake and the time between these events. He needs data. He needs to find a computer.

Robertson

ROBERTSON CHECKS HIS EMAIL. BUG fix, bug fix, DNS change. Fifteen minutes until the meeting. It practically vibrates on his calendar: Employee Visioning and Vision Board Executive Core Team. He wonders if he should get more coffee, if being awake and overstimulated would be better or worse.

He looks around the office. They haven't replaced Mowery and they were already two people down when the lottery happened, and the empty chairs and abandoned desks are a daily reminder that he could be a millionaire. Mowery didn't even bother cleaning out his stuff and his "It's Five O'Clock Somewhere" sign, printed in Comic Sans no less, is a constant reminder of exactly how stupid this entire situation has become.

At least it is quiet, he thinks, no Kenny Chesney blaring out of Mowery's idiot speakers, no constant chatter about making America great again. He looks around. It is almost too quiet.

"There he is!" He starts at the sound and as soon as the scare passes, he is filled with dread. If he could choose between Mowery and his MAGA hats and Chad Stephenson and his employee visioning, he would surely put Mowery back in that seat. He is nostalgic for the very recent past, when his days were filled with work tickets and virtual servers and DNS changes and Mowery talking about lunch at ten o'clock. It was all so simple.

"Finishing something up here," he says. "See you at the eleven?" Chad Stephenson does not respond. "The meeting?" he says. "Just gotta…"

"I was hoping you and I could hit it first," Chad Stephenson says. Robertson is fighting the urge to turn around. He is pretty sure Chad Stephenson is making that namaste thing with his hands.

"You thought we could hit it?" he says.

"Chat. Talk. I was hoping we could talk before the meeting."

"I have to…" He searches his mind for some reason, some terminology he could throw out. He once saw Mowery describe the full process for merging code onto a test server instead of discussing how he had been neglecting simple DNS tickets, a masterful performance that he knows he should not revere, but still.

"Look, I know you have lots of work," Chad Stephenson says. Robertson finally turns around. He is not making the buddha thing with his hands, but he has turned the chair around and sits astride it like an earnest teacher in a nineties high school drama. Robertson considers whether he would be able to take a picture to share with Jessie. He is wearing the Steve Jobs outfit again today, with the mock turtleneck. "But I see something in you," Chad Stephenson says. "We see something in you."

"You what?" Robertson is legitimately surprised for maybe the first time since the whole thing happened with the lottery.

"It's not a crazy idea," Chad Stephenson says. "You're young. Smart. You work in an area that is constantly changing, where there are all these demands from different people."

Robertson checks the computer. "Meeting is in two minutes," he says.

"Do you like your work here?" Chad Stephenson says. Now he is making the namaste thing again.

"Do I like it?" Robertson says. It is the most ridiculous question in the world, like asking a duck if it likes the electoral college. The concept is just not part of any equation. He comes in and he does his work and he gets paid. Liking it was just never part of the equation.

Chad Stephenson makes the namaste hands again. He scoots closer. Robertson fights the urge to back up. The meeting reminder flashes on his screen.

"What if I told you..." Chad Stephenson starts. He pauses. He is very comfortable, Robertson thinks, with long pauses and eye contact. It is a cheap trick, shameless. This is the problem with this corporate world—it rewards the shameless, the people who are too stupid to be embarrassed by trying so hard and so obviously and so poorly. He is still staring right at Chad Stephenson's eyes, which are a kind of slate green and kind of pretty. Everything about Chad Stephenson seems like it comes from the near future—slightly overdesigned, expensive, ornamented but not overly so. Robertson looks at his own scuffed Doc Martens and Levi's, his tee shirt from the last DrupalCon. His black hoodie is from prAna and he feels that Chad Stephenson himself may have a similar hoodie tucked away for weekend wear.

"Hey the meeting," he says. He clicks the reminder and it disappears. He checks his email. "We better..."

Chad Stephenson slams a hand on the arm of the chair. "No!" he says. He stares. Robertson makes eye contact again, looks away, looks back. His heart is racing, his face is getting hot. None of this is okay. He should be doing bug fixes, closing tickets, texting Jessie about where they are going to meet for lunch, and checking the Reddit thread on the new shitty *Star Wars* movie. Now he is engaged in...something, with this consultant with weird eyes and Nick Saban hair and an apparently bottomless monthly retainer.

"I'm sorry, but I'm not sorry," Chad Stephenson says, finally. "When I see a...when I see potential. A young man like yourself. Howard graduate, taking master's courses, technical proficiency and people skills." Robertson's glasses are fogging up. He has never told Chad Stephenson that he went to Howard. He has never told anybody at work that he is taking online courses toward an MBA, has never even told Jessie about the MBA part. What the hell does Chad Stephenson know about him?

"I have to call bullshit on it," Chad Stephenson says. "The whole thing. The whole culture. Not just Keystone but all of us. All of it." He scoots up his chair. "Did you know the average American worker spends fifty hours a week at work, sixty-three if you count commuting? That's the average. We spend more time here"—he waves his hands around and Robertson takes in the sad empty cubes—"than we do with our families. Our families." Robertson is worried that Chad Stephenson is going to start crying. What is the office protocol for when another person starts crying in your cubicle? Maybe they actually have a protocol for this in Marketing or Creative, but crying is not supposed to happen in Systems Administration.

Chad Stephenson's phone dings. He stares at Robertson. "There is a better way," he says. He pauses as if he is considering something. He actually closes his eyes, bends his neck as if he is praying. Robertson hopes he is not praying. He is positive there should not be praying at work. He stuffs his hands in the pockets of his hoodie. "I can show you," Chad Stephenson whispers. His green eyes are wet. He wipes a tear. Robertson looks at his laptop, his phone. How will he ever describe this to Jessie? The air is thick. He feels like he did in high school, when he was trying to impress a girl and wound up accidentally joining a church youth group, a meeting that started with icebreakers and ended with a plea to stand up and "accept Jesus Christ as your personal savior."

Chad Stephenson looks at his phone. He stands and types a message. "I really mean this," he says.

"Okay," Robertson says.

Chad Stephenson walks out of his office.

CRAVER

CRAVER SITS IN THE CAR. It is raining and cold. The Badlands is a more than appropriate name. He checks his phone. A Van Morrison song is finishing, one of the lesser ones from the late nineties. He flashes back on that night with Chastain at the bar, the night those assholes won the goddamn lottery. "It will be like a Springsteen song," he had said. He had been holding it in, trying not to put his cards on the table, poke his neck out through the Bubble Wrap of irony.

"A Springsteen song?" she had said. She looked at him. God, he loved her sloe eyes, the crow's feet just starting to show in the corners. "Which one?"

"'Thunder Road,'" he had said immediately, surprising even himself with the firmness of the answer.

"The screen door slams," he whispers. "Mary's dress waves." A car pulls in next to him and a bus next to that. The monument is blurry through the rain but there is certainly no mistaking it. God, it is huge. Washington, Jefferson, Roosevelt, Lincoln.

He likes the way the rain slants across the windshield, the visage of the presidents looming in the distance, the late-morning darkness of the

Badlands and the tourists wandering toward the information plaques in the distance. It looks pitiful and cold, everybody so far away except the slish slosh of the windshield wipers. He doesn't have to think about the numbers, just lets his fingers tap in the familiar rhythm and hit send. So he is doing that again. A twenty-four-hour break, some jalapeño poppers and three free margaritas, a hookup with a Chili's waitress and now he is doing this again. He types "Rain. Also four large white dudes" and hits send. Okay.

Washington, Jefferson, Roosevelt, Lincoln. He wonders how old they were when they were elected president. He pulls up a browser on his phone, types in "Mount Rushmore," and enlarges the picture. He stares out through the windshield. Those are young men depicted in that granite. Lincoln and Roosevelt look like they could be tight ends on a football team, Washington and Jefferson like the bass and keyboard player in some second-rate imitative hipster band. "Mount Shushmore" they would be called. It would be ironic.

He checks his phone and then closes the browser. This project may have worked better as a Twitter project, but he hadn't really intended to make it a project at all until he'd sent maybe two hundred texts and realized that he would not be filling up the expensive moleskin journals with poetic ruminations on his soulful days and ecstatic nights on the road. Soulful days and ecstatic nights. The idea embarrasses him. It looks like Roosevelt is crying, like Lincoln is looking straight at him. Jefferson looks like he is going to hand you a bootleg cassette tape.

Another bus pulls in and he stares as the passengers embark one by one, most of them wearing cheap plastic pullovers emblazoned with "Badlands Tours." Where would they be coming from? Did they leave the safe confines of Philadelphia or Winnipeg or Tokyo to stay overnight in some dreary Hampton Inn in Rapid City just for the purpose of communing with the dead presidents that loom up on the mountain?

He should get out of the car, at least. Everybody is wearing long pants, though, hiking boots and long-sleeve shirts and rain jackets. Craver had packed optimistically, California in his mind. He had packed like those young Springsteen heroes—no raincoat, sensible shoes, Zone bars and undershirts and suit jackets. Just ambition and gasoline—maybe some Bugles and Diet Coke and David Sunflower Seeds.

The heat in the car is so nice. Really toasty. The tourists from the first bus are starting to wander back. He gauges their faces and finds relief, exhaustion, confusion. No joy. Nobody is having a soulful, ecstatic experience at Mount Rushmore today. He imagines what they would be doing if Chastain had come along. Sitting there making fun of the tourists, on their way to a new life on the West Coast. Or better yet, Chastain's practical nature would have taken over and they'd have skipped this stop altogether, still under the covers in some hip hotel outside Denver, looking for apartments in San Francisco, walking down Lombard Street or the Haight hand in hand, laughing about the losers who won the lottery.

He thinks about the waitress from the other night. She was nice. Young. Blond. He remembers the way her back curved down into her backside, the slight Midwestern drawl.

He picks up the phone and starts texting. He should be clever, insouciant. "Mount Rushmore…" he starts. The rain has picked up and in the windshield everything is blurry, the presidents are a gray hulk. The tourists are moving back to their buses now. A lone woman, Asian and pretty, walks along the path toward the monument. He wonders if she is with a tour group or on her own. Where is she from? What strange path has put them both at this strange and unlikely place on this shitty day?

The first bus closes its doors. He watches the lone woman walking further down the pathway. He could open his door. He could follow down the path, avoiding puddles, the rain cold on his bare arms. The second bus pulls out and he notices a pale-green Prius a few rows away, the only other car in the lot. It is hot in the car now. He picks up the phone. "Mount Rushmore" is all he has typed. He thinks about time signatures, the way they can follow you anywhere from your cell signal. He is in the middle of nowhere but certainly there is a cell tower somewhere on this mountain, a national landmark. He puts his hand on the door. He opens it and stands. The rain is cold and it feels good, good to be out of the car, to be doing something. The woman is a speck in the distance, rounding a turn. He is nervous, hesitant. He takes a few steps and then feels for his phone. Nothing. He pauses. The woman is gone around a turn. He wonders how far you can walk up the mountain. She did not seem to be dressed for a hike. He feels again where his phone would be in his right pocket, turns, and heads back to the car.

russell

RUSSELL PULLS INTO THE PARKING lot. It is 8:54. He was supposed to be here for an eight thirty and if he walked up the back stairs probably nobody would notice that he was even late. Probably nobody would notice if he just drove back home and spent the day watching *Band of Brothers* again. He takes a sip from his coffee. Miles Davis plays slow and cool, melancholy and slinky. He could go to the diner, get some eggs and corned beef hash. He could sip his coffee and read the western in his briefcase.

He looks at the entrance and almost jumps when Sarah comes out. He fishes in his bag, turns off the car, acts like he has been looking for something. When he looks back up, she is getting into her van. Of course she never even noticed him. Why would she? He is sitting in his car in the back of the lot, watching the clock. 8:58. Sarah is supposed to be leading his eight thirty. That could mean two things: the meeting is canceled, or Lawson will be leading it. In either case, he doesn't really need to be there.

8:59. He can't help himself and looks to the top of the building again. Five floors up. Fifty feet. Sixty feet. There, to the right is where it happened, where he did it.

Sarah probably went to a meeting downtown. Russell had a brief moment when he went to meetings downtown, when he was up-and-coming, a young executive. He went to conferences, subscribed to magazines, networked without feeling the least bit uncomfortable about the whole thing.

Up on the roof it is like nothing ever happened. Down on the ground they have planted a fresh row of flowers but it is not a memorial, nothing there to recognize Yoder's years of labor, the meetings and reports and extra hours to get through this project or push toward that key performance indicator, nothing more eloquent than simple ground cover. That is how it works, the entire machine. A man jumps to his death and a day later they are back in the exact spot, putting in a fresh batch of mulch, a row of daisies to cover up the man's very existence, the place where he chose to end the charade they are all sleepwalking through every day.

If Sarah is downtown then Lawson will be running the meeting, or more likely even, Lawson will cancel, say they know everything they need to know and don't we all want an hour of our lives back? Lawson is fine. Sarah is fine. Everything is fine. He wonders what it was like in those last moments, the ground rushing up. He turns the key, puts the car in reverse, and drives out of the parking lot.

CHASTAIN

CHASTAIN FOLLOWS SARAH INTO THE room. This is not what she thought they would be doing when Sarah suggested "blowing off a little steam after work." She can feel the adrenalin, the nerves. But she trusts Sarah, believes in her even, so she has assented and signed the forms and thanked Sarah for paying the fee for an hour. She is flushed, fogging the tops of the safety goggles. Sarah has told her that this is all normal, par for the course, expected and even part of the reason they are here in the first place.

The range is long and low. It is utilitarian. A place where they can fire guns at targets and nothing else, no feints at being a lounge or a club or something other than what it is. Still, it is clean, well-lit, clearly a safe and orderly place or Sarah would certainly have nothing to do with it.

"So," Sarah says. "This is fun. I find it to be a good release."

Chastain nods. A good release. She feels for her phone and then remembers, again, that they have left their phones in a lockbox upstairs. "Best to have no distractions" is what Sarah had said.

"So let's go through this again," Sarah says. "It's pretty simple." She picks up the gun, a Beretta M9 is what she called it, and aims it at the

114

target fifty feet away. "I'm going to lock my feet, keep my knees bent just a little. My arms are straight. And then I'm going to pull this trigger."

"Okay," Chastain says.

Bam. Sarah checks her target. There, near the middle, in the yellow circle, a small hole. Bam. Bam bam bam. Four more holes.

"Holy shit," Chastain says.

Sarah is smiling. "Right?"

The last four are right around the bullseye.

"You're pretty good," she says, trying to mask the surprise in her voice. Of course Sarah is pretty good at this, like she is pretty good at everything.

"You ready to try?" Sarah says. She places the gun on the counter in front of her and stands aside.

Chastain steps up. She takes hold of the gun, aware of Sarah now moving behind her. "I can just…"

"Yep," Sarah says.

The gun is heavy and it feels good in her hand, a solid tool. It is warmer than she thought it would be. She remembers that Beatles song. She wonders how many texts she will have from Craver when she retrieves her phone from the lockbox. It is so strange how different things feel now. She sights the gun.

"Arms straight, legs set, ready for some blowback," Sarah whispers. "Whenever you're ready."

She locks her legs. Her arms are straight. She feels strong. It is so funny how things feel so different. She pulls the trigger.

Gibbons

GIBBONS PUTS DOWN HIS COFFEE and his bag. He turns on the computer. He shouldn't be mad. He needs to not be angry, to not make a big deal about this. But still, why would they do it in the first place if they didn't intend to follow through? He opens his yogurt. Vanilla. He really prefers raspberry but it just seems strange to buy a week's worth of the same kind of yogurt. He should be the kind of person who likes variety, the kind of person who vacations in foreign countries, marks them on a map, always looks forward to something new and different.

So today's new and different thing is vanilla yogurt.

He opens a Word file and types, "Where has the milk frother gone?" He makes the font huge, thirty-six points. But no, that is too much. He searches for an emoji, but all he can find is a milk bottle, a cow, a cup of coffee unfrothed. Unfrothed. It just looks so empty now. Why would they give them oat milk, dark chocolate almond milk, whole milk from the dairy, and then just take it all away?

He changes tack: It won't do to be angry. Sarah and Lawson and Chastain are trying to right this ship. They are trying to steer it away from angry seas in the boat of overcommunication, of breathing exercises and visioning. This is exactly the kind of sentiment they are rooting out of Keystone, the thing the consultants have been brought in to address in their consultancy way. He writes "Missing: Milk Frother," adds the unfrothed coffee emoji and below it writes, "I'm lonely and no longer as delicious!"

He clicks on print and then imagines himself walking through the office to retrieve the sign, past conference room 431 and Spontaneous Teaming Area Teal, through what used to be the receptionist's desk, past Sarah and Lawson and Chastain, down the hall and into the supply room. It is a minute walk, maybe thirty seconds if he really hustles. All that time, that sign sitting there on the printer. What if he walks into the supply room to find Sarah herself standing there, looking at his sign while monthly projections print out beside her? It is best to not be the kind of person who hangs anonymous signs in the office. It is best to be quiet and efficient and he is lucky to be in a place where those qualities might be recognized, to be working for people who are smart enough to notice quiet and efficient over loud and overconfident, or worse, too stupid to know what you don't know.

It is best to not be a person who puts up signs in the office. He clicks cancel. But still, why would they build up this expectation only to take it away?

He has been casually wandering into the kitchen when people are in there, asking if they know where the milk frother is, if there is still vanilla oat milk in the refrigerator.

He scans the entryway, pops his head down the cubicle aisle, and opens up Amazon. He types milk frother. The bestselling frother is twelve ninety-nine. The one they had in the kitchen was four ninety-nine. A five-dollar milk frother and they took it away? He has started to add oat milk to his groceries, but they do not have the same brand at his grocery store, so he has come to think of Oatly as some kind of exotic product, something from Trader Joe's or Aldi or even Whole Foods. He googles Whole Foods. Whole Foods is headquartered in Austin. The closest one is seventy-eight miles away.

A desktop notification from Slack. He checks the campaign channel. More deadlines are being pushed, this time the Amphitheater project. Their deadlines are real, though, concerts and events, the second year of a music festival that is the primary reason Keystone got the business in the first place. This is something he will need to address.

He opens the direct message with Lawson. He hates to communicate up but this is one that merits the initial notice. "Saw the note on Amphitheater," he writes. "Will get Creative, Production, Purchasing together AGAIN and work through it. May have to bump the bank (first thing that comes to mind) but will check schedules and take care of it."

He clicks over to the Amazon window, adds the recommended milk frother to his cart. It doesn't make any sense what they have done, but he will take care of things on his own. He will start bringing in a small cooler, find the local store that sells Oatly. He can have a whole spread right here, in his cubicle.

Another notification from Slack. Lawson has added a thumbs-up emoji to the DM. Okay.

Would it be sad, though, to have a little coffee station here? In the cubicle? Is that the kind of thing that leads to casual questions, light concern, and then your name is on somebody's mental list?

The heart of the ship, the heart of the ship, you are working in the heart of the ship.

He goes back into Amazon, deletes the frother from his cart. He closes the window and opens Slack. "On it," he types, beneath Lawson's thumbs-up.

Yoder

YODER WAKES UP ON HIS feet. Goddammit. He is in a kitchen, but something is wrong. He waits a moment and steadies himself. There is no table here, no walls, only a half-finished outline of a kitchen—beams, pipes, fixtures, a rough wooden floor. He is in a half-finished house.

There are takeout containers on the counter, a few bottles of wine, an opened sleeve of red Solo cups. He hears music and low talking coming from somewhere. He wants to sit but there are no chairs, no table. He feels his pockets but knows he will not find his phone there. On the counter there is some change. He puts a quarter in his pocket. If it is there when he next wakes, in some other asshole's asshole house, then at least he will know that he can keep things, which would mean he can write down information and save it, add to it later, let it accumulate until he can draw some conclusions. He has a problem to solve, and he needs data to solve it.

He thinks about the ghosts he has seen in movies. It never seemed like a good situation but at least they knew the rules, the basic parameters of their existence in the world, or the world they used to know.

Jimmy Stewart had that wingless angel to lead him through his wonderful life. Warren Beatty had Mr. Jordan in that movie from the seventies. Patrick Swayze had Whoopie Goldberg. And Yoder has nobody, nothing. They should have some kind of new employee orientation to at least let him know where he is, what he is, whether he can access Google Drive if he happens to find a computer, whether he can hurt people or just throw things, or if he going to spend the rest of eternity wandering the houses of these idiots who did a dumb thing and got unbelievably lucky. He hasn't really thought about hurting anybody, but if this is what the afterlife is like he may need to reconsider.

And whose house is he in now? He looks around. It is going to be nice, big and roomy. He wanders down a long hallway with tile samples laid out—nice choices, tasteful and dark. He always liked tile floors, had imagined that eventually he might retire to Arizona, where he would live in a house of brick and glass, tile everywhere, a simple place but nice and tasteful, different than the apartment he lived in up until however long ago it was that those assholes won the lottery. He realizes he had always looked at the apartment as some kind of way station, the place he was living in before he lived in the place that would really be his own. He was so stupid. It was all so stupid.

He follows the voices. At first he thinks they are children, teenagers who sneaked into a house under construction. There are two of them, a boy and a girl or, now that he looks closer, a young man and woman. They are sitting on a blanket, eating Subway subs and drinking something out of red plastic cups. At first he struggles to place either one of them. He walks into the room and notices that he does not expect them to react. He is getting used to this. A data note, something to remember, a clue that can help him put together all of these pieces.

They sit side by side, whispering and giggling. Yoder gets closer. They are slim and attractive, dressed in shorts and tee shirts. The woman is blond and, like all blond young women, reminds Yoder of Caroline from Ocean City. He wonders if some day he will wake up in her kitchen. He should be so lucky. The man is…he gets closer. He recognizes the face now. The new guy. Reichert. He had only been working for Keystone for how long? A few weeks? A month? He remembers an email. Jesus Christ, kid has his entire life in front of him, he is young and good-looking and he's sitting on the floor drinking wine out of plastic cups with a woman who looks like Caroline from Ocean City and he is a millionaire?

Yoder sits down and the floor creaks. "What's that?" the woman says. She looks into the hall. "I told you we shouldn't be doing this before the closing," she whispers.

The man stands. He looks at where Yoder is sitting. "I thought it…" he says, and then follows her glance toward the kitchen. "Probably just the house settling. That's a thing, right? You hear that."

"The house settling," she says. "Our house settling."

The young man sits back down. "I still can't…" he says.

"I know," she says. "I just don't know if we should have bought one so big. I mean…"

"It's not like cars, though," he says. "If we get freaked out, or it's too big, or it takes longer than we think to…"

"Don't say it out loud," she says, and Yoder has the feeling this is a topic they have covered before, because the tone in her voice is tender. Jesus Christ, they are adorable and nothing is fair. He stands and the floor creaks again.

The woman jumps. She looks straight at him. Her hair has fallen down over her left eye and he fights the urge to push it back for her.

"Just the house settling," Reichert says. He taps the floor.

"Maybe we better get out of here," she says.

"It's going to be ours in…" he consults his watch, an Apple Watch that Yoder had spent a day checking out online, reading reviews and looking for coupon codes. "Six weeks."

Yoder tries to do the math. How long does it take to build a new home? How long after the lottery would they have even been able to make a down payment? There would be paperwork, waiting, bank accounts to be confirmed, transfers to be made. "We will take the one-time option and not reveal our names" is how every single one of Garner's lottery emails had ended, but they didn't say anything about how long it might take to get their money.

"Okay," the woman says. She puts her sandwich into a plastic bag and unrolls a sleeping bag on the floor. She unbuttons a button on her shorts. Yoder takes a step toward her. She unbuttons another button. "Wanna come over here?" she says. Yoder takes a step. He can smell her—jasmine and lavender. Caroline from Ocean City smelled like green apple shampoo. Yoder puts a hand out and wonders if she could feel it if he made contact. She lets her shorts drop onto the floor. He pauses for a moment. He doesn't look down. He walks through the door and back toward the kitchen to wait for wherever he will be next time.

Robertson

ROBERTSON SIPS HIS DRINK AND watches the entrance. Why did he agree to this? Why couldn't he have just thought up some excuse? I have softball practice. I have a date with my girl-friend. My parents are coming for dinner. The cat is sick. Now he can think of a million of them, but at that particular moment in time—Chad Stephenson and Nicole Stetler-Stephenson standing there in the elevator, their backs to the door, both of them so tall and slightly futur-istic and vaguely chemically good-looking—he had gone blank, simply nodded his head and given them the thumbs-up.

"Sweet," Chad Stephenson said. "Let's do Legends down in Hotel Nicholas. You know it? They make a great Manhattan."

He had just nodded, again given them the thumbs-up. His mind was already racing, adrenaline flushing a too-late fight-or-flight instinct through this stupid body.

Now he is here, choking down some sweet bitter concoction that he supposes is a Manhattan because like an idiot that is what he ordered. He takes a big sip. Would it be okay to bail and order a beer? The bartender is a steampunk in a vest and top hat who Robertson has seen at the game store playing Magic the Gathering with a few other like-minded, like-dressing locals. Robertson chokes down the rest of the drink. He wishes he had a chaser, a glass of milk or a Milky Way bar to clear out the bitter whiskey. He motions to the bartender and then feels a hand on his back. He jumps, knocks over the Manhattan glass and it shatters on the bar.

"I'm so sorry," he says, and moves to pick up the pieces. He takes a large shard in his hand and immediately slices the soft space between his thumb and forefinger. He lets the glass drop and watches a gap appear in the skin and then steadily fill with blood until it is dripping onto the bar.

"Oh man," Chad Stephenson says. "Are you okay?" He sounds like he really cares whether Robertson is okay and he registers this fact along with the other increasingly discordant facts he has assembled about Chad Stephenson.

Nicole Stetler-Stephenson reaches across the bar, takes a towel, checks it for cleanliness, and then places his hand flat and expertly wraps it in the towel. She looks him in the eye. "You're going to be okay," she says. "I used to be a nurse. I don't think you'll need stitches." He looks at her eyes. There is a lightness there. She is younger than Chad Stephenson, maybe ten years older than Robertson, thirty-five or so. She smiles and taps his hand. "But I do think you're going to need another drink."

Chad Stephenson and the steampunk bartender have disposed of the glass and are now chatting about something called bitters.

"Could we get another Manhattan and…I'm guessing a beer?" Nicole Stetler-Stephenson says, looking at Robertson quizzically. "Yeah, a beer," she says finally. "Whatever he wants," she points to Robertson and he nods at the bartender.

"Founders," he says.

"Founders and two Manhattans up with Templeton Rye," says the steampunk bartender.

Robertson settles in as best he can. He presses the towel to his hand. "You sure I'm not going to…" he starts.

"I don't think so," Nicole says. "If it's still bleeding in an hour then maybe. That kind of thing, you can usually put a butterfly bandage on it, too. Or just superglue it."

"Superglue?" he says.

"See this?" she says, putting her hand over his and drawing a line down a short scar running for about an inch. "Superglued. We were on our sailboat, way out in Narragansett Bay, further than we should have been of course, which is a Chad Stephenson specialty," she looks to Chad, checking his phone a few stools down, and Robertson laughs along with her, an in-joke, just the two of them.

The steampunk bartender brings their drinks. Robertson takes a long pull, surprised at how thirsty he is. He will probably never try another Manhattan in his entire life. He looks around. Just normal people having normal drinks after a normal day at the office. "So how..." he starts, "how long are you going to be around the office? How long does your... retainer? How long does your retainer go?"

"Are you trying to get rid of us, Andre Robertson?" she says.

This time he can tell she is joking. He thinks. "No I just..."

"I know," she says. "My goodness, you Pennsylvania people are earnest."

"Earnest?" he says. It is a word he has never been called, except maybe by Jessie.

"You might be surprised if you were standing in my shoes."

He looks down. She is wearing some kind of platform sandals. As usual, they look like something you would have to drive hours to buy, something from the near future, or some slightly more hip dimension. "Those shoes?" he says.

"These shoes have seen some things, Mr. Robertson," she says. "Some things that might surprise you."

He takes another pull from the beer. He is starting to feel it, something in his head unlatching. She is really very pretty. Chad Stephenson taps at his phone, holds it to his ear, and walks toward the entrance. "What's up with him?" Robertson says.

"Just Chad things," she says. "He...takes his work seriously, you know?"

Robertson thinks about the strange meeting the other day, Chad so emotional. "Boy, do I know," he says. "Is he always like that?" He is not really sure what he wants to know, exactly. The idea that somebody could care so much about what they do here, about actual work, this kind of work, Robertson's work, is frankly hard to swallow.

Nicole puts her hand on his. It is warm and dry. Robertson fights the urge to pull his hand back. He looks toward the door. He can see Chad Stephenson's black jacket in the picture window, jabbering into his phone, gesturing out at the street. "He's taking an interest in you," Nicole says. "Some advice?"

Robertson notices a ring on her finger, dark metal imprinted with a pattern of dragons. He noticed a similar ring on Chad Stephenson's finger soon after their first meeting. "What is that?" he says. "That ring?"

"That is a very important ring," Nicole says. "Maybe someday we'll tell you the full story."

"That's mysterious," Robertson says. He finishes his beer. Nicole motions to the bartender and Robertson notices her glass has emptied as well.

"It is mysterious, actually," she says, the lightness returning to her voice. If he didn't know better, Robertson might think she is actually flirting. "So some advice," she says, returning to her business voice. "An important person is taking an interest in you."

"Important?" he says. The bartender places another beer in front of him and he takes a drink, watching Nicole sip at her Manhattan.

"Very," she says. "You may think we're just consultants, but the work we're doing here, what we do, it is very important. It can be important to you. To your career."

"I never even think about... I mean, to even have somebody refer to it as 'my career' seems a little, I don't know."

"That's the thing," she says. She puts her hand on his again and looks him in the eye. She is closer than he would like, closer than a colleague would position themselves, close enough that he can smell her, some kind of essential oil that smells expensive and exotic. "You deserve it," she says. "You deserve to be happy, even at work. Especially at work. Now I know those wheels are turning all the time in there." She taps him on the side of the head. "So, while you're thinking about what me and Chad are doing at your work, think about what you're doing there, too." She taps him again on the side of the head. "Think on that."

Lawson

LAWSON SETTLES IN AND WAITS for the others. There are three of them in the group. Of course, they don't seem like the kind of people he imagined he would be working with in this short fiction workshop. Of course, they all have more experience and seem better at this than him. He checks his phone, where he has written their names: Dorothy, Sam, Bimal.

Dorothy, Sam, Bimal. Dorothy is an older woman, close-cut hair, jeans, and lots of beaded bracelets. She is cool, the kind of cool that it is hard to maintain as you get older, the kind of cool Lawson himself would like to be as an older person. Perhaps that is why he is doing all this. He has realized he is operating on a kind of momentum that he doesn't understand but has learned to trust because it feels so counterintuitive, so opposite to every decision he has made to this point, large and small and in between.

Sam is a younger man, probably in his early thirties, who Lawson would describe as squirrely in his less generous moments. He is quiet, reserved, with a strange energy that seems always on the verge of boiling over. Bimal is a fiftyish man from Nepal who is writing in English, his fourth language.

Dorothy has published a book of poems with a small press. Sam has published four stories in literary magazines. Bimal has published six short stories in literary magazines, including a few that Lawson thinks he even recognized, the this Review, the that Quarterly. They have gotten friendly, the four of them, talking during breaks and even going for coffee after the last workshop. They are all fascinated with Joe, the instructor. They construct elaborate fantasies about his life—Joe is a spy, a government bureaucrat, a best-selling author working under a pseudonym.

He stirs his coffee. This would be better if they could do it in a bar, have a few drinks to loosen up a bit. He is still nervous about giving his feedback, and especially about hearing feedback from the others. He checks his phone. He is a half hour early. He looks at the cookie he bought solely because it didn't seem quite right to take up this much time and space for a two-dollar coffee. He breaks the cookie in half. He has gained eight pounds since the group won the lottery, something that, judging from his colleagues, is not unusual. They are all affected in different ways, but they are all indeed affected. How did Chastain put it? We're all kinds of fucked up. For Lawson it was like a near-death experience, coming face to face with the for-real idea that he was half-way done with his life. A wake-up call. He pictures himself on a stage, being interviewed about his latest book. "It's a funny story," he will say. "These people in my office won the lottery..."

He opens his laptop, then decides to look again at the stories they're talking about tonight. Bimal has written a lovely piece about a girl coming of age in Kathmandu and something called the monkey temple. Sam has written a weirdly confounding story about a man whose girlfriend can pull veins out of her arms. Lawson is sure he doesn't understand what exactly is happening in that story. Is it a metaphor, an analogy, is it supposed to be real? He has no idea but he can't stop thinking about it and when the girlfriend first pulled her veins out, even though in the story she kept on insisting it was a magic trick, Lawson actually started crying and had to get up and walk around for a while. He wants to sit Sam down and ask him questions, to really figure out what Sam is doing with this story, why it feels so visceral, so strange and moving. There is something happening there and Lawson wants to be able to make it happen in his own work.

His own work. At least, he thinks, he can honestly say that he has work. He has written four short stories and read more short fiction in the past month than the entire previous forty-two years, has read *Bird by Bird* by Anne Lamott and *On Writing* by Stephen King. He has subscribed to *Poets & Writers* magazine. He has twenty tabs open in his browser, most of them various literary magazines or blogs or something in between. He is not sure, but he is trying. That is more than he has done in the past. He wonders at how much time he had before. What did he do with all that time? Fantasy football and *The Bachelorette* and the analytics blogs. Well, he is still reading the analytics blogs.

He puts the stories away. Behind him, a group of teenagers are talking about something called Fortnite. He wonders at all the things he does not know. Indeed, the world is full of things he does not know, monkey temples and Kathmandu and women who pull the veins right out of their arms. He feels like he is opening up, like he is learning a new language, like he has found some other dimension that was there all along and he just hadn't noticed. He feels like he is pretty bad at all of this, really, but at least he is trying.

Twenty minutes. He should read the stories again. He checks his phone. Twitter is full of dogs today. He wonders if it is some kind of dog holiday. Should he get a dog? He likes the idea that he could pack up and leave at any moment, but when was the last time he actually did that?

He sees Bimal in line at the head of the store, Dorothy chatting with somebody outside. They are all early. Has he found his people? Huh, he thinks, putting away the laptop and straightening the printouts. He may have found his people.

russell

RUSSELL IS ON THE "EXECUTIVE Core Team."
From what he can tell, that means he goes to meetings once a week
and watches the consultant with the hair dye justify the surely ridiculous amount they are paying him. Russell has heard that they are on a
monthly retainer. He has heard the contract is a sixteen-month contract.
He remembers because the length seemed so strange. Who signs a sixteen-month contract for anything?

One perk of being on the Executive Core Team is donuts and good
coffee. Russell had forgotten about this meeting and brought his own
breakfast, his own coffee, but he will be damned if he is going to leave
any opportunities on the table, and he forces another bite of donut into
his mouth, stirs his Dunkin coffee and watches the creamer swirl while
the consultant writes on the whiteboard. Russell wonders idly what he
is writing and then puts it out of his mind. The man draws a circle and
then another one inside, another inside that. He goes on and on. At
first, people look at one another, then they titter. The consultant keeps
on going. Russell understands that is the point of whatever this is—they
are to suspect, then to laugh, then their interest will be drawn further

into whatever this is, only to be released eventually with the revealed understanding that they are all on the same page, that there was some grand plan in the consultant seeming to make an idiot out of himself.

He has three donuts in front of him and he goes up to the table and retrieves three more. He adds a chocolate cruller. He wonders if the crullers are more expensive than the donuts, why whoever buys the donuts would have even thought to add four crullers in on top of a dozen donuts. Does the consultant himself buy the donuts? Or maybe the wife? Do they have an unseen assistant?

He takes all the crullers, piles them on top of one another, and returns to his space at the end of the table. The consultant is still drawing on the board. Everybody is looking at their phones or laptops. He wonders when it became officially okay, not only tolerated but encouraged, for everybody to be looking at their devices in every meeting. He takes a bite of the cruller. He will go on a diet soon but right now the important thing is maximizing this dumb Executive Core Team opportunity and that means crullers. It means the good Dunkin coffee, real sugar and cream. He takes a bite of cruller, adds a bite of donut.

"And that…" the consultant says, "is basically the Universe." He pauses. People actually sit up in their chairs. Russell forces another bite of donut into his mouth. If this meeting goes long enough, maybe they will order lunch. The consultant gestures to a tiny spot in the center of his drawing. "And that is us," he says. There are wows and huhs and knowing chortles. It is exactly how it was planned. Of course, Russell knows this could not be anything like the shape of the Universe, an impossible thing to know. Also the consultant has located them, the company, the Visioning and Vision Board Executive Core Team and himself, of course, exactly at the center of the Universe. The slip, or even worse, implication, would be outrageous if it wasn't so consistent and predictable. Of course, the consultant with the Steve Jobs hard-on would locate himself at the center of the fucking Universe.

He looks around for somebody to commiserate with, but everybody seems to be buying into this bullshit. Jesus. He looks around again, nods at Robertson, the young kid who does something in IT. He is the only one also gauging the others' level of engagement. Russell nods and the kid raises his shoulders in an "I don't know" gesture. At least that makes one more, Russell thinks.

He looks around again. There are the usual department and group heads, the up-and-comers and brown-nosers and the people whose good intentions collude to put them on every ridiculous internal team and committee. And then there is Robertson, the young African American kid. There is Perez. There is Sheila, the very out lesbian. There is Shrestha. And then there is Russell. It dawns on him all of a sudden: he is the old people's representative on the Executive Core Team. He sits up in his chair. The consultant says something about shared responsibility, about being your own star. Russell puts all of the peanut donut into his mouth. He chews. Maybe he will have a reaction to something and they will have to take him to the hospital. Maybe they will have to pay him disability for the rest of his life. Maybe he should take his donuts up to the roof and follow in Yoder's footsteps.

He is the representative of old people on the Executive Core Team. He is more sure of it than anything. The consultant is high fiving somebody in the front row, a younger woman who does something with the Google buys. The consultant is not much younger than Russell but he seems less like a peer than a totally different species, a similar entity from some other time and space.

Russell takes another bite of donut, then another. He stuffs the entire donut in his mouth and for a moment he can't breathe and the feeling is a brief thrill and then embarrassment as he chews, chews, swallows. He can breathe again. He has three donuts in front of him now.

He started noticing around fifty that he seemed to always be the oldest person in the room. The question at that point was how to maintain his dignity, how to not fade into the background as everybody else became younger and leaner and stranger. If Yoder was here...but no, if Yoder was here, there would still only be one of them on the Executive Core Team, one old person's representative to space out and eat donuts. He takes the chocolate cruller and dips it in the coffee. He takes a bite.

The consultant is passing out pieces of pink construction paper and crayons. Jesus Christ, crayons. Russell wonders what they have been talking about. "So we'll just break up into small groups. Let's do…" he acts as if he is counting, "threes. Groups of three."

Russell eyes the donuts. He cannot break up into groups of three. It is that simple. He stacks the donuts. He pictures them falling from the roof, the gentle sway and then the light explosion as they hit the concrete. He picks up his phone, puts it to his ear. "Hold on," he says. "Of course. Of course. Just a minute." He gestures to the room, but they have already fallen into groups of three and are chatting earnestly among themselves. He stands at the back of the room, phone at his ear, donuts in his hand. He waits for somebody to call, to notice, to care that he has removed himself from the group. The consultant is chatting in the corner with Robertson and his partner. Russell puts the phone back in his pocket. He takes the donuts and slips out of the room. He lets the door shut behind him as he makes his way to the stairs.

Yoder

YODER WAKES UP ON HIS feet. He sighs, closes his eyes. Goddammit. He checks his pockets. No quarter. No phone. Nothing. He is in a kitchen. A big kitchen. Bright. He hears people talking in another room, footsteps. He glances at the microwave. It is 9:48, earlier than his usual visitations, or awakenings, or whatever they are. Hauntings? If these are hauntings, he has a feeling he is doing it wrong.

Mancus walks right past him and Yoder jumps, backs up against the counter. Mancus moves to the refrigerator. In the next room, Yoder can hear music, some kind of modern country, the kind that sounds more like Britney Spears than Johnny Cash. He can identify it as modern country only from the singer's low drawl and the presence of some kind of synthesized guitars that bear the faintest whiff of twang and his immediate hatred for the song and the singer and everything about it.

"Chew tobacco chew tobacco chew tobacco spit!" the singer says. Mancus closes the refrigerator and walks past with a beer in his hand. Yoder doesn't recognize the label. He never really had much of an opinion about Mancus, but he finds that he looks forward to developing one.

134

He glances around the kitchen. Interesting that he hasn't even thought of drinking during these wakings. If he is being honest with himself, and there is literally no reason not to be, since he seems to be some kind of singular isolated ghost who only exists in the kitchens of assholes who have won the lottery, he had been kind of an alcoholic for the past however many years. Ever since the thing with Ruth didn't work out and he started thinking way too much about Caroline from Ocean City. There was a point where he was tending his wounds, definitely pouring extra to avoid thinking, to get into that dead-drunk sleep, to stop himself from picking up the phone late at night and asking the questions he knew he would never find answers to. Then there was a period where it was boredom or frustration that there was nobody else like Ruth coming along, or that he would even have these bottled-up memories, this undeniable and sad Thing for Caroline from Ocean City after all these years. Then there was a time when he started to worry, woke up with regrets, joined gyms and volunteered and made lists. Then he just learned to accept it, keep his foot on the gas, lean into the late nights and foggy mornings because what difference did it make anyway?

If he would have known then what he knows now, he would have stepped off that ledge when he first started to notice the slippage. Or maybe not slippage really but a lack of momentum, a fading into the background socially, professionally, in all ways, as if he was literally slowly vanishing from the face of the earth, one cell at a time, one meeting, one request for vacation time, one all staff email, one awkward elevator ride, one key performance indicator at a time.

Yoder looks around. Chew tobacco chew tobacco chew tobacco spit? It is like a parody of country music, the search engine optimization of music—random keywords tangentially associated with a thing, as opposed to the thing itself. He never had anything against Mancus, but now he is wondering if he should have. Mancus. Tall, quiet, nice enough but not in an annoyingly outgoing way. Mancus did something with research, always seemed on top of things but also not fully engaged in a way that Yoder could respect. But still, chew tobacco chew tobacco chew tobacco spit?

Yoder wanders into the living room, where Mancus sits with two women, both drinking white wine. The resemblance is clear and Yoder assumes they are sisters. One of them taps at her phone and the music changes to an old Van Morrison tune. "I told you that song was real," she says. "Unfuckingbelievable."

"Chew tobacco chew tobacco...what was the rest of that again?" Mancus says.

"I think it might be, um, chew tobacco, um..." says the woman closest to him, slightly younger than the other, longer dark hair.

"Was it, spit?" the other woman says, and they all laugh.

Yoder takes in the scene: three attractive adults, two of them married and one obviously the sister of the wife, sitting in a nicely appointed living room—nice but not fancy, the word that comes to mind is tasteful—enjoying a drink and making fun of awful music. He spent most of the past decade sitting on his cracked leather couch, drinking Franzia and watching *Star Trek*. He could put a scare into this situation, do some old-fashioned haunting with blood and gore and things smashing against the walls.

If he had known he would wind up in this situation, he would have watched more horror movies.

"So how is your class this year?" Mancus says.

"Oh they're so cute," the younger woman says. "The usual, a few of them having some troubles but eight-year-old troubles are also kind of lovely and heartbreaking. And funny."

The house is nice. Clean and normal. It is the kind of place Yoder would have guessed Mancus would live in—solid upper middle class, nothing showy, nothing stupid.

The younger woman sits up and takes a sip from her wine. "So you two really doing this?" she says. "Really?"

Mancus sits up. "Maybe?" he says. "I mean, we filled out a form. That's all. So we're committed to being in the Peace Corps CRM and getting emails and phone calls from somebody and that's about it for now."

"We have an appointment," the other woman says. "With a recruiter."

"Who is probably like twenty years old," Mancus says.

"I don't know why you're hung up on that," his wife says. "The website says they're looking for older volunteers, couples, grown-ups."

"Do you have any idea where you'd go? How long?"

"It's two years," Mancus says. "You can tell them where you want to go or you can let them do the matching, and we decided to just throw those dice and see where we might wind up."

"So where do they need people to make mixtapes and chili and drink wine and make fun of terrible country music?" the woman asks.

"Right?" Mancus says.

"Seriously, where would they put a computer person?"

"Maybe Eastern Europe," Mancus says. "Africa."

"We're hoping Africa," says his wife. "I mean that's kind of the Peace Corps thing that we grew up talking about, right?"

"I still can't believe you fucking won the lottery," the sister says.

Mancus just shakes his head and holds up his hands in a helpless gesture.

Goddammit, Yoder thinks. He was really looking forward to hating Mancus, especially after getting a look at the wife, at the sister, at this tastefully appointed home that's only a tile floor away from the one Yoder pictured for himself in Arizona or New Mexico or Ensenada.

Where would they put a computer person? That's right. Mancus is some kind of technical person. Yoder walks down a hallway. Bathroom, bedroom, bedroom. He thinks about poking around in the bedroom and then he sees the office. On the desk, a laptop. He moves the mouse and the screen lights up. In the living room they are still talking. The music switches over to the first Lyle Lovett album. Jesus, he even likes their music. He pauses and imagines himself sitting on the couch with his arm around the younger sister. A smell rushes into his memory—green apple shampoo. Caroline from Ocean City.

I'm really dead, he thinks. A ghost. Or something. Maybe he will wake up in Caroline's kitchen someday. Maybe like that Warren Beatty movie he will get a notification that it was all a mistake, that he has another chance to do it all over again in somebody else's body. He notes that no matter where Warren Beatty went in that movie, no matter whose body he accessed, he still looked like Warren Beatty.

If he is going to figure this out, find his way station or supervisor or angel or some kind of interdimensional exit, he is going to need data. He sits down in front of the computer. He opens a browser.

CRAVER

CRAVER PULLS INTO THE HOLIDAY Inn and checks behind him again. He could have sworn somebody was following, a white sedan like a cop car in a seventies detective show. He tells himself that it doesn't make any sense. He has driven three hundred twenty miles. He has done nothing wrong. He is just a marketing associate breaking out on the Great American Road Trip.

Is that still what he is doing? He will need to figure out what he is doing, but that will come later. As his mother used to say, things have a way of sorting themselves out. He is sorting himself out. Things are happening but they are happening slowly, more an evolution than anything else. He is aware of things he wasn't aware of before. It feels like he is coming through the before part and soon it will all be after.

He watches the rearview. The lights of the strip glow in the near distance. Meineke, Chick-fil-A, Panera, Burger King, Applebee's, Chili's. It is the same as the other places. He is not sure whether this is reassuring or disconcerting. A car creeps past and parks a few spaces away. A man gets out and stretches. He is wearing a suit. Craver checks the car, tries to act like he is fiddling with the radio. It is a white sedan, but a newer one. The man is tall, big, like a pro quarterback, as if you took a normal person and put them in Photoshop and expanded to one hundred and twenty-five percent. Craver realizes that his car is still running. On the radio, the Eagles sing about a peaceful, easy feeling. The man checks his phone. He looks around, stretches again. Is he a man casually getting his bearings or a man pretending to casually get his bearings?

Craver wonders what would happen if he just backed up and drove away. He has not checked in anywhere. He has done nothing wrong. He worries again about the phone in his pocket, the signals it is constantly sending, the GPS working all the time, tower to tower, town to town, state to state.

The man nods at Craver. He walks toward the car.

He has done nothing wrong. He paused at Mount Rushmore. He got out of the car. He watched a woman disappear behind a pathway and he thought about following her. There is nothing wrong with that. Are these normal things to worry about? He should just go home. He should drive all night to San Francisco. He should post his résumé on whatever the new job search websites are and see what happens.

The man smiles and makes a gesture like rolling down a window. Lawson hits the button. He wonders at how many gestures are leftovers from a pre-digital world. How many more generations will make this motion for rolling down a car window? What would happen if he just backed out and left right now?

"Howdy," the man says. "You from around here?"

Act normal. He has done nothing wrong. "No," Craver says. He tries to smile but worries that it is coming out wrong, like he is baring his teeth.

The man walks to the front of the car. "Pennsylvania," he says. "You're a long way from home."

"On my way to San Francisco," Craver says. His phone dings and he wonders if it is a text message or a Twitter mention or a Facebook like or some other indication that someone in the world has interacted with something in one of his profiles.

"You need to get that?" the man says.

Craver realizes that he has been staring at his phone. An email. From the office. They have been sending paperwork. He needs to sign a statement of separation. He needs to turn in his key fob and parking pass. He needs to work through a list of things they have sent along as a PDF attachment. "No, it's fine," he says, putting the phone down. "Work."

"Where's that?" the man says.

Craver looks at the man again. "I don't..." he says. He is getting annoyed now. He has done nothing wrong. He should be sitting on the bed at the Holiday Inn, checking Twitter for whatever it is he checks Twitter for. He should be taking a shower, looking out the window for the closest chain restaurant. "Is there something I can do for you?" he says.

The man steps back. He reaches into his pocket. Craver flashes on the woman walking back toward Mount Rushmore in the rain, the slope of her tapered pants from her backside to her thighs to her ankles. He has done nothing wrong. The man pulls out one of those airport bottles, something dark brown. He takes a sip and then another. He drops the bottle onto the parking lot and Craver fights the urge to pick it up. The man holds his hands up in a helpless gesture. "Just new in town, thought I'd ask if there's any place around here to...you know...go have a couple Coca-Colas."

He actually winks at this last thing and Craver takes the keys out of the ignition and opens the door. He grabs his duffel and his backpack, makes a show of locking the car. "I'll pass," he says. As he moves past the man, he can smell sweat, road grime, and the sweet tang of secondary alcohol.

"No problem, partner," the man calls after him. Something about the way he says it is obscene, laced with something. "Maybe we'll meet again further on down the line."

CHASTAIN

CHASTAIN TELLS HERSELF AGAIN THAT
she should not be nervous. It is just a conference. They are just normal
people. Worker bees. Marketing professionals just like her. She can hear
Sarah's voice in her head: Hey, you're pretty good at this. It was an off-
hand comment, not even a performance review or official feedback, and
she is embarrassed—the part of her that used to look at everything so
cynically, at least—by the fact that she has found herself repeating the
simple phrase to herself every now and then.

Hey, you're pretty good at this.

It was Sarah's idea, of course, this presentation. They have started
to "hit the circuit," the handful of conferences devoted to regional digital
marketing. At first it was just Sarah, with Chastain along more for her
own professional development than anything else, but after the Higher
Ed Marcom conference, where she asked Chastain to come on stage to
answer the HR questions, it has been the two of them trading off. They
make a good team. Sarah, the seasoned professional and Chastain, the
person who started the process of, as Sarah describes it, stepping up. The
presentation starts with the data: thirteen lottery winners, eight point

eight million each, one death, fifteen vacancies, a company in complete and immediate turmoil.

Hey, you're pretty good at this.

She has the presentation on her laptop, on a flash drive, saved to Google Docs. She has her business cards and her suit and a bottle of water. She has done her half of the presentation five times. She practiced twice in front of the cat last night. She is ready. This is just a one-day for the Pittsburgh Area Marketing Association.

"Word is starting to get out," Sarah said. They didn't submit for this one, but were contacted directly. A thing that is starting to happen. Another thing is the book—"our book" is what Sarah calls it now. A book that doesn't exist yet in any form but already has some publishers interested, according to Sarah.

Chastain sits in the front row, listening to the conference organizers walk through some housekeeping. She goes over the beginning of the presentation again. If you can get the beginning down, Sarah says, you're going to be just fine.

Hey, you're pretty good at this.

She has no idea about the book thing, whether it is real, could be real, what it might possibly mean for her, for Sarah, for the both of them. "Our book," as Sarah says. She wonders what Craver would think of her now, sitting here in the Squirrel Hill Marriott conference room A/B waiting to be introduced to a hundred local marketing professionals. God, it is just the kind of the thing the two of them would have found tragic. She checks her phone. Nothing. The texts from Craver have started up again, but the tenor or something has changed. She wonders if something has happened to him, if he is running out of money, out of time, energy, whatever. She doesn't want to read too much into the texts, but something is different.

The conference organizer is working her way toward Chastain's introduction. What is she doing here?

Hey, you're pretty good at this.

She walks to the side of the stage. She is smiling, professional. She makes eye contact with the conference organizer, nods. She hears her name. She walks up the stairs and shakes hands with the organizer. "My name is Jennifer Chastain. Does anybody want to play the lottery?"

russell

RUSSELL TAKES A STEP TOWARD the edge. His
stomach turns and his fingers tingle. He flashes to high school, waiting in the locker room before a basketball game, that feeling of dread
and excitement and anticipation. Has it been that long since he has felt
adrenalin?

In the distance he can see the campus, the stately brick and the
football stadium looming like a UFO. He has spent the majority of
his life in this place and what has it gotten him? However many years
before retirement, a few hundred thousand in his 401k, a belly and a
gray beard and a certificate for twenty-five years of service on the wall
of his cubicle. Twenty-five years of his life and they give him a certificate printed off the printer in the supply room. Sarah hides them in her
desk but he has seen the stack of blank certificates, the folder labeled
"achievement awards."

He takes another step. It is colder up here, brisk. It feels good. He
should come up here more often, have a drink at the end of the day,
stretch his legs, get a look at all that green stretched out before him, the
hills in the distance. It is beautiful. He looks down and the butterflies

stir in his belly. He stepped through yellow police tape to get to this place. He wonders if he is the first person who has been up here since the police closed whatever case they had to make. He is fairly sure that he is not here to jump. He just kind of found himself here, wandered up the stairs after another ridiculous meeting. Jesus Christ. He is almost glad Yoder is not here to see all of this.

If they had known about this place when they were younger, maybe they would have snuck a few beers up here, a flask, a joint. Did they do that kind of thing when they were younger? He remembers it all being better, looser, fewer expectations, but the details are starting to fade into a kind of eighties movie montage.

He wonders about Chad Stephenson. Was there a path that would have taken Russell toward that kind of job? There was a time when he could have done anything, and then there was a time when he was making the most of the path he had chosen, and then there was a time when he was just on that path, and now the time when he is coasting, waiting it out for another decade or so to…what? To retire? To stop? To die?

He looks down. A few guys are vaping on the sidewalk, exhaling huge plumes of cotton-candy vapor. Another ridiculous modern contrivance. Just smoke fucking cigarettes. He could spit on them from here. He could drop a quarter on one of their heads. He could hit the ground at however many miles an hour and scare the cotton-candy vapor right out of them.

Visioning exercise. He has been through three department reorganizations, countless "belt tightenings," the reign of four executive directors, and a run of management consultants in the nineties that must have cost millions of dollars, but this is as ridiculous as it has ever been. Visioning. They are writing down words, cutting pictures out of magazines like thirteen-year-old girls. The IT kid said he wanted to be rich and Chad Stephenson fawned over him like he was the newfound Dalai Lama.

He kicks at the gravel. He had never thought about what was on the top of this building. It seems odd that it would be gravel. Probably something to do with rainwater, the environment. Did somebody have to lug bags of gravel up the stairs? But no, this building is not that old and it is all done by machines now. A crane put that gravel here. He picks up a pebble, feeling his belly push up against his belt. He needs to get back to the gym. He needs to go to the dentist. If he took two steps forward right now, he would never need another thing.

His phone dings and he jumps. He backs up a few steps. In the distance he sees a plane moving through the blue sky. A text. Ginny with a grocery list. Milk, lemonade, paper towels. How many more rolls of paper towels will he buy? When does it end? If they found him, they would look at that text and it would be profound and ordinary. Milk, lemonade, paper towels. He walks toward the stairs and notices the sweat under his arms, on his back, his forehead and neck. Was he really going to do it? What was he doing up there if he wasn't thinking about it?

Milk, lemonade, paper towels. "No problem," he texts back.

Yoder

YODER WAKES UP ON HIS feet again. He is in a kitchen, a familiar kitchen. He is in Pappas's kitchen. Jesus fucking Christ. He looks for a computer but of course all he sees are empty bottles and shopping bags, Best Buy and Walmart boxes. The idiot wins eight point eight million dollars and he goes and spends it at Walmart.

There are five Pizza Hut boxes stacked on top of the stove, and Yoder registers the fact that this doesn't even make him hungry. He opens the top box. Meat Lovers. He wonders what would happen if he tried to eat a slice. There are voices coming from far away in the house, laughing and shouting, a low twang that he suspects is modern country music. Chew tobacco chew tobacco chew tobacco spit.

He walks into the living room, now nearly covered in Best Buy boxes. They seem to have metastasized, filling the room with virtual reality headsets and gaming systems and unidentifiable gadgetry. He scans the boxes. Not a laptop or a simple computer in the bunch. He walks down the hall, peers into what looks like an office. No computer. He searches the bedroom. Nothing. He needs to find out what day it

147

is, enter the data so he can start figuring out exactly what is happening to him.

He sits down on the bed. It smells terrible in the room, a mixture of sweat and beer and pizza, a fraternity smell. Why doesn't he just pay somebody to clean the place? What is wrong with these people? Stepping off that ledge is the best decision he ever made. He would do it a hundred times out of a hundred. If he had known what was going to happen, how useless it was all going to be, he would have jumped off that building years earlier. He would have taken some of these millionaires out with him.

The voices are getting louder and then Pappas is walking past the doorway, moving into the kitchen, opening the refrigerator. Yoder follows him and another man through the doorway. They are warming up pizza. Two Corona bottles sweat on the counter. Pappas's friend is exactly who Yoder would have thought Pappas would hang out with: beard, beer gut, graying hair, baseball hat. Right out of central casting.

"I swear," Pappas says, "that ass is…"

"I hear you," the other man says.

"Like the man says, grab 'em in the pussy."

The two men laugh and clink bottles. Yoder steps into the kitchen. He walks right up to Pappas, stands in front of him. Pappas walks right through him and moves to the refrigerator. He takes out two more beers. "Grab 'em in the pussy," he says, the tone in his voice fond, as if he is recalling a favorite aphorism.

Yoder picks up a Corona bottle. He throws it against the wall. An explosion, and Pappas shouts, "The fuck!" and then everything goes still. Yoder takes another bottle and throws it against another wall. "The fuck!" Pappas shouts. "What is…"

"I don't…" the other man says. They are both staring at the wall. Pappas is actually shaking. He seems as if he might cry. The country music is still playing somewhere in the further reaches of the house.

"It's a fucking…"

"No. There has to be some…"

There is some spare change sitting on the counter and Yoder shoves it onto the ground.

Chew tobacco chew tobacco chew tobacco spit.

Pappas jumps and then runs out the living room door. His friend follows. Yoder can hear them out in the street shouting "what the fuck" at each other. Yoder feels fantastic. This is as good as he has felt in years.

He walks to the living room, where he can see them staring at the house. Pappas is pacing. He pulls out his phone and types a number, then puts it back. Yoder feels like he could dunk a basketball. His Achilles tendons don't even hurt. He opens one of the boxes, takes out a small Bluetooth speaker. It is shaped like a football, small and compact and heavy. He weighs the heft in his hand. Pappas and his friend are framed in the window, both of them just standing there. Yoder throws the speaker as hard as he can, a perfect spiral right through the picture window. The smash is a symphony. Pappas passes out. His friend starts running down the street. Yoder will turn off that goddamn country music and find a computer. He will enter the data. He will figure this out eventually.

CRAVER

CRAVER STIRS HIS COFFEE AND watches the door. The waitress is chatting in Spanish with two chubby men at the counter. Elvis is playing on the jukebox, the steady bump mixing with the hiss of the fryer. He can see the cook making his cheeseburger. Sweat drips down his back. He checks his phone.

The Elmore Leonard novel he bought in El Paso sits open in front of him. Everything is hot, drenched in sunlight. Ever since he got off the interstates it's been like this, too bright, too hot, everything gone slightly askew. He feels like he has stepped into some movie from the seventies.

At least he hasn't seen the man in the white sedan. Or, he doesn't think he has.

He checks his phone. The text thread with Chastain is the only thing he's been managing these past few days. He thinks again about how the phone works, how he's stringing along a series of electronic breadcrumbs, cell tower to cell tower. Ping ping ping. I was here. And here. And here.

The burger comes and he nods thanks to the waitress, watches her walk back toward the counter. She is young, possibly Native American, maybe Mexican. A black ponytail bobs lightly against her robin blue uniform. She retakes her spot at the counter, says something that makes the two chubby men laugh. He wonders if she is talking about him but nobody turns. It wouldn't matter.

The cheeseburger looks good—a hand-formed patty crisp with grease, centered on the plate and haloed with fries. He takes a picture and texts it to Chastain with a single word: AMERICA.

The door opens and he jolts, almost chokes on the burger. A woman and her daughter come in to a round of greetings. He realizes that everybody in this diner knows one another except him. He wonders again if the joke the waitress made was at his expense. He thinks about her walking to the counter, the dress punching back and forth. She is probably twenty years old. She is beautiful.

He can see the road from here, a weathered gray line receding into the distance. Not a highway, definitely a road. He would like some mustard for the burger, but as soon as he started eating he realized that he had been famished, and it is nearly gone. What kind of waitress doesn't come back to check if everything is okay? He used to go to lunch with Cowens and Pappas and remembers how Pappas would simply not eat if he didn't have ketchup. They spent fifteen minutes in a Chili's at the mall one day just watching Pappas's food while he watched the waitress doing everything but bringing him ketchup. Craver himself had to go grab a bottle off the bar and he was still twenty minutes late for a meeting with Sarah and Lawson.

Jesus Christ, Pappas and Cowens. They are millionaires. He wonders what the office is like. Same as it ever was, he imagines. What kind of dumb things is Pappas doing with eight point eight million?

He has looked at the paperwork but only on his phone. He cannot imagine a situation in which he locates a printer, a fax machine, a spare half an hour to explain the nature of his severance. He does not know what happened to his key fob. When he tries, he can only imagine a few of their faces, Sarah with her glasses and ponytail, like a pretty robot from some movie set in the future. He can see Mowery and his stupid Make America Great Again hat, his pressed jeans. He can kind of picture Garner, Pappas, Cowens. He can definitely still picture Chastain, that night at Kirkpatrick's wedding.

He really thought he had played. He can picture the email from Garner: "When we win, we will take the cash payout and not reveal our names."

The waitress retrieves his plate and leaves the bill. "That was great," he says. She nods. That was great. He is an idiot. He watches her walk back toward the counter, her dark legs rippling against the smooth nylon of her uniform. When she settles at the counter, she says something in Spanish and the men laugh again. One of them looks his way and quickly looks out the window. A car pulls up in a cloud of dust. A police car.

I have done nothing wrong, he thinks. He sips at his Diet Coke, picks up the novel. He will find something different in the next town, something spacey and sci-fi, or something with dragons and elves. Elmore Leonard is great and fun but not right for his head right now. The man in the white sedan could have been conjured right out of an Elmore Leonard novel himself. He wonders if that really happened. "See you on down the line," the man had said. Has he been reading too many Elmore Leonard novels?

He has done nothing wrong.

The police officer is a young woman, dark-haired and slim. She stands outside the car, looking at her phone. She enters and hugs the waitress. It is obvious they are sisters. She greets the chubby men. She looks up and down the diner. He nods his head. Has the waitress called her sister the cop because he was looking at her ass? He pictures them standing and turning his way, slowly walking toward him in the back of the small room. The chubby men, the mother and daughter, the two sisters, the cook. They all know each other. Nobody would ever know he had been here.

But nothing happens. The policewoman sits at the counter and her sister pours her a coffee. They chat in Spanish. Every now and then the woman's walkie-talkie buzzes and somebody says something cryptic. Craver stares at the novel. He texts Chastain a cheeseburger emoji. He puts a ten-dollar bill down on his six fifty-seven tab. He will stand and walk to the door, nod at the chubby men and the policewoman. He will say "Thanks!" and then move down the stairs, and into the Civic. He will keep on driving west. He will probably never see the man in the white sedan again. He has done nothing wrong.

Lawson

LAWSON WONDERS HOW MANY POEMS each
person is going to read. It seemed like a lot of people on the Facebook
event, but he is new to this and was happy that Joe had thought enough
of him to reach out. Maybe all poetry readings have twelve poets. Maybe
that's normal. Poems are short, right? Maybe that's not even a lot.

They are in a bar, a dark one that he has been to a few times after
work. It's been a long time since they went to a work happy hour, he
realizes. Probably before the whole thing. It was Cowens who mostly
organized those outings, though, and Cowens is probably too busy
doing whatever you would do with eight point eight million dollars to
even think about Chili's or Applebee's or this place, Hank's Bar.

"So what are you working on?" Joe says. He places a beer in front of
Lawson. "You writing anything?"

"The usual. Some stories. Trying to suck less."

"You do not suck," Bimal says.

"I'm not so sure about that," he says.

"It all sucks in the beginning," Joe says. "We all suck."

Lawson takes a sip of his beer. People are clumped into groups,

153

talking about this or that. They seem like normal people, maybe a little younger, a little more tattoos than he's used to. Are these poets? At the front of the room, a tall, white-haired man dressed in jeans and a black jacket seems to be some kind of key figure. He has a thin mustache and beard and reminds Lawson of a train robber in a silent movie. People come in and hug him, they talk.

"Have you been to many of these?" Bimal asks Joe.

"I guess," he says. "There's not much of a scene, so this is, you know, this is the scene."

"Is that the main guy?" Lawson asks, nodding toward the stage, where the train robber is chatting with a group of heavily tattooed young women.

"Yeah that's Grey. He's a poet, some books out. He's the editor of *Gutshot*. Do you know that?"

"I think so," Bimal says.

Lawson is pleased that he does know. "I picked up a copy of that at Webster's the other day," he says. "They have that table that says Locally Grown with all the local writers?"

"Yeah it's good. Been around for a while. It's our local literary magazine, I guess."

The train robber moves to the front of the room. "How long do these usually go?" Lawson asks. He has work to do, but it is just for the ridiculous visioning exercise the consultants have them doing. He will give Sarah just about any benefit of the doubt, but he is starting to have some real doubts about the consultants.

"Can't quite tell. An hour? Hopefully they all read pretty quick. I know a few of them and they're good. Funny."

"Funny is not what I was expecting," Bimal says. He says it the way he says everything, flat and final.

"I know, right?" Joe says. "Some of the poets are funny, though."

The people in the front of the room look like they are settling in— hugs and chatting and handshakes. Eventually seats are taken. The train robber moves toward the stage.

"I got some good news this afternoon," Lawson says. He has been dying to tell them and the idea that he might have to wait until twelve poets read however many poems is simply not tenable.

"What's up?" Joe says. He scoots forward. Lawson can tell that he read somewhere that you should try to give your sole focus to people, to be in the moment. He imagines Joe has taken more than one improv class.

"I think they are starting up soon," Bimal says.

"I got a thing accepted," Lawson says. "One of the stories we work-shopped in your class, Joe. The one about the—"

"Hello everybody, thanks for being here," the train robber says. He is standing next to the microphone but not using it. He walks up a step and stands in front of the microphone, just in case anybody has not noticed that he doesn't need the microphone. "I'm Tommy Grey," he says. "On behalf of everybody at *Gutshot*, I want to say thanks for being here and welcome to our…fifth? Is this our fifth?"

He turns to the group of heavily tattooed women assembled to the right of the stage and one of them shouts "Seventh!"

"Our seventh," he says. "Seven? Where the hell have I been?" His voice is clear and almost high, a professor's voice.

"Where?" Joe whispers.

Lawson gives him a look. Where?

"Your story," Joe says.

Lawson starts to speak, but right at that moment the train robber announces the first reader, and one of the poets stands. She is tall and young, wearing a dress, her right arm covered in a sleeve of tattoos. "Later," Lawson mouths.

Joe scoots forward. "Congratulations," he says. He holds his glass out and they clink. Bimal gives him a fist bump.

"Oh she's funny," Joe says, pointing to the stage, where the poet is hugging the train robber. "This is going to be good."

CHASTAIN

CHASTAIN STIRS HER DRINK, A gin and tonic with extra lime. Another sits to her right, nearly untouched, Sarah having been out on the street talking to the consultants on her phone for the past ten minutes. Chastain wonders if she could finish her drink and order another one before Sarah is back, what it would be like to be caught doing it. She wonders at the fact that she cares, but she definitely cares.

She takes a sip. She is not used to pacing herself at happy hour. She is used to happy hours with Craver, where the whole point was to get drunk enough to start smoking, then to figure out whether she was going to drink enough to make out with Craver.

She checks her phone. Three texts. A cactus, an improbably large bag of Funyuns, a selfie of Craver in front of some kind of roadside store, a shack really, with a sign that says "Gas, Guns, Sandwiches." Something about Craver looks off, but she puts it out of her mind. He is probably not scared, not sad, not going a little weird in the eyes. Probably he is playing the part like usual, his every word or gesture filtered through a layer of irony so thick that it might as well be a second skin.

She watches Sarah pace on the sidewalk. Sarah is always calm. Always cool. This could be a huge thing that's going to affect them all or it might be nothing. Sarah continues talking. Chastain drinks half of the remaining drink, motions to the bartender. Sarah walks down the street, still talking, hands gesturing as she moves. Chastain finishes the drink, the burn of the gin buried in the extra lime. "Another," she says.

Robertson

ROBERTSON WAITS UNTIL EVERYBODY HAS left the room. Chad Stephenson is chatting with Taylor and he notices how close they are standing to one another, the way Chad removes his glasses whenever he is talking to one of the younger women, the way Nicole Stetler-Stephenson watches whenever this happens as well, sideways glances while she puts the materials back into the carrying cases. The materials are ridiculous, but he has grown used to them: scissors, magazines, glue. They could be kindergarten teachers or they could be management consultants working on a sixteen-month retainer contract.

Nicole looks to him and he smiles. She shrugs. They are waiting for Chad Stephenson and somehow, at some point, waiting for Chad Stephenson has become a usual part of Robertson's workday.

He needs to check the New Relic report, see what's been making the conference site crash every night for the past few days. He needs to do his goals for the year, look at résumés for the three programmer/analyst jobs they posted this week. He needs to do a lot of things and he is standing in room 210 and waiting while Chad Stephenson flirts with the Senior Marketing Associate for Digital Media Buys in front of his wife. He will give her one of his patented hugs, put his glasses back on, and join them with some remark about something insightful Taylor has said, some way in which her career path might be brightened through this visioning exercise or some kind of focused workplace mentoring, through Yoga for Business or watching a TED Talk or learning to code. How did this become a normal part of his day?

Nicole Stetler-Stephenson motions and he takes a seat. "Should just be a minute," she says, and they both chuckle. It will be more than a minute. "How did you like the exercise?" she says.

"It was interesting," he says. He is not sure what to say, where the line is between friendship and work. They are definitely becoming friends, but they are undoubtedly now at work. These people are high-paid consultants here to do a very difficult task and he has been careful to remind himself that they may seem like friends, but they are still not his friends. "I mean, this is all interesting to me I guess. Being in meetings with people talking is different. I'm used to..."

"Administering to the systems and not the people," she says. This has become a running joke between them. Another indicator that maybe they are Actual Friends and not just work friends or even colleagues. She pulls out an envelope and puts it on the table. "We have..." she starts. She steals a glance at Chad Stephenson.

Chad Stephenson hugs Taylor. He puts his hands in the namaste sign and Robertson cringes inwardly. "Thanks so much," Chad Stephenson says. He puts a hand on Taylor's shoulder. He squeezes. She leaves the room and Chad Stephenson turns to Robertson.

"We have something to discuss with you," he says. "We think you're ready."

CHASTAIN

CHASTAIN ROUNDS THE CORNER. SHE is almost back at the apartment. Two point seven miles. Yesterday she stopped at the shoe store, and today she has told herself that she won't stop. She passes an old man walking his dog, muttering lightly. "Come on Cosmo, it's okay Cosmo." The dog is nearly as old as the man. Before, she would have thought it was tragic, or stupid. She would have thought something nasty, maybe even said it under her breath. Before, she wouldn't have been out of bed at six forty-five and she sure as hell wouldn't have been running.

Her phone buzzes, and she checks to make sure it isn't Sarah or somebody else from work. She has been getting notifications when the servers go down, a bother but another sign of her advancing responsibility. Sarah has noticed that she is good with the technical people, good when things break down and everybody is still trying to assess blame, good in the time between when something has gone wrong and they figure out what to do about it.

A text from Craver. Jesus, what time is it on the West Coast? Is he on West Coast time yet? The last photo he sent looked like the desert.

She realizes she's not even sure where that part of the country starts and makes a note to spend some time googling later on in the day. You can never tell what kind of information might be useful.

This is a picture of a dark parking lot, a Chili's sign glowing orange in the distance. As always, he has only written one word: AMERICA. She waits at a red light, jogging in place. She used to think this was ridiculous, showy. You really can't stop at the corner? Really? But she told herself she isn't going to stop on this run and she sure as hell isn't going to stop now, with two point five miles of her two point seven in.

She would like to see a picture of Craver. She wonders if he is growing out his beard, his hair. She pictures him lean and suntanned. She remembers the picture he kept on his bulletin board, Jack Kerouac and Neal Cassady standing on some fire escape. He had been careful to point out the *Brakeman's Guidebook* stuffed in Kerouac's pocket. She had just nodded at the time but now she wonders at what kind of significance that held for Craver, sitting there in his desk all day, taking a smoke break every now and then, doing work when he could no longer avoid it and never quite caring about any of it, any of them, not even the work. She wonders if he will come back, what that would be like now, what he would think of her jogging in place at this intersection at six forty-five in the morning.

She has had to admit that she misses him, but only every now and then—lunch breaks, the times when she used to go out and smoke. Now, she almost never takes those breaks at all. Every now and then a snarky comment sneaks into her thoughts and she wishes there was somebody to turn to, somebody to send a Slack comment to, but more often than not the person in front of her is Sarah. Another thing Craver would surely not believe.

The light changes and she jogs across the road. She is feeling good, strong. She will need to stop smoking cigarettes eventually, but for now the idea that she can still have a few nighttime smokes and run her two point seven miles in the morning feels just about right.

The sun is fully up now, everything glowing like it is lit from within. This is the time they call the golden hour and for the first time she understands why. She never used to see this time of day, was either still asleep or looking at her phone in bed. She is surprised at how alert she feels after she runs, how she enjoys even the feeling of her aching muscles.

They have an interview at nine, then another one at eleven. She and Sarah are meeting their digital advertising consultant for lunch at Panera. The phone dings again. Another photo of a parking lot. She shakes her head. If he came back, he wouldn't even recognize her anymore.

She pushes past a couple carrying coffees and keeps the shoe store sign in her sights. She is twenty, ten, five yards away and then she is crossing that homemade finish line, walking, her breath coming fast. Her legs feel tight and useful. She is more awake now than any other time in the day. The phone dings again. Another picture of the same parking lot. She stuffs it in her pocket.

russell

RUSSELL PAUSES. "HOLD UP A sec," he says. He is breathing heavily, heavier than he expected, even on the Valleytop Trail. He has been playing it cool for most of the hike—how long have they been out? Jesus, only like twenty minutes—but now his heart is racing, his glasses fogging up. He needs to stop before Ginny has to carry him down, before a helicopter has to carry him to the ER.

Ginny is up ahead of him about ten yards. She stops, takes a drink from her water bottle. "You okay?" she says.

He breathes in as deeply as he can. It is not enough. He has not had this feeling before, like he can't get enough air, like he can't stop sweating, like stopping the hike won't even make his heart rate go back to normal. "I'm fine," he says. He breathes in again. Slightly better. Should he keep going?

Ginny puts her water bottle away. She checks her phone. He is going to have a heart attack on a trail that isn't even outside their cell service.

"Just a few minutes," he says. If he sits down, will he ever be able to stand up again? He is aware that he is standing spread-legged like Superman. He is aware that he is a far, far cry from Superman right now.

Ginny walks back down toward him. She puts a cool hand on his chest. "Maybe we should call it a day," she says.

"Nah," he says. "I'm fine. I'll be fine. Maybe shouldn't have had that last glass of wine last night."

He breathes in again. It is too hot for this. They should be sitting in the house, finishing the rewatch of *Mad Men*. They have been hiking Valleytop since they moved to the valley thirty years ago and it has never been a problem until just now, this time.

"Okay," Ginny says. She turns and starts walking. He breathes in again. Breathes out. They have done this hike how many times? He will get the NordicTrack back out, start doing push-ups in the morning. If you start with ten, do ten a day for a week, you move up to fifteen, do fifteen every morning, eventually you can build up to fifty each morning. He has done this before, when was it? The nineties. He had gotten down to a thirty-four waist, was doing the Atkins diet, taking the buns off his cheeseburgers and eating chicken wings for lunch.

"You sure you're okay?" Ginny says.

He has been just standing there. "Yeah, sorry," he says. The worst thing is the real concern in her voice. No animus or scorn. She is worried about him. "Yeah, I'm fine. Just fine."

She takes a step toward him, almost loses her balance. She grabs a tree and spins in slow motion, twisting the branch as she sinks to the path. She lands gracefully on the trail and lets go of the branch. She turns to him and laughs.

God, he loves her, loves how her first instinct in this kind of ridiculous situation is to laugh. To look to him and laugh. He is lucky. He smiles and nods and makes a face that he hopes will suffice.

He is still breathing heavily, unable to quite catch his breath. Is this one of the signs of a heart attack? Is it better to tell her he might be having a heart attack and have it turn out to be a false alarm, or to hold his tongue and just hope it all works out?

He imagines the scene. He would fall to the ground, clutching his chest. She would call 911, an ambulance, but where would it drive? A helicopter, but where would it land? She would have to wait with him, sitting here on the trail, watching the life drain out of him second by second. How long would it take? She would sit there by his side, crying while the trail stones jutted into her bottom. She would stand, finally, when they came to get his body. She would ride with him in the ambulance, a slow trip with the lights on, the urgency of the siren unneeded. She would have to fill out paperwork. Would they take her into a separate room, or leave her in some waiting area full of children and parents, husbands and wives, entire families waiting to hear the fate of a loved one? Would she have to take a taxi home, an Uber, listen to the driver's chatter about the football team or the roadwork while she thought through their lifetime together, while she compiled lists, memories, opportunities they would never have? When she got home, how ridiculous would it feel to exchange money, to click a fifteen percent tip on the app? To go into the kitchen and have to see all of his things there—the fantasy baseball magazines and his phone charger, his coat on the chair, and his winter boots still sitting by the door? Would she change her clothes, pour a glass of wine, take a bath, call her sister?

"Well," she says. "Come on over here and help me up."

She reaches out a hand and he steps forward. "You know," he says. "Maybe it's just not the day today. I'm feeling kind of off." He tries to put as much levity into his voice as he can, as much as his depleted lungs can breathe into him, breathe out, force into being despite everything, like an annual report or performance goal. He can do this.

She puts a hand over his arm and pats him a few times, as if he is a dog who has done a good job. "Let's go home," she says.

CHASTAIN

CHASTAIN STIRS HER DRINK. SHE checks her phone. Two texts from Craver. She has no idea where he even is right now. They are both pictures, both with the message "AMERICA." If she is being honest, she has lost interest in his project, suspects he has lost interest as well, and these last hundred or so texts, each with the same message, each some safe blend of ironic and vague, seem like the final rote breaths as he limps across the finish line of the Great American Road Trip. The Great American Road Trip. She is embarrassed to even be thinking the phrase.

Shouldn't he have gotten to San Francisco already?

She takes a sip and looks around. Nobody she recognizes. In her pocketbook there is half a pack of American Spirits. Old habits die hard, like this thing where she likes to get to the date spot a half an hour early, have a drink or two, be sitting there so she can watch Stan's face when he sees her from across the room. She likes to watch him arrive, watch as he makes his way toward the bar, through the door, as he assesses the situation calmly, then finally sees her there across the room. She likes the involuntary smile of recognition, the way he nods to recognize her habit of always being early, the way he never mentions it when he settles in at the barstool she has saved for him.

He kisses her on the cheek. His hand lingers briefly on her arm before he motions to the bartender. "Beer and another one of those," he says. "Gin and tonic, extra lime."

"So," he says. "How are things? What's going on with your sister?"

"Oh Jesus," she says. "Do you really want to talk about that?"

"Seemed like a Thing last time we talked."

Sally is pregnant again. Chastain finishes what's left of her drink and thanks the bartender for the new one. She takes a sip. She thinks about the cigarettes in her pocketbook, wonders if Stan would disapprove. This is their fifth date. The last two ended with some pretty good kissing in the parking garage, but that is as far as it's gone so far. Her phone buzzes and she ignores it. "The thing is," she says. "Oh god there are a lot of things but somehow, this time, I mean there have been like a lot of things with her but this time, for once, I kind of don't care?"

Stan laughs. He takes a drink. "You don't care?"

"I know," she says. "I'm surprised, to be honest. Maybe I didn't even really know that until just now but actually I don't give a shit."

"I like that," he says, raising a glass. "Here's to not giving a shit."

"It's wonderful," she says.

"That was the thing," Stan says. "When I turned forty? Maybe forty-two."

"Forty-two?"

"I know. It's very specific, but forty was just kind of a freak-out, you know? Like oh shit I'm forty."

She nods, sips her drink. The phone buzzes again.

"You need to get that?" he says.

"So forty-two?" she says.

"Forty-two was like, oh I'm actually in my forties now."

"Are you dropping wisdom," she says. "Is that what's happening here, old man?"

"You'll get there," he says. "At some point."

They have not discussed ages but the dating app gives a range. She is younger and he is older and it is all within the guidelines of what she has generally deemed to be acceptable. He is forty-two but fit and handsome in a daddish kind of way. An ex-wife but no kids. What seems like a reliable job that he doesn't talk about much. He is kind and nice and funny and smiles when he notices her across a crowded room.

"And when I get there, there will be some kind of wisdom?"

He laughs. "I wouldn't go that far," he says. "Laziness maybe? Set in my ways? Somehow I just stopped caring so much about, I don't know. Everything?"

She thinks about Sarah. Sarah cares so much about everything: the way time is tracked in the system, the way tasks are labeled on Basecamp, the people who are in the meeting, the people who are not in the meeting, the fact that nobody throws away the whiteboard markers when they go stale. She cannot think of a thing that Sarah doesn't have a careful and precise opinion on. "What about work?" she says.

"Well that's tricky," Stan says. "I try to do a good job. I mean, I'm proud of that. I work hard. I'm good at what I do."

"But."

"I don't know. I need another beer." He motions to the bartender. "At some point I realized that everything's basically going to be fine. Everything is going to keep on moving along almost no matter what and if I freak out about something, the only thing anybody's ever going to remember is that I freaked out."

She replays this in her head. The only thing anybody is going to remember is that I freaked out.

"I mean," he says, "I know you have been dealing with some serious shit at your office. Most offices, for sure mine. Everything is generally going to be just fine."

The only thing anybody is going to remember is that I freaked out. She thinks about the book they have started to outline. She will go home and open up the Google Doc, try to flesh out some of the bullet points in the hiring chapter, the visioning exercise. But this. The only thing anybody is going to remember is that I freaked out. She almost wishes she could share it with Sarah, but it is not Sarah's way—it is not Sarah's way to freak out or question any reaction to work other than stoic steady progress. She puts that in the back of her mind. You can never tell when something is going to come into play.

"What are you looking at?" Stan says. "Do I have beer on my nose or something?"

"No," she says. "No, you're good. You're very, very good."

CRAVER

CRAVER WATCHES THE REARVIEW. VAN truck car car car. No sign of the white sedan. No police. He passes a sign: Roswell 45 miles. New Mexico is desert scrub and the occasional gas station. He should have stopped at the McDonald's an hour back. He should have packed some sandwiches, bought a cooler, checked the balance on the Visa while he still had Wi-Fi at the hotel. He should have played the goddamn lottery.

He could be in San Francisco now, should have been there months ago. He could be sitting around a bohemian outdoor cafe with his new friends, laughing and talking about literature and pop culture and whatever those kinds of people talk about. He could be walking confidently down Lombard Street, his face set in a resolved grin, knowing that he made it. He could be interviewing for jobs, working on his novel, learning how to make his own kombucha. But no. The misdirection was necessary, a good idea. He has done nothing wrong but the white sedan, that young police officer and her sister, the whole idea of San Francisco, of being in a specific place at a specific time, it was like he had been dragging something behind him and now he is free.

He sees the image again, the woman walking toward Mount Rushmore in the rain, her slim figure retreating, the empty parking lot, the feeling like anything could happen, like he could do anything.

The signs are starting to lean strongly toward alien kitsch: visit the UFO Cafe. This was a good idea for the text potential alone. There is nothing in the rearview, nothing up ahead on the road. He checks his phone. Another email from the system administrator, that kid Robertson. "I'm sorry I can't activate your account." He has cc'ed Sarah and Lawson.

Up ahead, a rest stop. He pulls to the right and slows. He is starving now but will probably have to wait until he gets closer to Roswell to eat. He imagines eating an alien burger at the UFO Cafe. He will text Chastain a note that says only PHONE HOME. But that might make her think he is making some kind of gesture, asking for something, for help in some way. He will text ELLIOTT.

The rest area is a low building and a gravel path. Two cars sit in the parking lot. Off to the side, a woman walks a small dog. Craver parks and checks his phone. His battery is down to twenty-two percent. The woman with the dog is talking on the phone, shouting at somebody. She gestures with her free hand, pointing off toward the desert. She ends the call and stares straight up at the sky. Her fists are clenched, mouth open. She is practically vibrating with rage. The little dog pulls at the leash but the woman remains still.

A man walks out of the building, zipping his fly, and nods to Craver as he walks past. Craver pretends to be looking for something in the glove compartment. He regards the knife he bought at a truck stop outside Albuquerque, a Jeff Gordon NASCAR signature knife that he told himself was a joke, or protection, or something funny to mail to Chastain as a souvenir. He takes it out of the box and holds it. The handle is curved and hard plastic. It is heavier than he would have thought. A tool. Seems to be a pretty good knife.

The woman is moving slowly along the gravel pathway. The dog sniffs and waddles, its little tail twitching in delight. The woman is tall, wearing dark jeans and a white shirt. She is dressed like she is going on a date. It is twelve forty-five and Craver wonders where she would be going dressed like that. She is lean, dark-skinned, good-looking. He wonders if she is Mexican. Honduran? What is it like in Honduras? He could keep driving, just go down to South America. That is a thing he could do. He could do anything he wants. He deserves things. He has done nothing wrong.

The woman is still walking. She is blowing off steam, gathering herself. He wonders who was on the phone. All these phones sending all their signals all the time. Ping ping ping.

There are only two cars at this rest stop. The woman drives a BMW, a small one, black. It looks new. She has run out of sidewalk now and is walking in the rocks and scrub. The dog sniffs and waddles. The woman is pretty. From this distance she looks young but he guesses she is about his age. He sits up and puts the knife in his pocket. The highway is empty, nobody coming or going. He puts a hand on the door. He wonders what Chastain is doing. Probably standing outside, smoking. Maybe she has found somebody new to hang around with, somebody new to tease, to lead on. Were they ever really friends?

The woman is coming toward him. Toward her car. She is about his age, mid-thirties. Pretty. She is really pretty. He gets out of the car and stretches. Acts casual. He is not sure what he is going to do. It has been a few days since he has talked to anybody. He remembers the waitress in the diner, whose sister was a cop. This woman could be their older sister. Everybody in this part of the country is Latino. He realizes he needs to go to the bathroom. That is why he pulled into this rest stop in the first place. Tell yourself that, he thinks. He pulled into the rest stop to go to the bathroom.

The woman is really pretty. He puts his hand on the knife. The dog stops to smell something on the sidewalk and the woman picks it up. She talks to the dog in low Spanish. "Chichi something something, Chichi something something something."

"Cute dog," Craver says. His voice is scratchy.

The woman nods. She picks up her pace and Craver turns around. Should he follow? He takes a step, thinking for reasons why he might be going back to his car. He pats his pockets as if he is missing his phone. The woman picks up her pace. She is a few yards from the BMW and he could run, sprint, meet her hand on the door. He is still patting his pockets when she gets into the car, locks the doors, and speeds away.

Robertson

"A WHAT?" JESSIE SAYS. SHE has paused the game, Office Mail, and the character's arm remains extended, a red file marked "Top Secret" dangling tantalizingly toward the mean-looking cartoon boss. "Like a multilevel marketing thing?"

"No. I don't think so. I mean…"

"The Emerald Dragon Society?"

"I think it's more like a lodge? Like an Internet version of like, the Masons? They call it EDS."

She takes out her phone. "URL?"

This is what he was worried about. He never should have told her. "They've been like really nice to me, though."

"U. R. L." She points to the phone. "I need to check this shit out. I love this shit."

"I need to. I mean…These people have been really nice. They recognize my value."

Jessie sits up. She actually turns away from the monitor. "They recognize your value?" she says. The concern in her voice hits a register that

173

he knows he should be worried about, a signal that he can hear but can't quite interpret just yet.

"I don't have one point four million fucking YouTube followers," he says. He wants it to land like a joke but the minute it comes out he realizes how whiny that sounds. "I'm sorry," he says.

She gives him the look and returns to her game.

"Is that the Office Space game?" he says.

"Office Mail. And you are not going to distract me from this Emerald fucking Dragon mumbo jumbo."

He sits down on the beanbag chair, stretches, pushes his legs out and his fingertips toward the wall. Do they ever really talk? Could he explain to her how this all feels? "So, you just walk around and give out mail in that game?" he says. The arm is still extended. What kind of office would have a folder that says "Top Secret?" Where would you even get that folder? Would they be sitting around in the copy room? He wonders if Sarah has a stack of Top Secret folders. Or Chastain. Chastain would be the one to have the Top Secret folders now.

Jessie has been growing out her hair and she strikes him as especially beautiful from this angle. "I have to finish this for Los Angeles tonight but I am not gonna forget."

Robertson sits up. "What's that?" he says, pointing at the screen.

"I said I am not gonna forget this Emerald Dragon business," she says. "EDS."

"No, what's that? That…is the Office Space guy wearing a ring?"

"Office Mail," she says. She clicks the mouse and the screen focuses in on the hand.

"Yeah kind of funky now that I look at," she says. "Was that an eighties thing?"

He looks out the window. There is nothing out there but the street, the usual cars driving past. It can't be.

"Jessie," he says, but he can't finish.

"What?" Now the concern in her voice is clear, throwing a red alert. She pauses the game and it freezes on a close-up of the mean boss, with his mustache and slicked-back hair and white collar button-up.

"That ring?" he says. "Is that…"

"What?" she says. "You need to calm down. You need to communicate."

"A fucking emerald dragon ring," he says. He is sure of it now, the ring is pixelated and rough but it is dark brown with some green, maybe some kind of thing etched into the side. It is impossible to tell at this resolution. "Do you have the original files?"

"You know these things don't come with original files," she says.

Could they have planted the ring in the game? Do they have that kind of reach? What the fuck is the Emerald Dragon Society and why is it not on the Internet? Is not being recognized by Google an indication that something doesn't even exist, or does it mean that thing is on some whole other level? Nicole called it a whimsically named investment group, but that ring is real and what kind of investment group gives itself a *Game of Thrones* name?

"Right," he says. He looks outside but there is nothing but the regular traffic moving past on the street, and what did he expect? Chad Stephenson and Nicole Stetler-Stephenson standing by the lamppost like spies in a fifties movie? "Of course," he says, his mind reaching for something to change the topic. "So what happens when you hand off that Top Secret folder?"

"Only one way to find out," Jessie says. She clicks a button and the handoff is made. "We're going to talk about this later," she says.

Yoder

YODER WAKES UP ON HIS feet again. He looks around. He is in a familiar kitchen. He sits down on a chair. When was the last time? Pappas? Cowens? He feels his pocket, but even as his hand moves down, he understands there will be no phone there.

There are sounds coming from a nearby room, low talking, music playing. The kitchen is neat, orderly. It is nice but not too nice. On the counter there is an array of liquor—Tito's vodka, Buffalo Trace bourbon, the gin in the green bottle. An orange box of wine. A few six-packs.

"Well," a voice says. "I guess we should get started?" Yoder recognizes the voice. He pauses, feels again where the phone would be. There are nacho chips and salsa and hummus lined up on the counter. No laptop, no computer. "So we're the thirteen. I just thought, you know, it might be a good idea to..." the voice stops. It may be Mowery. Or Czuba. He places the man in some kind of technical support position, bullshitting him about why they couldn't do one thing or another, that move that he used to hate, the tech people just dropping a series of technical terms and then shrugging.

176

"It's been," the voice continues. He thinks it may be Mowery. "It's been weird, right? And kind of…"

"Lonely?" Cowens. He sounds drunk already, much more drunk than Mowery. There are a few muffled laughs.

"I don't know about lonely." This is Garner. "It's been different, I guess."

"You're still working, though?" Cowens's voice slurs and it comes out like all one word: yourestillworkingthough.

"Laurie wouldn't know what to do with me if I didn't have someplace to go," Garner says. Yoder knows immediately he has said this a hundred times, a thousand. He realizes all of a sudden that he hates Garner, has always hated Garner with his dumb gadgets and his inane chatter. He is sure Garner's credit score is perfect. He is sure that the man has never missed an appointment with the dentist, the dermatologist, the doctor, the accountant.

"So I had an idea," somebody says. Yoder stands. There are too many of them and it has been too long. He can't tell anybody's voice anymore. He wonders if he is losing something, if his brain is not as sharp as it once was. He is, after all, a ghost. Or a specter. Or a poltergeist. No, he thinks, a poltergeist is a totally separate thing. He is pretty sure of that. Is he a demon? He does not feel demonic. He runs his hands along his head, his belly, his back. He can still feel the bald spot on the top of his head, the hairs coming out of his ears, the belly pushing out over his belt. Physically he is almost the same, with the notable exception of the invisibility. He tugs at his shirt, unbuttons a button. If he had known that he would be wearing the yellow Van Heusen shirt and his gray dockers for eternity, he might have reconsidered his usual Monday outfit. If he knew those assholes were going to win the lottery, he would have reconsidered a lot of things.

There is no computer in this kitchen, no smartphone. No technology of any kind. This is a normal house, though, Garner's house, and he is sure there is a desktop or a stand-alone unit somewhere.

"This isn't the Yoder thing, is it?" a voice says.

Yoder jumps.

"It is," the other person replies. He is fairly sure this is Cowens.

"It's a scholarship? In Yoder's name?"

"A scholarship to what?"

"The guy killed himself. And we're all so lucky."

"Rich."

"We're all rich and the guy...he..."

Yoder stands. He picks up a beer bottle and then puts it back down. He could go in and spook them all, could send them running out to their brand-new BMWs and motorcycles and Ford goddamn trucks.

"He's dead," somebody says.

Yoder waits for the laughs but none come. He can hear music bubbling in the background, Sade singing about love. Not what he would have chosen, but at least it's not chew tobacco chew tobacco chew tobacco spit. He walks down the hall toward what he assumes is the living room. He looks down but cannot see his feet waddling slowly forward. He feels his belly but cannot see the yellow Van Heusen shirt pushing out over the seam of the gray Dockers. Where do I go when I'm not awake? he wonders.

He sees shoes, jeans, a pair of flip-flops, a beer bottle sitting on the floor. And then he enters the room and they are sitting there, the thirteen, or most of them, at least. Cowens and Pappas and Mowery and Czuba and Squillante. The young kid who they hired to do some kind of thing with Google is sitting next to the guy who always tried to bullshit him about his IT tickets. The woman who used to make popcorn in the microwave every afternoon is chatting with the guy who drove the Rav4 with a Foo Fighters sticker on it.

"So what would this even be?" Mowery says. He is wearing brand-new jeans and what Yoder takes to be expensive cowboy boots. He is wearing aviator sunglasses inside.

"I don't know," Cowens says. "Like a scholarship. A fund. You know what I'm talking about." He finishes his beer in two great glugs and then stomps toward the kitchen. Yoder almost follows him. He never would have guessed that Cowens would have given him a second thought. He wonders if he has misjudged Cowens all along. Sounds of the refrigerator, a beer being opened, and then another.

In the room, there is low talking, idle conversation about the heat and football, the things they are doing and buying and the emails they are still getting from the company. They seem nervous and strange. Uncomfortable. None of them really had anything in common other than the office, the work, the meetings and small talk and key performance indicators.

"I heard Sarah is writing some book about it," Squillante says.

"About what? Us?" the popcorn lady asks.

"More about them. The other ones," Squillante says. "You know Sarah. She just kept on going."

"I heard they're doing some kind of vision quest thing?" Pappas says.

"All I know is the servers keep going down," Mowery says. "I never stopped the uptime notifications and now I just kind of..." he trails off. "Do any of you," he says and then pauses. He drinks half his drink, something clear and fizzy. "Do you miss it at all?"

Cowens comes back, sits down, drinks half of one beer and sits the other one on the ground. "We should do this more often," he says. "Like a regular happy hour or a dinner or something."

"A book club," Squillante says.

"We can read Sarah's book," Pappas says.

"I would read that book," Cowens says. "I feel a little bad about, you know, just quitting like that?"

"Bad?" Pappas says. "Why the fuck would you feel bad?"

Yoder wishes he could have a drink. He wonders how long it's been since he last awoke. When was that? Mancus's house? Where does he go when he is not awake? He has a sudden thought. It can't be. No. But then so many of the pieces fit together. He backs into a corner and slides to the carpet.

What if there is a god?

Jesus Christ, what if there is a god and this is what the afterlife is like? What if there is a god and this is what has been chosen for him, this is what he has earned. It is unfathomable, the idea that what is happening to him is something other than random, a glitch, an unidentified bug in the system. He stands, then sits again.

"So how would this work?" Mowery says. "This scholarship or whatever."

"We'd have to, I don't know, figure out where to do it. Like what did he like?"

"Pop-Tarts," Pappas says.

Yoder will take note of this the next time he wakes up in Pappas's house.

"Let's be real," the popcorn lady says. "I mean. Do you really think he deserves a scholarship? Deserved?"

"Deserved? We won the lottery," Mancus says.

"I don't know about you, but I worked for everything I have," Pappas says. "I sure as hell deserve it. We all do."

"The dude's dead, man," Cowens says. He finishes his beer and gets up again.

"He okay?" Mowery says, nodding to Pappas.

"Fuck if I know. He's got eight point eight million dollars. Can't imagine why any of us would not be okay."

"I think he liked ice hockey?" Czuba says. "He had a Flyers thing up in his cube?"

"I was just saying he used to eat Pop-Tarts a lot," Pappas says. "He did. I saw him in the kitchen a bunch of times. He would heat them in the microwave. It was a weird move." He turns to Mowery. "You bought the Kentucky Fried Chicken?"

"What's so weird about heating your Pop-Tarts in the microwave?" the popcorn lady says.

Jesus Christ, Yoder thinks. He spent thirty years at that company, worked alongside some of these people for decades, and they don't know a thing about him. Pop-Tarts? Ice hockey? This is what they remember.

"I don't know about the hockey thing. I think that's..." Pappas says.

"The other one. Russell?" Cowens says.

The other one? The other what? Yoder stands. He wonders if he can shout. He realizes he's never tried to say anything to any of them. He is shit at haunting, or whatever this is.

"Yoder liked country music, right?" Mowery says.

"Country music? What are we going to do with that?" Pappas says. "Donate to the Dolly Parton Hall of Fame?"

Yoder moves into the kitchen. He picks up a knife. He could throw it in there and really put a scare in them. He may be able to actually stab one of them, the idiots. But what if this is the test? What if there is somebody watching him? He is failing even at this.

"A scholarship would be simple," Mancus says. "To the university. I don't know if he was one of those bleed blue and white people, but he lived here almost his entire adult life, right?"

"A country music scholarship?" Pappas says.

"I'm fairly sure there is no Dolly Parton Hall of Fame," the popcorn lady says.

"There's Dollywood," Pappas says.

"We're not talking about country music," Mancus says. "Just a scholarship. For a local kid. They have to be used to this kind of request, right? The development people. The probably have a whole brochure or something they can send you."

Yoder puts the knife down. A scholarship. It's not what he would choose, or maybe it is. He has to admit that he had never really done any charity work, any giving other than the years they were in DC and it seemed like everybody was involved in one thing or another. Jesus Christ, a scholarship.

"Are you joining the Peace Corps or something?" Pappas says.

"We applied," Mancus says. "We might."

"So a scholarship?" Cowens says. "A scholarship."

"I'm just saying I think there are the mechanisms in place to do that. If that's what we want to do," Mancus says.

He pauses and there is a general grumbling assent, yeps and sures and nods.

"Okay, a scholarship," Cowens says. He is still slurring his words but he seems less burdened than before. "Maybe one of us can follow up and then send out an email or whatever, or we can meet in a few weeks, do a happy hour, a planning thing."

"I'm keeping what I deserve," the popcorn lady says. She parades past him, grabs a coat, and is out the door.

"A planning thing," Pappas says.

"I'll follow up," Mancus says. "Remember Poston? He worked for Lawson for a while. English guy?"

"The one with the super green car?" Pappas says.

"I don't know, I guess. But he's in development now I think."

"He won the fantasy league that one year that Drew Brees went crazy."

"Oh yeah," Squillante says. "He was a good guy. What happened to that guy?"

"I think he's in development now," Mancus says again. Jesus, Yoder thinks, they are all so goddamn stupid. Poston is in fucking development now. Were they all this stupid when he was alive?

"Okay, so I'll do that," Mancus says.

"I'll email about happy hour," Cowens says.

Yoder leans against the counter. A scholarship. If he closes his eyes he wonders if he will go back to sleep, will wake up again in some celebration hall watching Sarah announce the Arthur R. Yoder Scholarship Fund. Or the president of the university. Or Terry Bradshaw or Dan Rather or Bruce Springsteen.

In the living room they are still milling around, chatting about this and that, not sure that they are able to just up and leave yet. Yoder always hated this part, the part when it is over but for some reason nobody feels like they can just leave. Nobody cares if you just fucking leave, he thinks. What is that called? Ghosting. He almost laughs. Ghosting. He sits down in a chair. Cowens wanders in and opens another beer. He stops on the way out and takes a drink right out of the vodka bottle. He looks ragged, unwell.

The Arthur R. Yoder Scholarship Fund. Isn't that something?

CHASTAIN

"A WHAT?" CHASTAIN SAYS. "A scholarship? For Yoder?"

"Well, in his name," Sarah says.

They are sitting in the Spontaneous Teaming Area, otherwise known as "the cushy chairs." Chastain swirls her double macchiato. "Who knew his name was Arthur?" she says. "Arthur."

"I thought it suited him," Sarah says. "Kind of old-school elegance to it."

"A scholarship."

"It's nice. He didn't have any people, you know. The funeral was kind of rough to be honest."

"I heard," Chastain says. What she heard is that it was tragic, a short story of a funeral, Russell and his wife and Sarah and the guy from his dry cleaners. She recalls wishing that Craver was still around so they could break it down, especially the detail of the dry cleaner, just the kind of terrible/sad/hilarious thing Craver would have loved. They could have done an entire happy hour just putting together the story of the dry cleaner.

"So here's the thing that could kind of screw us up here," Sarah

says. She leans in close. "They're going to do a launch party thing. An
event. I think they're actually calling it a gala."

"Who? The university? The development people?"

"The lottery people. They're going to hold a gala."

"A gala?" Chastain is trying to picture Mowery and Cowens even
saying the word. "They win eight point eight million dollars and all of a
sudden they're holding galas?"

"Well, all of a sudden ten months later, I guess, yeah."

Chastain takes a sip of her coffee. She knows Sarah well enough
now to know what she is worried about—work, the office, the visioning exercise, the book, all of it. "When is it?" she says. She takes out her
notebook and the day planner she has started using recently.

"Two months," Sarah says.

"The one-year anniversary?"

"It's going to be tricky for us," Sarah says. "We should talk to Chad
and Nicole, make sure we have a plan and we're proactive."

"The one-year anniversary of his death? Is that a thing you do?"

"Well," Sarah says. "For them it is the one-year anniversary of the
lottery. But no, this doesn't seem like a normal thing you would do. A
scholarship, though. I think you would have to call that objectively a
nice gesture."

Chastain marks the date. Jesus Christ, it might be the worst possible thing that could happen. Now they not only have to recognize the
anniversary, but will need to be happy about it. All of this effort to push
forward and now they have no choice but to look back.

"Another chapter, I guess," Sarah says. "Assuming we get through
it okay."

Chastain writes the date and then starts making a list of everything
they will need to. A gala for the Arthur R. Yoder Scholarship Fund. She
may have to actually call Craver on the phone.

They hear chatting far off and then getting closer. Chastain recognizes Chad Stephenson's baritone, Nicole's light southern accent. And
there he is in his black jeans and New Balance sneakers, like the ghost
of Steve Jobs himself. "Hey friends," Chad says. "I understand we have
a Thing."

Gibbons

GIBBONS PUTS DOWN THE COFFEE and turns
on the computer. He takes the frother out of his bag and lays it on the
back of the desk. There is no reason to be embarrassed about improving
the life of the office. There was a frother and then there wasn't and now
there will be again. Still, is this the kind of thing that would get Sarah's
attention? The consultants? Is this a mild rebellion or just somebody
taking it on themselves to make the office a slightly better place? Sarah
likes initiative. Doesn't she? This is the kind of thing that should earn
a high five from Chad Stephenson. Or is this the kind of thing Chad
Stephenson is supposed to be doing himself? Could this be a threat? It
is just a frother.

Seventeen unread emails. Test test test spam spam meeting invitation meeting invitation meeting invitation. He deletes them one by
one. There are two notifications of Slack messages and he notes that
they are both from Lawson. Probably no big deal. They are, for the first
time since the lottery, almost back to schedule, nearly back to capacity
in Creative and Production and Purchasing.

He could just put the frother in the kitchen drawer with the can openers and the thousand packets of Chinese takeout mustard. He could do it without saying anything. The important thing is the frother itself. But no, that is not the case. The important thing is he has a job and he is moving up the ladder, slow and steady. He doesn't hate it. He doesn't make a lot of money but it is fine. Everything is fine.

He checks the cubicle entryway, scans the aisle, and then opens up Yahoo fantasy football on his browser. He completely panicked in the draft and wound up with way too many New Orleans Saints. Not a typically recommended strategy but the Saints are having a crazy year, running up points, undefeated, throwing and catching and running like they are in a video game from the eighties. He enjoys adding and drop-ping players, one area where his natural tendency toward data, math, schedules, and planning actually pays off. His wide receivers are not returning the dividends they could, so he reduces his search to WR, and then to the past three games. Their league is a point per catch league and he knows most of his friends from college are…how to put it? Not as attentive to data. They don't understand that receivers who catch a lot of balls, slot guys who do not score a lot of touchdowns, little guys like Julian Edelman or Chris Hogan can be more valuable under this point scheme than the big traditional receivers who might catch two balls a game but one of them for a touchdown.

A desktop notification. There are four available receivers averag-ing more than seven catches a game. That's as good as a touchdown. He looks at their per catch average, at touchdowns. He filters based on total points, then total points over the past three games. Another desk-top notification. Hopefully this is nothing. He will need to do a little more research, check quarterbacks, bye weeks, injury histories for each receiver.

He could just not make such a big deal out of everything, just slip into the kitchen and put the frother on the counter, slip the vanilla oat milk into the refrigerator. There is no reason to feel strange about doing something nice for everybody, but there is also no reason to rock any boats, not now, with the consultants and their breathing exercises and all staff meetings. Not with them almost, but not quite, back to capac-ity, back on schedule. He wonders what the quarterly projections look like for Sarah and Lawson. Above his pay grade, but he gathers from their tone that they are making progress but are still on shaky ground even now.

He has one email from Lawson, checking in on the Mattress campaign, another from some salesperson, or a bot pretending to be one, a meeting invitation to something called the Arthur R. Yoder Scholarship Fund Gala. Yoder? Gala?

There is no save functionality in Yahoo fantasy. He is going to have to do all of that filtering, drilling down, all over again. He holds his cursor over the window. "Hey are you at your desk?" A message from Lawson. He opens Slack and checks the messages that are waiting there. Creative is missing another deadline. He was really hoping to get through today without being hassled but this is something he will need to deal with. The awning account is new and strangely demanding, but also very committed to traditional media, which means they are a veritable gold mine and Keystone needs all of the veritable gold mines it can get right now.

"Yep just looking at the awning deadlines," he types.

"Stop on over when you get a chance," Lawson writes.

Gibbons holds his cursor over the window for Yahoo. He will add when he gets back. He stands up, grabs his notebook and a pen. He looks at the frother, still in the box. He puts it back in his bag.

russell

RUSSELL STIRS HIS DRINK AND watches the door. Why is he nervous? Because they are rich? Because he hasn't seen them since it all happened? Or maybe because they are going to talk about Yoder and he is expected, he supposes, to represent Yoder's interests in this thing, make sure, as Cowens said, "it comes out how he would have wanted it to come out."

He sips his drink. What are the chances that they are just fucking with him? Cowens sounded sincere in the email but still, the idea that they would be doing this for him, that Cowens would have even noticed that a man died on the same day his life got awesome, it all seems a little far-fetched. He puts the odds that it is a put-on at five percent.

But they wouldn't have invited Sarah if wasn't real. Maybe that is why he is nervous, a social work engagement that involves Sarah is the kind of thing most people in the office would be genuinely terrified about, even with this new Sarah, the hands-on, how are you doing with real empathy in her eyes, consultant-hiring, book-writing, visioning-exercising Sarah.

"Hey." Russell jumps. "Sarah can't make it so she wanted me to be here." It is the girl who went from being a put-upon admin assistant to Sarah's doppelganger in a matter of months. She sits down. "Are those guys here?" she says.

"Not yet." Her name is Jane, or Jennifer. Something with a J? He is starting to forget names, words, exact memories. He should tell Ginny about this but he knows he never will.

Chastain sits and motions to the bartender. "Manhattan," she says. "And whatever Mr. Russell here is drinking." Russell takes another sip of his gin and tonic. He had been wondering how socially acceptable it would be to order another but that was when he was expecting Sarah.

"So, this will be interesting," Chastain says.

Russell sits up. "It will, won't it?" he says.

"Have you seen any of them since?" she says

"Not really. I mean, around I guess? I heard that Siegel bought a boat? And he's sailing around the Caribbean? And Mancus joined the Peace Corps."

"That one kind of makes sense," she says. The bartender brings their drinks and she takes a sip. Russell watches her. She is pretty, not as young as he had thought. He likes the way she seems comfortable, at ease with herself. Like Sarah, there is something purposeful in her carriage, like she has decided to be a certain way in the world, a carefulness that he thinks of as old-fashioned, something from his parent's generation of real grown-up adults.

"And Fitzgerald bought a camper and they're just driving around, visiting national parks. Got one of those passport things. I heard that was the plan all along and the eight point eight just moved it up some."

"It's weird, though, right, that most of them just stayed around?" she says. She takes a sip of her drink. "Did you play? The lottery, I mean."

"I never did," he says. "The odds…it just seemed so…"

"Stupid," she says, and smiles.

Russell decides that he likes her a good deal. It's no wonder that Sarah has seen whatever she has seen in the woman. "You were friends with Craver," he says. "Are friends."

"Yeah, we were work buddies, I guess. Let's be miserable together. Something like that."

"And he moved somewhere out West?"

"San Francisco. Although I think he kind of turned it into an extended road trip? I get texts from him. Sometimes. Although lately it's more like pictures of food and road signs."

Russell does not understand these Millennials and their Facebooks and selfies. The boy is driving around the country sending pictures of his food back to this lovely young woman?

"So, what do we do when they get here?" he says.

"I guess we just need to plan this thing out, see however they think it's going to go. I think they want Sarah to say a few words?"

"The Arthur Yoder Memorial Scholarship Fund," he says.

She pauses. She wants to ask him something but she is holding herself back.

"Hey, there they are," somebody says. It is Cowens and Pappas, both of them holding two drinks. Cowens looks ashen and drunk. He flops down in a chair. Pappas puts his drinks down, holds out his hand, and Russell shakes it. Were they friends? He does not think that they were friends.

"So," Cowens says. "Let's throw a fucking party."

CRAVER

CRAVER IS CONSIDERING FINALLY GET-
TING out of the car when the email vibrates into his phone.
Cowens? What the fuck would Cowens be emailing him for? He has a
moment of dumb animal thrill—a quickening in his pulse, everything
goes blurry and he closes his eyes. They have reviewed everything and
determined that he did play. He was right. He's a millionaire. He leans
back in the seat, the motion—left hand hitting the seat recline, right
pushing back—as familiar as hitting the elevator button to floor four
used to be. And then something registers, a blip: the word "Yoder" in the
subject line. He sits up again. Yoder?

In the back of his mind he registers that the woman he had been
watching has come out of the rest area and is looking at a large outdoor map of Arizona. She picks through the flyers in the Sun State
rack, looks at the soda machines. She is maybe college age, light skin,
curly blond hair cascading everywhere. Craver turns the knife over in his
pocket. He is doing nothing wrong.

A scholarship fund in Yoder's name? Jesus Christ. He tries to picture Yoder, but all he remembers is the way he always wore gray pants

and a yellow shirt on Mondays. A scholarship is a pretty nice gesture, though, and he did seem like a fine person. Bit of a sad sack. Kind of a bore. Yellow and gray just don't empirically go together. But still, a scholarship seems fine. The woman yawns. She seems to be thinking, considering some course of action or another. She checks her phone, scrolls. Craver is doing nothing wrong. He has done nothing wrong. He is a…can he even call himself a marketing associate anymore? It's been a long time since he has been much of anything. A traveler. A gawker. A voyeur.

They have invited everybody from the company and that does make sense in a way. It makes sense. Will he drive from here back to Pennsylvania? He files the question away, something to be answered the way he's answered the rest of the questions for these past ten months— with a turn of the wheel, a casual veer northward or southwest, a pretty woman in a sensible car mouthing the lyrics to some pop song.

What would he tell people he has been doing? What would he tell people that he does?

The woman walks back toward her car, a green Honda Civic with brand-new tires. Craver scans the parking lot. There are only two other cars, no people walking either to or from the rest stop.

Hey Craver, what have you been up to? I've been driving around the southwest kind of stalking women in rest stops. Oh no, no I haven't done that yet but I have been thinking about it. What's that? I guess the usual reasons, you know, I'm kind of lost, kind of not making much of a mark here in life, kind of angry that these assholes I used to work with— no offense, of course—won the lottery and kind of tilted me down this path that I didn't really consider or plan but now feels kind of inevitable.

He reads the email again. Jesus Christ, he had almost forgot about Yoder. Yoder who he really didn't think much about. Yoder who is a fucking hero now that he thinks about it. Yoder who, when faced immediately with the bullshit heart of the stupid, random world, decided to eat the sidewalk instead of live one more day in a universe where fucking Cowens and fucking Pappas and fucking Mowery and all the fucking rest of them are millionaires, rewarded for ritual stupidity. He is immediately sure that Yoder would hate this idea. He did not know the man well but anybody who made that choice would bristle at hearing his name in Cowens's mouth: the Arthur R. Yoder Scholarship Fund.

He flashes on the event, pictures the VFW where his cousin had her wedding party. A makeshift bar, balloons strewn around, a framed picture of goddamn Yoder, the sad stuff from his cubicle. He will sit in the car and watch them arrive, the eight point eight lottery winners and the sad idiot rest of them, Sarah and Lawson and Chastain and…god he can't even remember anybody other than those three. He will drink from the flask. He will come in late, cause a ripple, a disturbance in the awkward small talk and all of it, the reports and the meetings and the button-ups and sensible socks, the lottery and the constant driving, always moving, ping ping ping, it will all be over. They have been living in before and he will deliver them to after.

When he pictures himself walking into the room, he is carrying a gun

CHASTAIN

SHE CAN HEAR CHAD'S LAUGH booming down
the hallway while she waits in Spontaneous Teaming Area Topaz. She
closes her laptop, takes out a notebook. Sarah hates laptops in meetings—too distracting, half working is not working.

She writes down "10:30, STA meeting Chad." She can hear the
meeting down the hall drawing to a close, somebody talking to somebody about a grocery list further down the row of cubicles. She can
hear Chad Stephenson's voice getting closer, the series of greetings
he booms out in front of him like a carnival barker. She leans back as
a heavyset man in a three-piece suit walks down the hallway with a
briefcase in his hand. If she is being honest, she is not a huge fan of
the Spontaneous Teaming Areas, or the idea of naming them after
obscure and annoying colors from the nineties: Spontaneous Teaming
Area Teal, Spontaneous Teaming Area Topaz, Spontaneous Teaming
Area Florescent Yellow.

She checks her phone. Nothing. It's very strange that Craver has
stopped texting. She has heard only one thing, a reply to her "you okay"
that just said "yep," for the past few weeks. The cessation should be a

relief but something about it feels strange. She had gotten used to it, these messages coming in a steady stream. It was comforting to know he was out there, doing his thing, following whatever vision drove him west and then south and then southwest and then... at first the airport texts stopped, then he stopped telling her where he was, although the images he was still sending seemed southwestern, cactus and desert and the occasional mountain. Then they dribbled to a stop altogether. The last message she got was some desolate rest stop, a woman in the distance looking at a giant map. It was the very first with no accompanying message, and she wondered if it was a mistake.

"Hey there, friend!" Chad Stephenson holds his arms out. She stands and hugs him, a quick embrace she has mastered: chest pulled back, arms reaching out for a quick shoulder embrace, and then a full step back before he has a chance to lengthen the hug, morph it into a shoulder squeeze, a semi-embrace that extends into a kind of shoulder massage conversation. She sits down and Chad nods his head.

Three women walk by that Chastain recognizes from the Analytics Department. "Diane, Daphne, Daisy, the three D's!" Chad yells. They stop and comply with his open arms. She notices they all employ versions of her own self-defense hug retreat.

Lawson nods and sits down. "How's it going?" he says.

"Good," she says firmly, as if it going good was a precondition of her existence here, at work, in the office, every day. She has noticed the way Sarah says this, each small interaction a gentle affirmation that they are all in the right place, that everything here is of course fine and okay and even more than that, good.

"Excellent," he says. She steals a glance. He is watching Chad Stephenson chatting with the three D's, something about a band she has never heard of. Lawson has a look on his face that would have to be described as bemusement. She has not seen this look in the office since Craver drove out west to wherever. She wonders briefly what Craver would think of Chad Stephenson and his visioning exercise and his Spontaneous Teaming Areas. She knows what Craver would think.

Lawson has grown his beard and upgraded his glasses to modern blocky black ones. It looks good. She had never really thought of

Lawson as anything other than a reliable if uninspired colleague, a nine to fiver. He's wearing jeans and black Doc Martens, a checked shirt with a brown jacket. He looks like a college professor, and it suits him. She almost asks the question on the tip of her tongue but then he looks back and she realizes she's been staring.

"This guy," he says, smiling and nodding at Chad Stephenson. Despite herself, Chastain thrills to the conspiratorial tone. It has been a long time since she heard that sound in this office. "It's like he's in some kind of parody skit from the nineties but he doesn't even know it," he sits up. "Or more like, he knows it but he just doesn't care, which is fascinating. Like he's a Labrador retriever who also just happens to be a management consultant."

Chad Stephenson bumps fists with each of the three D's and makes a different noise each time. "Explosion, rocket ship, siren," Lawson whispers. Chastain stares, genuinely surprised. "He does those same three, that order, almost all the time."

"I never noticed that," she says.

"He's very big on explosion," Lawson says. He says all of this with a kind detachment that she would not have associated with him five minutes ago.

"Sometimes he mixes in a dog bark, or a zoom kind of sound. Hey Chad," he says, waving. Chad Stephenson opens his arms for a hug. "I'm good," Lawson says. He reaches his hand out for a fist bump and mimics Chad's explosion sound. He smiles pleasantly, gestures at Chastain. "Should we start?" he taps where his watch would be. "I have an eleven thirty if you don't mind."

Chad Stephenson stands for a moment. He smiles, allows something like recognition to cross his face. "Right, right," he says finally, folding his hands together in the yogi thing that he does. Sarah has taken to doing this back to him and Chastain has a visceral reaction to this, a jerking away that she is finding hard to camouflage. Lawson is still staring at Chad. "Right, right," Chad says, dropping into the empty Teaming Chair. "Love the way you're always moving forward, partner."

"So, this celebration," Lawson says.

"Arthur R. Yoder Scholarship Fund Dinner Gala," Chastain says.

"Of course," Lawson says. She looks to him but the air of bemusement is gone. "Scholarship Fund Memorial Dinner. Gala. Do you get to many galas, Chad?" he says.

Chad has been looking at his phone, but with the mention of his name he snaps to attention. Chastain can see him rerunning the conversation in his head. "Galas," he says. He is clearly stalling for time while he calculates whether the right answer is yes, I am a sophisticated management consultant from Boston and of course I go to a lot of galas, so many galas, gala this and gala that; or whether the right answer is no, new Pennsylvania friends, I am just like you and do not have the opportunity to attend galas on the regular. "I'd say a normal number of galas," he says.

"Right," Lawson says, as if this is exactly the answer he was expecting. "Well, this will be a first for me. Gala virgin right here."

"Well," Chad says. "I think you'll find it suits you, partner." He has taken to calling everybody partner and Chastain is secretly very much dreading the day when Sarah starts parroting this back to him.

"On that note," Chastain says. "Since we only have a few minutes here…"

"Right, right," Chad says. "I know I was tasked…we were tasked with drafting some talking points for Sarah." He makes the hands again and Chastain turns away, focuses on a whiteboard in the cubicle across from the Teaming Area. "Optimize" has been written in red ink and circled. "But I had a wild idea and let me run it by you," he says this last phrase as if he has only just now coined the idea and the phrase, "before you say no."

Chastain had pictured an anecdote about Yoder, a note about his service, about the need to continue their important work even in light of the terrible tragedy of his death, maybe insert a joke in there about how the company is getting along just fine despite its sudden proliferation of millionaires, maybe a joke about the retirement plan in there, maybe not.

"I think I should be the one to speak," Chad Stephenson says. He says it like he says everything else, as if the idea just sprang up out of the ground like an oak tree, obvious and impervious to argument, and also like he has been rehearsing just the right way to say it for quite some time.

"What?" Chastain says.

"Hear me out," Chad Stephenson says. "I think an outsider. Somebody who has a certain kind of viewpoint might…"

"Outstanding," Lawson says "Perfect. Let's do it."

Gibbons

GIBBONS PUTS HIS COFFEE DOWN and turns on the computer. He checks his phone. Fourteen new emails. Spam spam spam test meeting invitation Slack notification. He takes a sip of his coffee. It is strange how the froth makes a difference, but it definitely makes a difference, even this way, frothed at home and carried the fifteen-minute car ride to the office. He knows the froth is not frothy anymore but somehow he can still taste it.

There is a reminder for the Arthur R. Yoder Scholarship Fund Gala in his email and he dutifully checks the day and time, accepts the event again. There is no upside in rocking the boat at this point and the rumor is that this will be an open bar event. "Opulent" is what Lawson had said, but lately he is having trouble figuring out when Lawson is joking and when he is serious. It is a strange development and he senses a kind of pulling back. If Lawson leaves, will he be promoted? He managed to make it through the lottery shake-up with no change in his position, but he knows that this is exactly what Lawson and Sarah were aiming for, no shake-ups, just a steady righting of the ship until they were back to capacity.

He goes into the kitchen and retrieves his yogurt from the refrigerator. Raspberry today. It is going to be a good food day. It is all wide open. He could get pho for lunch, or Korean, or a burrito from the new place out by the mall. The food truck will be over by the library and eating at the food truck always makes him feel slightly hip, almost urban.

Opulent. The gala will be opulent is what Lawson had said, with special emphasis on the word gala. It is, after all, at the VFW. So that must have been a joke. When he thinks about the word opulent, he pictures sheiks, kings, shrimp cocktail, and crab legs. He is already planning to not eat before the gala. He wonders if it will be weird when he does not show up with a date. There was the option to bring a plus one, like a wedding. There was an invitation, with something like calligraphy.

There are three messages in the campaign channel. More delays. There are always delays, he tells himself. The important thing is that they prioritize, make the right decisions for the future business. It is like a game of Jenga, all the small pieces holding the structure of the thing together.

He checks his phone. He opens Twitter and then closes it again. It is nine fifteen. He has a ten and then an eleven. A two and a three and a four. He will need to run out and grab something for lunch. He could go to the good grocery store and get something hot, or call in for Chinese. He will be asked for numbers for the eleven, the Awning campaign. They have been doing well with traditional media, and he is excited to share the numbers in front of Lawson and Sarah. They are doing well with digital as well, the Adword buys returning leads at a rate that surprised him when he reviewed them with Cooper yesterday.

A gala. Is he expected to wear black tie? A tuxedo? He google image searches "gala Pennsylvania" and scans the rows of pictures of people standing with politicians. They are wearing suits, sometimes not even ties. He breathes a sigh of relief. He is fairly certain there is still a program for his cousin's wedding in the pocket of the blue suit.

A desktop notification. Lawson checking in on the numbers for the eleven. "They are good," he writes, with a smiley face. Lawson responds with a thumbs-up.

"Are you ready for the GALA?" he types. He is not sure why he is putting the word in all caps but Lawson definitely finds something about it to be funny.

Lawson responds with a crown emoji. Then a noisemaker. Then a ticket.

Gibbons ponders these emojis. Isn't it strange that he would be communicating with his boss in this way? He answers with a thumbs-up. "See you at the ten," he types. He finishes his yogurt. He stands and then sits back down again. He opens another window in his browser.

Yoder

YODER WAKES UP ON HIS feet. He is in a kitchen again, but this is different. Industrial. The smell of grease is the first thing that hits him: warm, salty, thick. He knows it would have made him hungry before but now it just registers like the tiled floor beneath his feet, the stainless steel triple sink to his right, the whirr of machines and the chatter of people in the near distance. A fryer crackles somewhere close. The smell is…chicken? Fried something.

He leans against the sink. There is music playing, Kenny Loggins singing "Footloose." Loose, footloose, rip off the Sunday shoes. Sunday shoes? At least he still knows the lyrics, still remembers Kenny Loggins. Decay, slipping, any kind of loss of intellect would be bad news.

He takes a few steps toward the crowd noise and sees a cashier in a red shirt, black hat. A heavyset woman faces him, her attention on the menu.

Jesus Christ, he thinks. I am in a Kentucky Fried Chicken.

He wanders toward a room in the back that he assumes must be the manager's office. There would be a computer there. A toilet flushes and Mowery emerges, wearing his own KFC shirt, his name stitched on the breast with the word "Owner" underneath. Mowery took his eight point eight million dollars and bought a goddamn Kentucky Fried Chicken.

"What the…" he says under his breath. Yoder registers again that he has gotten used to not being seen, is not even nervous when Mowery stalks toward him, nodding his head, swearing lightly under his breath. "Jaime!" he shouts. "Jaime!" He walks to a back door and sticks his head out. "Jaime," he says, his voice the forced calm of an airline pilot. "We talked about this, bud."

Yoder can hear the response, a young person unworried and laconic, a light Latino accent. "No," Mowery says. "Once every two hours. Every two. And it's ten minutes. I have Latisha out there with a line and nobody on the fryer, buddy." He steps out and the door snaps shut.

Yoder can hear them outside, a back and forth. He walks into the manager's office. The computer is on but sleeping. A tablet sits on the desktop, a phone in a charger. He swipes a finger across the tablet and a password reminder appears. He clicks the mouse on the computer, considers grabbing the phone.

The door opens and Mowery and a young Latino boy walk back into the restaurant. "I don't know, man," the boy says. "I mean, there are a lot of jobs. The economy is good. I could be driving an Uber, listening to my music. I can't get with this grease, these burns on my fingers all day and you busting up my break time."

Yoder remembers how much he hates young people. This last generation, the last few, Millennials on down to whatever this boy is, have been nothing but lazy and self-interested, obsessed with taking their own pictures. Fucking selfies. He should have taken one before he took his last step. That would have been something to accompany the story, get some viral marketing out there. He remembers again placing the cell phone and the wallet next to his shoes. Why did he take his shoes off? If he hadn't, would he be wearing them now? One thing about the ghostly afterlife, he thinks, make sure you bring sensible footwear.

"Well I wish I could convince you otherwise, Jaime," Mowery is saying. The boy is taking off his apron, his baseball hat. He hands them to Mowery like a peace offering. They shake hands. Mowery watches the boy walk through the door.

"Hey guys, I need this number four," a small African American woman appears in the glassless opening between the kitchen and the restaurant. "And two small fives, with mashed. They've been waiting."

Mowery stares at the back door. He has his hands on his hips and his face to the floor. "Goddammit," he says. "God fucking dammit." His voice is more sad than angry and for a second Yoder has a twinge of pity for the man. "Fucking beaners," Mowery says, and the pity goes away. Mowery reaches into a cooler and pulls out a package of indistinguishable meat. He separates the pieces and drops them into the fryer.

russell

RUSSELL WATCHES HIS FEET ON the trail. He
watches the retreating figure of the person in front of him, the kid from
IT who is like Chad Stephenson's reluctant pet project. He watches
Chad Stephenson far ahead, leading this hike. The last time he was out
on this trail he was with Ginny and thought he might actually have a
heart attack and now he is back with the entire goddamn Executive
Core Team, all of them slogging up the trail in their Dockers and sensible shoes. Well, some of them seem to have had some kind of advance
warning, but who would read a meeting agenda before the meeting?
What kind of kiss-ass even opens the emails Chad Stephenson sends
them constantly?

He can feel his Achilles tendons tightening up, small beads of sweat
starting up in his crotch and on his back. This is ridiculous. Team building for a group that is supposed to be cutting pictures out of magazines
and putting them up on posterboard. He is getting short of breath. The
process of aging has been disappointingly predictable. At every point
he knew what was going to happen and it happened. He started to feel
out of place. He started to drift away from his friends. He started to

notice the way his muscles, never much to speak of, had started to atrophy and slide into fat. He started to notice the way he would get short of breath after walking up even a flight of stairs, the way he woke up more hungover after a night of drinking, the way his legs would ache after even a drive longer than two hours. He expected all of it, and it arrived right on time. What he did not expect was to be the old people's representative on some kind of ridiculous consultant boondoggle, for a bunch of idiots to win the lottery and force his old friend over the side of the building.

He can actually hear his breath. Not a good sign. Up ahead they are pausing, a few of them talking, a few looking his way. Oh Jesus. Literally the only way this could possibly get worse. He waves, nods, tries to make a neutral expression. He wonders how red his face is, if they are talking about whether they should cut everything short already and send him home, send everybody back to work, send them all to the goddamn bar. That was team building, when they used to all go out to happy hour every Thursday, him and Yoder and Avery and Old Snyder. Now where are they? Avery will be in Florida soon. Old Snyder has been gone for a long time. Yoder to be celebrated with a scholarship fund paid for by a bunch of idiots who won the goddamn lottery, of all things.

He is getting closer to where they are grouped. A few of them, that kiss-ass Williamson and his buddy Griffin, have positioned themselves back on the trail, eager to get started again. Why would anybody be hurrying to do anything when it is the middle of the work day? Don't they understand that the entirety of the game is just putting in the time, running out the clock, that no matter what they do they will still need to do it again tomorrow, the next day, the day after that, every goddamn minute of every goddamn day and the only point of the whole thing is the time, clocking in when you punch that elevator button and clocking out when you pack up that bag and slink out to your car and back home to your wife or husband or kids or dogs or video games or off to look at pictures of other people's dogs or kids or feet in the sand on your phone or tablet or desktop or whatever is next? They are idiots, pushing widgets around the office and up into the cloud, tracking their key performance indicators, making better widgets, tracking the improvement and the budget and all the while keeping one eye out for the next thing they will need to push up into the cloud and get all worked up about. All of them worrying so hard. Demonstrating so hard. Look at me working. I am an up-and-comer. I am coming. I am here.

He has gone from lightly sweating to being engulfed in it. He is soggy and tight. He cannot imagine going the rest of the way but he will have to do it. If he dies, will the company owe Ginny some kind of insurance? Would she sue them if he collapses right here on the Valley Trail? He wants to text her, to let her know she should sue them, but that would start off a whole other thing.

"How you feeling, guy?" Chad Stephenson says. He is smiling, as if they are sharing some kind of joke, as if the impending heart attack or heat stroke will serve as some kind of Yoda-like lesson in Business.

"Guess I better get back to the gym," Russell says, wiping sweat out of his eyes with a handkerchief.

"Ah, you're doing great," Chad Stephenson says. "We get there together as a team, just like everything we do."

Russell notes the use of the word "we." He wonders again how much they are paying these people. He supposes that Chad Stephenson is getting paid ten times what he will make in this same amount of time. He supposes Chad Stephenson has never played around with the retirement calculators and found that he will be able to retire when he is ninety-seven years old. He imagines Chad Stephenson lounging on some boat, checking his portfolio, dragging and dropping and making money off his money. He imagines Pappas and Cowens and Mowery sitting on some beach, taking pictures of their feet in the sand and sending them back to Central Pennsylvania through Facebook and Twitter and Instagram. He wonders if they feel like they deserved to win and then he puts that idea out of his mind. This is Chad Stephenson's fault today.

Russell's breathing has returned to normal. He looks around at the forest, the steep slope moving up the mountain, the trail winding down through rocks and trees. It is lovely. He wishes Ginny were here instead of the goddamn Executive Core Team. But at least they are out here and not in the office. At least they are getting some exercise, even if it has to be in service of some kind of ridiculous team-building effort led by a preposterous pretender on a monthly retainer.

"Let's get rolling," Griffin says.

"Okay," Chad Stephenson says.

The IT kid, Robertson, has drifted behind him. Russell has noticed how still the young man is, full of none of the constant chatter or phone-checking nervous tics he sees in the rest of that generation. He seems comfortable being quiet and Russell has come to appreciate that—he seems to engage in neither the ridiculous office small talk patter or the pretentious business talk that flows constantly out of Chad Stephenson.

"Onward!" Chad Stephenson says. He says it the way he says every-thing, like he is mostly for real but withholding some percentage just in case, like an earnest talk show host setting up a joke.

Russell and Robertson wait for the rest of them to start moving. Russell feels like the kid expects no small talk, no weather or football or lottery chatter. They just stand. Finally they start up. Russell motions for the kid to lead but he defers. "Nah that's okay," he says. "I'm cool bring-ing up the rear."

"I get it," Russell says, and he starts up the mountain again. He wonders if the kid has taken this rear position to watch out for him or just to put some distance between himself and Chad Stephenson. Either way, he realizes, he appreciates the decision.

He concentrates on the trail, on his feet moving forward one step and then another. Ahead of him, the Executive Core Team moves slowly up the mountain. He tries to name them all: Williamson, Griffin, Chad Stephenson, Sheila somebody, Young Snyder, the woman who is Sarah's assistant now, or not even her assistant but a Manager? A Marketing Associate? Chastain. He likes that young woman a great deal. He is not sure what they call the people who are moving up the ladder on that side of the company but whatever they do, she is one of them. Then there is the Latino guy who does something with money, the fatter young man who occasionally says something funny, the guy who runs the fantasy football, and the one who always dresses in black.

He remembers now that Chad had mentioned something about their next meeting being outdoors, about bringing exercise clothes, maybe even something about hiking boots and water bottles. In these meetings he is mostly focusing on the donuts and the coffee, cataloging the running list of small outrages and indignities, the ridiculous breathing exercise Chad Stephenson forces them through before starting each of their meetings, the hangover looming in his head, the guest speaker Chad had invited—a Creative Director from a marketing company in town who spoke with an Austrian accent and seemed to think he had been invited to give some kind of TED Talk about Japanese auto factories.

He puts one foot in front of the other. It is a slog, work. He can hear his breath again, a light wheezing that he is no longer trying to mask. He can hear Chad Stephenson jabbering up ahead of them, Griffin and Williamson laughing over something ridiculous, wind whistling through the trees, and the steady scrape of his feet on the rocky ground below. He should stop, catch his breath. If he passes out on this trail, if his heart explodes and he is dead before he hits the ground, surely they would have to give Ginny some kind of settlement. He is not really sure how those things work but that sounds like the right word for it, a settlement. He wonders if they had to pay anything out to Yoder, or his estate, his people, if there were any people to raise the right questions, even. Should he have raised the right questions? Yoder doesn't have to worry about any of this anymore. Yoder is gone. A settlement might be just the answer, an escape route that might allow one of them to grow older with some semblance of dignity. He puts one foot in front of the other. He keeps on going.

Robertson

ROBERTSON SPENDS THE LAST HALF of the hike googling CPR on his phone, trying to surreptitiously bone up on exactly what they will need to do when the old guy, Russell, finally drops from a heart attack. It is torture, walking this slow, listening to the huffs and puffs morph into a steady wheeze, listening to him swear under his breath and then decide, apparently, that he needs to literally save his breath for...staying alive? Plotting revenge? He wonders if he should record this, if there is a lawsuit that can be brought against the company, against Chad Stephenson, at least, when the old guy drops dead right here on this mountain.

Somehow they make it up the hill and they find everybody else spread out along the overlook that gazes down into the valley. Chad Stephenson is leading them in the breathing exercises he makes them do before every meeting. Jesus Christ, the breathing exercises. Robertson steals a glance at Russell, who is sitting on a stump, staring right at Chad Stephenson. His face is red and wet and the look in his eyes is pure hatred. Robertson stares, wondering if the man is going to have a heart attack or spontaneously combust. Chad

210

Stephenson has pushed this whole thing a little too far here, even for Chad Stephenson.

He wonders what Nicole Stetler-Stephenson would think of this. Of course, she would have known. What he has found out is that Chad Stephenson is basically making all of this up as he goes along. There is no precedent for the situation they are in, and no roadmap or even scorecard for what Chad Stephenson is doing. As long as nobody else leaves or jumps off the roof, Chad Stephenson is succeeding, so he is just kind of making things up, staying the center of attention, making sure Sarah feels good about the way people are feeling, playing out his contract until it is time to talk through another contract, or write a book, or move on to the next company in such dire straits that they might find themselves cutting pictures out of old magazines, writing "RICH" on posterboard.

Robertson checks his phone. Chad Stephenson looks him in the eye and nods, gestures him into the loose circle they have formed. It is a summary of what has been happening to him for the past year. He has been gestured into Chad Stephenson's circle for reasons he could never fathom, against his will and all sense. All he wants to do is sit behind a screen and do his work. Chad Stephenson motions again but Robertson knows he will stop soon if he doesn't get a successful result. Better to pull back and maintain his air of confidence than demonstrate failure at even the smallest task. This is something Nicole Stetler-Stephenson actually told him the last time they were at happy hour, when she had one more Manhattan than usual.

Will he allow himself to be gestured into the circle? In so many ways it would be easier to be manipulated, to not think, just do whatever Chad Stephenson or Sarah or Jessie or whoever tells him to do. To move right right right like Mario. Jump when somebody presses two, roll when they press B. Pick this up, throw it at that. But has that been working? He is only twenty-four but he is so tired and all the available paths just look awful, embarrassing and corny, and so, so long. They look like Griffin standing there, dressed like he is going to run a trail marathon, eyes closed and chest swelled out, waiting for Chad Stephenson's next instruction. They look like Russell, still sitting on his log, looking like he is trying to make Chad Stephenson's head explode. They look like

Chad Stephenson, standing here on a mountain top, making a bunch of Marketing Associates and Business Analysts and Systems Administrators run through some breathing exercises in the name of Business.

Jesus Christ, he realizes, he should have played the goddamn lottery.

Chad Stephenson looks at him and smiles, indulgent, like he is a child who is acting out, a dog who has managed to get his leash on the other side of a tree and can't figure out how to continue his walk. Robertson nods, tries to make a neutral face, looks at Russell still sitting there just glaring at Chad, as if to say look we're all on the same page but this is a situation over here that might demand your attention. Russell has gone back to his normal color and is no longer wheezing. There is a calm about him that is actually more disturbing. This is the face of somebody who has been through something and come out on the other side, the face of somebody with a plan.

Robertson's phone dings and he feels for it in his pocket. He tries to make a habit of not checking it constantly, of only reaching for it when necessary, but this could be actual work, a server down or a denial of service attack. It could be Jessie. It could be Nicole Stetler-Stephenson texting from a hotel room somewhere.

He needs to get his shit together. Thinking of Jessie and Nicole Stetler-Stephenson even in the same category? Jessie is famous in certain circles, so good that she will never have to look for work again in her life. She is beautiful and funny and no doubt pecking away at the keyboard in the basement right now.

Robertson considers his options. Will he be drawn into the circle? Chad Stephenson is wrapping up his breathing exercises, moving into some light yoga. Sun salutations. Before all of this, the lottery and the consultants and the Executive Core Team, Robertson had never done a sun salutation in his life. The idea that he would be drawn into this kind of thing at work—sun salutations?—is insane, crazy, nonsensical. And yet here he is, walking toward the circle, Russell unmoving in his peripheral vision, Chad Stephenson smiling in his Steve Jobs cosplay outfit, leading them all in some kind of thing he saw on YouTube. Here he is, taking his place in the circle. Here he is, placing his legs at ten and two, raising his hands to the sky, stepping into the circle once again.

CHASTAIN

CHASTAIN CHECKS HER PHONE. THERE
are five messages from Craver. She stares at herself in the mirror. She
is not nervous because it would be stupid to be nervous and she doesn't
do stupid things.

But he can't possibly expect to pick up where they left off, wasted
in the middle of the street after day-drinking a Monday away. Jesus, that
day. The ambulances, the lottery, the eight point eight people partying
away in the conference room that has since been converted into Chad
Stephenson's "Teaming Center."

She has decided to dress as if she is going to a work reception. She
wonders what Craver will wear, if he even packed his work clothes, the
dark pants and gray button-ups he preferred. She flashes on him leaning against the copy machine, telling some joke, whispering gossip or
making his little comments about everybody in the office. She realizes
with a start that he is exactly the kind of person Sarah would be trying
to weed out or, in Chad's words, "emotionally rehabilitate." Emotional
rehabilitation, professional growth. It is practically a mantra.

Craver has been gone for a long time.

Where did she leave things with Stan? That is more complicated. She had been thinking about what he said. "If you get worked up all anybody will ever remember is that you got all worked up."

Something about it didn't sit right. She had been thinking about it for some time, at work and on her way in and on her increasingly long runs. She hadn't planned to talk to him about it, but he asked about the book and it just came out. "I think you're wrong," she had said. "About all anybody will ever remember is that you freaked out."

"About what?" he said. He seemed genuinely curious, lightly concerned.

"A thing you said awhile back. When we were at Peterson's, at the bar there."

"What is happening here?" he said. One of the things she liked about him was his light touch, his ability to disagree without necessarily turning everything into a Thing.

"I don't know," she said. "It just kind of stuck in my craw?"

"Stuck in your..." Stan said.

"It's just. You know how important work is to me right now. This book we're writing, I mean, Sarah has given me a real chance here. To make something. Last year I was miserable. Every other year I was miserable since maybe junior year of college."

He leaned forward. His eyes were kind, one of the things she likes about him the most. "I didn't mean anything by that. Not about you."

"I know," she said. "I know. I just. This is important to me."

Since then they have seen each other a few times but something had gone away that she knows cannot be replaced, a tension that had been let out, a question answered. What was she doing? Was she breaking up with a perfectly good person for Sarah? For the company? For some kind of ideal she had only come to feel over the past year?

Craver. She is not nervous, should not be nervous. She is proud of who she is now, her work with Sarah, with the company, the book for which they've secured a publisher. Craver is walking back into a whole new world, a whole new Jennifer Chastain. It's just been a long time. It's been a lot.

She takes another sip of wine and looks at herself in the mirror. She has grown her hair out, lost weight. She will refrain from drinking, will not kiss him, even if he looks just like the picture in her mind, tanned and long-haired, like a thoughtful beatnik surfer outlaw.

But no, that is Patrick Swayze in *Point Break*. She takes another sip of wine. Regardless, their lives have diverged. Craver doesn't even live here anymore, doesn't really seem to actually live anywhere. She has received five texts in the past five days, each of them nothing but an Arby's gyro held up in front of a highway. She is not sure what that is supposed to convey, but she understands it to be something about motion. He is coming back for the scholarship gala.

She imagines it is like this for everybody: lives divided up into before and after. Certainly it was like that for poor Yoder. Their work with the book has made her actually think about him as a person, not just some sad-sack old joke sleepwalking through every day until retirement. Chad Stephenson is ridiculous in almost every way but if his presence, his whole visioning thing, can save them one more person jumping off that roof, or drinking themselves to death, or even spiraling across the country like Craver, then it will have been worthwhile.

She imagines a before and after picture would be like looking at yearbook photos—the same people but changed so much they could scarcely even be thought of as the same. She checks her phone. Nothing. Two hours before she is meeting Sarah and Lawson for pre-event drinks.

She moves into the living room and turns on the TV. Should she be doing work right now? There are chapters to outline, the last four, but they have also decided that the story is not finished yet. They need to allow events to play out before they decide how to manage them in the manuscript, what lessons will be learned, what messages about managing change can be conveyed.

The book. Jesus, Craver will never believe that she is writing a book. A business book. A kind of self-help management guide to "surviving catastrophic change." He has been away for a long time.

Lawson has grown a beard, bought a pair of Doc Martens, and has begun gently mocking Chad Stephenson to his face. It is an interesting series of developments. She and Craver used to make up elaborate home lives for their frumpy and ridiculous colleagues and she struggles to recall what they may have made up for Lawson. Something about reading web analytics books in his spare time. That's right, she smiles, *Web Analytics Illustrated*. Look out for the annual swimsuit issue. There was a joke about key performance indicators that she remembers thinking was the funniest thing she had ever heard, she and Craver smoking cigarettes around the side of the building, the part half hidden by the dumpsters, the part where Yoder's body hit the pavement.

She turns on the television. Two blond women shout at one another in a restaurant. "You are disrespecting Logan!" the slightly older woman yells at the slightly younger one. Both have had the same plastic surgery and they look like squinty-eyed, big-lipped models turned out by the same production line. She wonders if plastic surgeons can be sued for plagiarism.

She finishes the wine and pours another. She will keep it under control. She will not kiss Craver.

The phone dings. Another text from Craver, this time she recognizes the location, the Arby's out by the mall. Behind the gyro, she can see the tire place where she got her oil changed two weeks ago. So he really is in town. She texts back six words: "You've been away a long time."

russell

THE GUN STORE ISN'T EXACTLY what Russell thought it would be. It is dingy, cramped, full of ammunition and scopes and tee shirts and hats and belts. It is more like a convenience store than an armory. Behind the counter, a young Latino guy scrolls through his phone. He scowls, shakes his head, picks at an order of carryout french fries. "Help you?" he says, with a nod.

Russell pauses. He has driven three towns over for a reason. "Was looking for something…I don't know."

The young guy puts down a fry. On his lapel, the word "Hector" is written. "First time?" he says. Russell nods. "Sport or protection?" Hector asks.

"Um…protection?" Russell smells mildew and cleaning solution and metal. He could leave now, turn around, get in the car and drive home.

"Just-in-case kind of thing," Hector says. "Got it."

Russell feels like he should correct him but he doesn't know what he would say. A car pulls in the lot and he feels his face turning red. His glasses are fogging around the edges. On one side of the store there is a display of snacks, potato chips and beef jerky and Bugles. How could there be Fritos in the same store where he will buy a gun, the place where the ending of the whole thing is just about to start?

Hector walks out from behind the counter. He is wearing sweatpants and a track jacket. He could be anybody, a kid walking past him at the mall, the UPS guy, a person in line at the 7-Eleven. He is so casual. Russell is not sure what he was expecting—MAGA hats and mustaches, camouflage pants and flannel shirts. He was expecting a group of people, a cabal, a militia of mustached men in paramilitary gear.

The door opens with a ring and a woman enters. She is young, twenties or thirties, dressed in office clothes. She could walk into any meeting at Keystone, sit down with her laptop and notebook and nobody would bat an eye. "Hey Hillary," Hector says. "It's here." He turns to Russell. "Be back in a minute. I just need to ring her up. That's the general place you want to look at over there." He points to the far wall, where there is another counter, handguns displayed in neat rows. "Kind of the out-of-the-box section. Be right back."

Russell wanders toward the far wall. He can hear polite conversation behind him, the casual back and forth of a simple sales transaction. It is all so normal, Hector in his sweatpants, Hillary buying whatever she apparently buys regularly, the barbecue chips and pretzels and chewing gum.

He could walk right out the door, right now, a ding of the bell and he would be gone. Hector would never think of him again, some old suburbanite who chickened out at the last minute. It must happen all the time. A trickle of sweat drips down his back and he remembers the hike up Valley Trail, the steady feeling of embarrassment morphing into disgust with every step, every trickle of sweat down his back, under his arms, on the top of his head. Standing there trying to get his breath while Chad Stephenson led the rest of the group in his goddamn breathing exercises. He had considered it then but he didn't have what he needed.

Yoder didn't have what he needed and all he could do was step off the building. Yoder left them all high and dry. Yoder was selfish, a coward. Yoder didn't have a wife, a grown son to worry about. Russell has five thousand dollars in credit card debt, three thousand two hundred overdrafted at the bank. He is still not even sure how that happened. How did they lend themselves money? Is that legal? And now he is on the hook for that plus interest, plus the overdraft fee every goddamn month? He must have signed something, but who reads the things they sign?

He leans over and looks at the guns. They have labels, names: Smith and Wesson M&P Shield, Glock G19, Ruger LCP. He is surprised to notice that the packaging carries the strong scent of marketing: somebody has market researched this name, the font, the description. Of course they have. This is big money. He imagines that his father would have simply gone into Sears and left with a common handgun without having to endure the indignity of sifting through some clever advertising professional's inferences as to what might motivate a man like him into purchasing this particular gun.

The door opens and closes and Hector makes his way back to the rear of the store. He is wearing boots with his sweatpants and this, at least, feels closer to what Russell was expecting. He wonders if the young man owns the store or just works here. "So…" Hector says. "Any questions?"

"This one," Russell says, pointing to the Ruger. "This one will do just fine."

Robertson

ROBERTSON SIPS HIS BEER. HE checks his phone. He is five minutes early and is surprised that Chad Stephenson and Nicole Stetler-Stephenson would be so late as to be merely on time. He takes another drink. The prospectus sits on the bar. A prospectus. He finishes the beer and motions to the bartender. He doesn't usually drink this fast but Jesus Christ, a prospectus?

Without thinking about it, his brain runs the numbers: two hours before the gala and he just drank one beer in five minutes. If he drinks twenty-four beers before the event he might actually tell Mowery what he thinks of him, finally.

He motions to the bartender. He opens the first page of the prospectus. A beer appears in front of him and the bartender leaves before he can even say thank you. A perfect transaction. A text dings into his phone. Chad Stephenson and Nicole Stetler-Stephenson are running late. He takes another deep drink. How did he get himself into this situation? He feels like he's accidentally made an in-person appointment with a car dealer or a mattress salesman. Up until six months ago he had spent the entirety of his adult life studiously avoiding in-person situations and then some idiots win the lottery and all of a sudden he is in a parody of a nineties movie, meetings and feelings and sun salutations and now this.

The prospectus promises a three hundred percent return on investment. It is tastefully designed and he supposes it must be expensively printed, with the raised text and golden trim, the thick, bulky paper that may even be handmade. Knowing Chad Stephenson, it was created by artisan craftspeople working in a converted warehouse in Brooklyn or Austin.

He has been careful to keep all of this from Jessie. First of all, she has money and no student debt. She is a savant, a gaming genius who started building her own portfolio at fourteen and had an agent at sixteen. One point four million followers on YouTube, and she barely even plays anymore. She has a savings account. The house is in her name, fully paid. He wonders again what she is doing with him. At least he has been careful enough to keep his own issues far enough removed from her that she has no idea about the mountain of student debt he carries around. He wonders if she would even understand, if she has followed the news, the stories about their generation and the way they have been saddled with this debt like a hunchback in a Pixar movie.

He takes another drink and notices idly that it is again halfway gone. He checks his phone: Chad has put in a drink order and Robertson hates that all he needs to read is "drinks please" to know that Chad Stephenson and Nicole Stetler-Stephenson would like two Manhattans with Basil Hayden's, up, with Griottines cherries if they have them, no cherry if they do not. How did he get to this place? All he wanted to do was system administration, making virtual machines or database backups, maybe worry about some web caching or CDN work. Now he is sitting here in the bar of the Hyatt ordering drinks with or without Griottines cherries for Chad Stephenson and Nicole Stetler-Stephenson, braced for the hard sell on a virtual pyramid scheme. Worse, he is not sure that he is going to say no, that he is in a position, even, to consider saying no to something that Nicole, especially, tells him can solve all his debt problems within a year.

Fucking Generation X, fucking Greatest Generation, fucking whatever generation Chad Stephenson is representing.

"There he is!" Chad Stephenson is squeezing his shoulder, giving him a hug. And then he is hugging Nicole Stetler-Stephenson and they are ordering Manhattans up with Basil Hayden's and a Griottines cherry. They are paging through the prospectus, one of them on either side, like parents and a child looking through college brochures. They are writing down numbers, smiling, ordering more drinks. Then he is saying yes, his lizard brain calculating what will get him out of this immediate situation, fight or flight on a dotted line. Then he is signing his name on a different paper. Then they are hugging.

CHASTAIN

CHASTAIN STIRS HER DRINK. SHE checks her phone. Three more texts. "So," Lawson says. "I have some news. I thought I should share it with you two first. Before, you know, Chad and Nicole get here. Or before the thing."

"What's up?" Sarah says. She takes a sip of her drink and Chastain fights the urge to mimic her. She sits up straight. "You're not leaving, are you?"

Lawson laughs and rubs at his beard. Chastain wonders if it feels funny, all of a sudden there is a beard there. "Not exactly," he says.

"Not exactly?" Sarah says.

Chastain feels like she should say something. She is surprised that she's having a kind of visceral reaction to this news. Lawson was just getting…interesting. "What's up?" Chastain says.

"I don't think you know this, but I've been doing some writing. Like I've taken a couple of classes. In my spare time. And I'm getting kind of into it."

"Writing?" Sarah says. She says it like it is a patently ridiculous idea, like he has just told them that he has been juggling or beekeeping.

"I know. It's crazy. Stupid," he says, but something in his voice seems like he doesn't actually mean it, a low-key confidence betraying his words. "But…" he says. "I've gotten a few things published."

"Published. Wow, that's great. A published author," Sarah says. She has processed the information now and Chastain knows that she will be kind and understanding moving forward, that she has indeed already moved forward and thought through whether she will promote from within or advertise. Chastain wonders if she is a candidate for Lawson's job. She considers whether she wants it and is surprised to find that she does indeed want Lawson's job, that she wants it very much.

"Nowhere you would know about probably, like, ever," Lawson says. "A few really short stories online."

"That's really great," Sarah says. "But that's not your news."

"Indeed," Lawson says. "I applied to a few master's programs. Low residence. I got into one in Pittsburgh, at a place called Chatham."

"Low residence," Sarah says.

"So it's almost all online, email. I'll be in person in the summer for ten days. All should be manageable with my workload.

"I just thought I should give you a heads up," he says. "With you two in charge, I think all is well. And how is your book, speaking of published authors. You two are the ones with the book deal."

"It's good," Sarah says. She nods at Chastain. "What do you think?"

Chastain sits up. With you two in charge. Interesting. "It's great," she says. "We have some chapters to finish but the editor says it's basically what she's been hoping for."

"She said the writing is, quote, better than expected but still needs some finish," Sarah says.

"Well look at us," Lawson says. "Just a bunch of writers, as it turns out."

Sarah laughs and nods. "You know we'll need to add this to seven," she says, turning to Chastain.

Chapter seven is the one about non-work-related effects and it is, to be honest, a little slim. They have, to date, satisfied themselves with the idea that the book is about work, but the publishing people keep on reminding them that it's really about people. "There might be a thousand managers who would buy this," Kelly has said to them on more than one occasion, "but there are millions and millions of workers." Or how does she say it, "Millions of people who are trying to manage work and money and life." The phrase, Work and Money and Life, is one of the working titles, with some kind of subtitle along the lines of "How One Company Survived Winning the Lottery."

"That's your chapter, right?" Sarah says, and Chastain snaps out of her reverie. Sarah knows very well whose chapter it is.

"Yeah, that's me," Chastain says. She has learned to pay attention whenever Sarah is even the slightest bit untruthful, when she pretends to not be sure of something, to not remember something completely.

"Well, maybe you wouldn't mind if we talked to you about this," Sarah says, looking at Lawson and putting on the voice she uses when she is about to ask for something, the voice Chastain has come to think of as the fetching voice. "If you could spend some time with Jen, kind of share your story?"

"My story," Lawson says. He looks at Chastain as if they are in on something together. She likes it.

"There's a chapter in the book," Sarah says. "And to be honest it's kind of…undeveloped right now? Through no fault of Jennifer's, but we just haven't had too much to work with."

Chastain finishes her drink and sits up. Her phone dings and dings again. "It's kind of the non-work part of it, the part about how the lottery affected people outside of work."

"Huh," he says. "Well sure, I guess. As long as you don't try to make this into some big success because it's all very small potatoes."

"That would be huge," Sarah says. "Thank you." She nods to Chastain, a slight smile playing around the edges of her mouth, slight enough that she would not have noticed it a year ago. She is fairly sure that Sarah has just set her up with Lawson. A book date.

"Well," Lawson says. "I guess we better head out to this thing?"

Sarah finishes her drink. "Do we have to?" she says.

"I'm pretty sure you're the person who can answer that question," Lawson says.

"We have to," Sarah says.

Yoder

YODER WAKES UP ON HIS feet again. He reaches for something but there is nothing there. He wobbles, puts his hands out, regains his balance. It is dark. He is in a large room, dying light peeking through darkened windows. He waits for his eyes to adjust. He would have thought that being a goddamn ghost, an apparition, a haunt, whatever he is—would have at least given him better eyesight. Better night vision. Shit, perfect eyesight. Perfect feet. Achilles tendons that don't ache with every ghost-step. But no. Of course not. Not for Yoder. Nothing for Yoder.

There is some kind of banner hanging, chairs set up in front of a stage, what looks like a bar coming into focus. He is in some kind of hall, a great room or concert venue.

He hears music playing from somewhere, the tinkle and clank of dishes being prepared, voices jabbering back and forth.

His eyes are adjusting now. There is a stage, circular tables set up with folding chairs, tablecloths, and table settings. The banner reads "Arthur R. Yoder Scholarship Fund First Annual Gala Dinner and Happy Hour."

He wanders to a table and sits down. He considers it for a moment, everything flooding back. Those assholes made a memorial scholarship in his name. Those assholes are having some kind of party to celebrate. Those…not assholes, those guys are actually memorializing him, putting some of their eight point eight million toward his memory, his name living on. He shakes his head. None of it makes any sense.

A gala? Sure, a party or a mixer or happy hour, but a gala?

He fights to catch his breath and hiccup chokes back a sob. And then another. He wonders if the people in the kitchen could hear him if he really let go, and then he cannot control it and the sobs come in soft hot waves. He can feel the tears pouring from his eyes, the watery rivulets running down his face. He looks at the table and sees nothing where there should be drops, where there should be a puddle of his own tears gathering.

Doors open and voices get closer. Cowens and Pappas are dragging a cooler. "I swear to god," Cowens says. "Gene Simmons himself. Standing right there not like ten feet from me. Nicest guy in the world."

"So how long was this?" Pappas says.

They carry the cooler over to the bar. Yoder stands. For a moment he forgets that they cannot see him. He holds a hand up in a salute and then sits down again. They start removing beer from the cooler, transferring it into the refrigerator behind the bar. "With Gene? Like I don't know, five minutes. Ten."

"No, the whole cruise," Pappas says.

Yoder remembers that they used to kind of hang around together at work, chatting by the coffee maker, goofing around near their cubicles. Now he wonders if they are actual friends or work friends. If you don't work, then what do your work friends become?

"Four days, three nights," Cowens says. "Fucking great, man."

Yoder feels for his phone even though he knows it is not there. Where does he go when he is not awake? How long between?

"Four days on a KISS cruise?" Pappas says. "I don't know, man. Really?"

"Four days on THE KISS cruise," Cowens says. "Gene Fucking Simmons standing there not ten feet from me, man. I'm telling you. Nicest guy in the world."

They really are idiots, Yoder thinks.

"Gene Simmons is Jewish," Cowens says. "You know that?"

"Jewish? What does that even have to do with anything?" Pappas says, real annoyance in his voice for the first time. Yoder wonders what Pappas is doing with all of his virtual reality equipment, if he has moved on and bought himself a Best Buy or stock in some kind of ridiculous company. Good god, he thinks, these idiots must have been like new-born fawns for the right kind of grifter. He almost feels sorry for them.

"Gene Simmons is six foot four," Cowens says. "He has a degree in economics from Northwestern."

"Cool," Pappas says. "So tonight, like, when the thing starts…"

"His parents were in the holocaust."

Pappas stops. He looks away, chugs half his beer. "In the holocaust. I don't know if you say somebody was, like, in the holocaust. Like it wasn't *Titanic* or something."

"That was real. I saw a documentary."

"I know it was real. I mean the movie, like saying you were IN the holocaust isn't like saying you were IN *Titanic*. Or *90210* or *Star Trek* or *Dazed and Confused*."

"But the *Titanic* was real, is what I'm saying."

Yoder wonders how far he could wander. Could he go for a walk around the block? Could he go check in at his old apartment, see what they've done with the place? These are the people who are memorial-izing him and they really couldn't give two shits about him. His name is on the banner, but the only name he's heard in the past half hour has been Gene Simmons. This is guilt. Lack of direction. They have bought a salve for their consciences like they are buying virtual reality headsets or autographed guitars. No more, no less.

But still, there is his name on the banner. There are the chairs and tables and a stage and a microphone.

They finish their beers and open another. Yoder walks closer and sits down on the floor, his back to the wall. His belly pushes up against his pants. His back is starting to stiffen up. He shouldn't be sitting like this.

"So, they're all coming tonight?" Pappas says.

"Yeah I think," Cowens says. "Craver was like super weird but I think even he's coming."

"He quit, right?"

"Driving around the country?"

"Huh," Pappas says, and Yoder can tell immediately that he wishes he was driving around the country. He wonders what could possibly be keeping him here in the Valley. With eight point eight million he could ride his dumb three-wheeler into whatever future he could imagine.

"Sarah and whatshername, the one who used to kind of hang out with Craver?"

Pappas pauses. "I think I know who you're talking about."

"It's weird, isn't it?" Cowens says.

"Weird?"

"Like how it was such a big deal, like one of the main deals in your life. And then this thing happened and it just kind of faded away."

"You mean working? Like at Keystone?"

"Of course," Cowens says.

"Fuck that," Pappas says. "I mean, didn't you just always think you deserved better? I knew I did. I don't know about you."

"I can't even picture most of them," Cowens says. "Well a few. Like Sarah obviously. Russell for some reason, and the guy who used to always be making soup in the break room?"

"Can you picture him?"

Pappas points at the banner.

"I can," Cowens says.

"Like before you started up with this whole thing?" Pappas says it flat, like he knows the answer.

"I don't know," Cowens says.

Yoder knows the answer. He has a flash, not his whole life, like they say, but an MTV video version: he is in fifth grade playing basketball with his father; he is walking into Central Columbia High School for the first time; he is on the bus home from a wrestling match in his sophomore year, all of them singing some heavy metal song; he is making out with somebody he will never see again in the lobby of his freshman dorm; he is sitting at the desk of his first job in Rockville,

Maryland, a red pen and a set of bluelines at his side; he is walking through Montgomery Mall, looking for work clothes; he is moving back to Central Pennsylvania, loading boxes into his first-floor walk-up apartment; he is giving a presentation at a regional marketing conference, making jokes, answering questions; he is waiting for the elevator, hungover, hoping nobody walks through the doors, wondering if he smells like alcohol, if he should turn around now or try to make it through another day; he is standing near the back of the holiday party, checking his phone and wondering what people talk about, when did he lose the ability to make small talk, to get along with people, to actually charm them, to just hold his own in a random bullshit conversation; he is sitting at his desk with his eyes closed, listening to the chatter around him, wondering if he could just get up and leave, if anybody would notice if he just stopped coming; he is listening to the shouts and whoops from the conference room and he knows immediately what has happened, what he needs to do; he is standing on that roof, the wind blowing against his cheeks, the chatter of the landscapers drifting up on the wind, his wallet, cell phone, and shoes lined up neatly behind him; he is walking up to the ledge; he is stepping off and then the ground is getting closer, closer, too close.

CRAVER

CRAVER DOESN'T EVEN REALIZE HOW much he missed the mountains until he is in them again, driving through rolling farm country in Ohio and then back in Pennsylvania. Back in Pennsylvania. Jesus. He doesn't feel anything like the person who drove out of town listening to "Thunder Road" half-ironically and desperately trying to text Chastain into running away with him.

He should be embarrassed but he has shed that skin, or covered it with road dust, distance, knowledge, with something. He has been through thirty states and back again. He no longer bears any practical resemblance to the Marketing Associate who spent his time stalking ex-girlfriends on Facebook and tracking email campaign key performance indicators and gossiping with Chastain.

He has done nothing wrong. He has done nothing wrong but he has thought about it, planned it, has decided on the right conditions and the way he would do it, the things he would do after, the stupid things people do to get themselves caught. He has done nothing wrong but there is a gun under the passenger seat, a knife in the glove

231

compartment, work gloves and bleach and a plastic tarp from Home Depot in the trunk.

He has done nothing wrong but he has had a lot of time to think, and he knows how he would do it.

He could do nothing, of course. It is always the easiest thing to do: stay the course, keep on keeping on, follow the leader, don't rock the boat. But that is how he spent his first thirty years. That is how he built up a legacy of spreadsheets and handshake dates and B-level performance reviews. He has always been a B—fine, almost good, insignificant, an extra and never a leading man. He sleepwalked from high school to college to work with Keystone, sleepover parties to frat parties to afterwork happy hours. Angela to Tracey to Chastain. But Chastain was never really his girlfriend. He can see that now. He can see everything now.

The distance is what he needed. It is like he had been in a corn maze, never seeing the end or even glimpsing the larger picture, just making the moves that would get past the corner that was right in front of him. This turn and then that turn and then this turn again. Turn turn turn and it is just more maze. Now, ever since Mount Rushmore, it is like he is floating above the maze, can see the way he was wandering around in it like a lost child.

He checks his phone. Chastain has started to reference a "we" in her messages about the event: we are meeting for drinks before, we will be at the firehall around eight, we are dressing business casual. She has snuck it in there, as if "we" were an existing condition on the day of his departure, the day after those idiots won the lottery, but he notices everything now and although the first time it shook him up a bit, he has noticed but he does not care. He supposes she is telling him that she has a boyfriend. He has been gone a long time. He has shed his skin and grown a new one on the blue routes and back roads of the American West.

He is coming up on a Sheetz. Back in Pennsylvania. He backs into a far spot and waits. It really is lovely here, the mountains rolling in the background, green-gray against the red Sheetz sign. He has gotten comfortable with waiting, watching. "We are dressing business casual."

What does that even mean? Gray Dockers and a Black Gap button-down? Khakis from Old Navy and a Banana Republic jacket?

A family gets out of an SUV and trickles into Sheetz. Two guys with beards and dirty jeans and matching tee shirts walk into the store. He checks his watch. He is planning to get there when the event has already started. A half hour late feels just about right for making an entrance.

The family loads themselves back into the car. The two guys come out of Sheetz carrying giant coffees. He waits.

He wonders what those idiots have done with the money. He wonders if any of them have blown it all yet, if any have moved, bought a bar, bought Jet Skis and electric guitars and dumb-people cars. Bought bought bought. He is almost out of money but that is fine, everything is fine.

He has done nothing wrong but after tonight he will not need money, or Chastain, or anything else. After tonight he will be done.

Gibbons

HE PARKS A FEW BLOCKS away and opens up the email invitation on his phone. The Valley Volunteer Fire Department, 223 Barnard Avenue. He remembers an elementary school birthday party, plastic helmets and a turn holding the fire hose and a vanilla cake with red frosting. But this is a gala. He wonders if they will be in suits and dresses. He is wearing his normal tan slacks with a brand-new blue button-up and a darker blue blazer.

The heart of the ship, the heart of the ship. You are working in the heart of the ship.

A few people trickle past but nobody he recognizes. He imagines Sarah and Chastain and the consultants walking by, himself hopping out of the car and joining their party, a grand entrance, champagne and shrimp on little skewers.

He checks his email. A proposed fantasy football trade. His starting quarterback for a running back that catches a lot of passes and a tight end who is leading the league in touchdowns. A fair deal. He could pick up another quarterback on waivers, but would that be smart? He does like making trades, the small thrill of risk. He will check the waiver wire after the gala.

He checks Facebook, scrolling through pictures and statements and memes that he doesn't quite understand. High school friends and college friends and a few people from the office.

His phone vibrates with another email. The trade offer has been retracted. And then another, a notification that a trade has been executed.

In the distance he sees a small group walking in the direction of the fire hall. Sarah and Chastain and Lawson. Sarah wears a yellow dress and walks a few steps ahead. Even now, even on her way to a gala, she looks businesslike and efficient.

He checks his hair in the mirror. He wonders if he should have worn a tie, if he should have eaten dinner beforehand. But food seems implied in a gala. Waiters carrying trays of things on sticks. He opens the car door and stands. It is too late to catch up with Sarah and her party. He will be a party of one.

The heart of the ship, the heart of the ship.

He checks the email one more time. He takes a step forward. It really seems unfair to offer a trade and then immediately rescind. If he went back to the house he might be able to offer his own trade. He has been looking at the tight ends and thinking about moving one of his running backs, a former all pro who is having a down year so far.

It is entirely possible that he is dressed completely wrong. He is unsure of the seating policy, if the tables have been prearranged or if they will have to arrange themselves. He should have worn a tie, a suit, perhaps even a tuxedo.

He gets back in the car.

Robertson

ROBERTSON REALIZES IMMEDIATELY THAT HE had forgotten about almost all of them. He follows Nicole Stetler-Stephenson through the door and almost turns around, but before he can even think, Mowery has enveloped him in a hug. The man smells like tobacco and grease. He certainly doesn't smell rich.

"Goddamn," Mowery says. "It's really good to see you, man." He turns to Nicole Stetler-Stephenson. "And this must be Jessica."

Robertson is stunned that Mowery would have remembered Jessie's name. He is still processing the hug, the decided smell of...fried chicken?

"Oh no, I'm Nicole Stetler-Stephenson," she says. She holds out her hand. "I'm just a friend of Andre's. I'm one of the consultants?" She says it like of course everybody would have known about the consultants, like I'm one of the Pips, the Celtics, the Rolling Stones.

"Okay then," Mowery says. Robertson can tell he has no idea what she's talking about. Something strange is happening in his head. Is he glad to see Mowery? Were they friends?

"So, how's everything around the shop?" Mowery says. He punches Robertson in the arm. "You keeping everything up and running?"

Robertson flashes on his last performance review, Mowery with his sleeves rolled up, leaning in and talking low and soft about his potential, about management, leadership, about how these jobs can't go away and somebody has to be in charge. "It's good to see you," he says. "What have you been up to?"

"Bought a Kentucky Fried Chicken," Mowery says.

"A Kentucky Fried Chicken? Like a restaurant?" Nicole says. She is smiling, amused.

"The one out on Connor? Near the Lowe's," Mowery says. "That's the one."

"I don't really live here," Nicole Stetler-Stephenson says. "We're in Boston. We're just here for this special engagement."

"So did they hire anybody?" Mowery says. "Or did you wind up outsourcing? Did you get the utility server up in the cloud yet? Wait, so where is Jessica?"

"Yeah," Robertson says. "I just didn't, you know, this isn't really her thing."

Mowery nods. "None of us, right? This isn't exactly our kind of thing neither."

Has Robertson missed Mowery? Jesus Christ, he realizes, in some kind of way he has missed Mowery. Or something about Mowery. Maybe it is just that he associates Mowery with sitting at his machine and doing his work, his real work of moving virtual things around a screen and not talking to people, of trying to keep systems up and running, making new systems, monitoring uptime and run speed and file size.

"I played that game of hers," Mowery says. "The last one she worked on? The Office Mail thing? Pretty trippy but I lived through the eighties so, well, the details were pretty impressive."

Nicole Stetler-Stephenson puts a hand on his arm. "I think we better move along," she starts.

"Well we better..." Robertson says. He realizes he would actually like to catch up with Mowery.

"You and Jessica still an item, though, right?" Mowery says.

"Yeah," he says. "I'm not..." he looks at Nicole Stetler-Stephenson but she is pretending that she has already moved on from the conversation and is looking forward with a smile on her face as if she has seen some-body, as if she is standing in line on a red carpet, greeting the reporter from the E! Network. "I'm still with Jessie," he says.

"Good," Mowery says. "You think of it, tell her that game was crazy. I mean crazy good. Weird, you know?"

"So you're good?" Robertson says.

"So much time to just…I don't know." Mowery moves a little closer and lowers his voice. "I don't know what I thought it would be like but nobody wants to hear about that. It's fine. So you keeping everything going, huh?"

Nicole Stetler-Stephenson returns and gives him a look. "I better…" he says.

"Sure," Mowery says. "Yeah, definitely. We'll catch up later." He nods, tucks his chin, shakes his empty Bud can. "Definitely."

Nicole Stetler-Stephenson puts a hand on his shoulder and leans over to talk into his ear. She smells expensive. Her hair brushes against his shoulder. "I do want to talk to you about Jessica," Nicole Stetler-Stephenson says. "I understand she's quite the influencer."

Robertson pauses. He pulls away. He didn't think they knew any-thing about Jessie. Quite the influencer? Is that…could that be what they were after all along, the whole thing, you are valued and you are worthy of happiness and your work should mean something, all for access to Jessie's one point four million followers?

"Oh my goodness," Nicole says, turning to the bar. "Something tells me they are not going to have Griottines."

Yoder

YODER CAN HEAR THEM GATHERING, the jibber jabber, chairs scraping, nervous laughs and shouts and conversation. They sound like a bunch of idiots. He wonders if a party always sounded this stupid. Snatches of conversation drift into the stairwell: *hey there he is, whazzzzupppp, great to see you, what have you been up to, oh you know we're getting by.* He can hear Cowens talking to somebody about the KISS Kruise, Mowery talking to somebody about the Kentucky Fried Chicken, two men talking about football nearby. The normal bullshit.

Every now and then a body blocks the doorway, somebody looking down the stairs to see if there is another room, some better place to be. He wonders what they will actually do. There is a microphone, a stage, a few rows of chairs. Who is going to do the talking? What the hell will they talk about?

He wonders if they had a funeral for him. Of course they would have had a funeral. But who? Sarah and Lawson and Russell? Yes, most likely. He looks up at the ceiling. If there was a way to influence events, if there was some kind of benevolent or even malevolent force at work

here, dictating his comings and goings, these random awakenings, certainly that person or entity, god or the devil or aliens would have put
him in that place at that time, right?

If there is not something moderating these events, then where does
that leave him? Is that better or worse?

He plods up the stairs. His legs are tired. He thinks as hard as he
can. Does he sleep? He wonders if he sleeps in a coffin, like a vampire.
But their legs are always straight and comfortable, arms folded at their
sides. He can feel the tightness in his calves, the ache in his Achilles,
how tired his thighs are despite the fact that he's been doing nothing
but standing in this stairwell for the past hour or so. He is not a vampire.

He slips through the doorway and along the wall. It is a party. Just
a normal party—disappointing and awkward in the ways all the parties
have been for the past, how many years? Twenty? He wishes for the first
time that he could have a drink. It would be easier to take if he could
have just a little wine, hit the fast-forward button on this whole thing.

They are all here, or most of them, at least. The lottery winners and
the ones who didn't win, who must have slogged back to work, or found
other jobs, or pretended the whole thing never happened. He wonders
what they think of him, but he doesn't really care. When he took the
step, he took the step.

There is some movement, a few of them shuffling toward the stage.
Pappas ambles up, knocks on the microphone. "Hi everybody," he says.
"I just want to say a few words."

CHASTAIN

CHASTAIN COULD USE ANOTHER DRINK
but she holds off. Too many work people. Too weird, too height-
ened a situation with all of them back in the same place at the same
time. Too much on the line with Chad Stephenson scheduled to
speak about who knows what? After Pappas and before Sarah, whose
main job—one that Chastain may be the only person who knows she
is unhappy about—seems to be to introduce Cowens of all people.
Chastain can only remember a little about Cowens, mostly how he
shrunk through the halls, never seemed to really be present or committed to the fact that he was actually here in this place at this time.
She remembers him getting too drunk at a happy hour once, saying
some super weird things that she later learned were references to the
movie *Super Troopers*. The idea that Cowens would be starting anything, much less a scholarship fund for Yoder was—how did Sarah
put it?—unlikely.

The idea that he would be a millionaire, retired at twenty-eight, or
thirty-three, or however old he was, was something she couldn't allow
herself to think about or she would wind up like the rest of them.

"Well I'm not going to talk too much," Pappas says. He is wearing a dark suit and no tie, nice shoes. He has a two-day stubble that does not look unplanned. She wonders what Pappas does with his time now. What did he do before? Something with research. Or support. She kicks herself for wasting so much time, so many hours, days, years spent half there, maintaining some kind of ironic bubble between herself and the company, her co-workers, the idea of work itself. Like she was slumming, biding time with office requisitions and scheduling meetings and moving paper around until some higher calling showed up at her desk. What was she waiting for? Some kind of talent scout to spot her in the drugstore, some Conrad Hilton or Jeff Bezos to saunter up and tell her he liked the cut of her jib?

Had it been Sarah she was waiting for all along? Thank you for being here today was all it took?

Sarah. She focuses. Pappas finishes his beer and smiles at somebody in the back of the crowd. He gives the thumbs-up and then reaches into his front pocket and pulls out a roll of money. It is banded, like she has seen in bank heist movies. "Like I said, I won't waste too much time talking," Pappas says. He takes the band off the roll and flips it as if he is about to start counting. She is unsure what kind of bills they are, but her mind registers that they are not small. "No reason to talk when the money can do the talking for me," he says.

A group of men she doesn't recognize at the back of the room whoop and laugh and high five. Pappas nods and puts the money back in his pocket. Groans go up and Cowens hops on stage. "The fuck you doing?" he says. "That's not..." and then he realizes that he is on stage, that the room has gone quiet and they are all looking at him. "Shit man just get back over there," he says, and Pappas walks off stage, rejoins the group in the back. They high five and laugh and Cowens waits them out until they finally quiet. "Look, that's not how this was supposed to go," he says. "We're just here to celebrate Arthur. Arthur Yoder who... but I don't want to get too far in front of us here." He looks for Sarah and when he sees her standing off to the side of the stage, the competent smile on her face, arms folded, he seems so relieved that Chastain actually gets a lump in her throat.

Sarah points to Chad Stephenson, standing just to her right. Nicole Stetler-Stephenson stands next to him, Andre Robertson next to her. Chastain is not sure what to make of their annexation of the young System Administrator. It is curious, and she regards this the way she regards everything having to do with Chad and Nicole Stetler-Stephenson, with intense scrutiny mixed with a kind of remove that eventually they will be gone and in the meantime the clear path forward is cooperation and light positivity.

"What?" Cowens says.

"CHAD," Sarah mouths. She makes the face she makes when she is trying to get somebody to remember something that they clearly agreed on earlier.

"Fuck," Cowens says. "Oh shit." The crowd giggles and Chastain feels the vibe in the room lighten. This is good. Cowens may just bungle his way into this evening working out. "Okay, now I'm going to introduce," he takes a piece of paper out of his back pocket. "Chad Stephenson."

russell

RUSSELL HEARS CHAD STEPHENSON'S
NAME and laughs. It is perfect, so fucking perfect. Finally Chad
Stephenson's all-consuming desire to take the spotlight, to be the center
of attention despite his mediocrity, or even because of it, to bullshit his
way into the lead role out of sheer shamelessness might actually be playing to Russell's advantage. He feels like he is Elmer Fudd and the rabbit
has somehow trapped himself right in his sights.

"Thank you, I'm Chad Stephenson," Chad Stephenson says. "I like
to think of myself as a corporate healer." Russell is happy to hear giggles,
a few groans. Pappas and his friends laugh right out loud and then head
to the bar. They are the kind of Central Pennsylvania people Russell
has been dealing with his entire life—mean, confident, half-smart. The
guys who teased him for his good math grades in elementary school and
then cheated off him in middle, the kind that pushed him into lock-
ers, slapped him on the balls as he walked through the halls of Central
Columbia High School, the kind who made comments on his Dockers
and his button-down shirts when he was back for breaks from Johns
Hopkins.

He reaches into his jacket pocket and feels the cool metal. He practices again looping his finger around the trigger, the way he would pull it out of the jacket without firing, without shooting himself in the foot, or drawing undue attention. Pappas is handing out shots. They high five. Somebody says something about Sarah and they all look at her standing there on the side of the stage. "I believe I would," a blond guy in jeans and a Life is Good baseball hat says. The rest of them laugh and slap backs, high five and fist bump. A thought enters Russell's mind and he forces it out. That is not what he is here to do tonight.

He finishes his beer and feels the alcohol swimming in his head. Should he get another one? He checks the stage. Chad Stephenson is doing his little TED Talk act, walking from one end to the other, making his little jokes, doing his Steve Jobs routine. Russell walks along the back wall and nods at the bartender, holds up his Yuengling bottle. He drinks half of the new one and then walks back along the wall toward the stage. He stuffs a hand in the pocket and feels the cool metal of the gun.

"So, we're just going to do some breathing exercises," Chad Stephenson says. He stands at center stage. At some point he has actually replaced the firehall microphone with one of those TED Talk headsets. He is wearing his jeans, New Balance sneakers, and black long-sleeve turtleneck. "Some healing breaths. Some community breaths." He is shifting into his yoga instructor impression. "We're all here together," he says in a singsong whisper. Russell finishes the rest of his beer. When he goes to set it down, he wobbles, puts a hand on a chair and steadies himself with a quick screech. People look but they continue breathing, arms out to their sides, heads back. "Let's be here together. Together. Be here," Chad Stephenson says. Russell puts his finger around the trigger, hand on the stock. He removes the gun slowly, keeps it at his side.

Chad Stephenson puts his arms up over his head. "Let's breathe in." He looks at Russell, walking slowly up toward the stage. He nods, smiles. "Long breaths. Community breaths. Breathe in…that's right. Very good. Community breaths. We're all in this together. All of us."

A door slams. Gasps. A scream. Somebody shouts "What the fuck?"

Yoder

YODER HEARS THE SCREAMS AND feels a shooshing, like he has been pushed gently in a sled, and all of a sudden he is above it all, looking down. He can see everything: Craver standing in the doorway with some kind of machine gun, Pappas and his buddies backing slowly toward the bar, a ripple forming in the crowd as Craver walks slowly forward, Chad Stephenson slipping toward backstage, Sarah walking toward Craver, a young woman he recognizes but can't place trailing in her wake, Russell edging along the side of the room, a gun in his hand.

Did he fly? Can he do that? How many times has he awakened and now, tonight, this is the first time he learns he can do something like this? Again, he thinks, all of this could have been addressed with a simple orientation, a webinar, a VHS found lying around somebody's house.

The crowd has formed as large a space as possible, everybody pushed against the walls, a few of them curled up into the corners, behind the bar. Craver waves the gun around and it causes a ripple, hands moving over faces, groans, cries. Some of them seem frozen in place, weeping silently or tapping final words into their phones.

Craver turns to an empty wall and squeezes the trigger and the entire room is pop pop pop and screaming.

"Put your fucking phones down," Craver says. "Down!" He waves the gun around and phones drop to the ground like ducks shot out of the air.

"Hey Scott," Sarah says. Her voice is purposefully calm.

Yoder can see everything at once: the consultant who had been leading that ridiculous breathing exercise skulking back behind the curtain, backing toward the exit, Russell continuing to move along the edge of the wall, Sarah taking another step forward. He wonders if he could keep on moving up, through the roof, over the building, into the clouds. Is this roof the only thing keeping him from strumming a harp with Jimi Hendrix? But he knows this is not true. He is not an angel. He will not ascend. There is no orientation. He thinks about that final step, the wind blowing along his face, the smell of fresh-cut grass drifting across the roof, the ground getting closer, closer, too close.

"Stop right there," Craver says.

The assistant, his buddy, the woman who is now trailing Sarah steps out from behind her. "Hey Scott," she says. Her voice mimics Sarah's overly calm demeanor, like an airline pilot announcing upcoming turbulence or a mother speaking with a toddler who is just about to melt down.

"What are you...why are you dressed like that?" Craver says.

"What are you doing?" she says. "Put that thing down. That's not you." She takes a step forward. Russell is still moving along the side, slipping behind the bar now. The gun is hidden behind his leg.

"You don't know what's me," Craver says. "You don't know. Everything is..."

"It's different," she says. "Right? I mean, you've been away for a while. I can see some things have changed. Same here. But you don't want to do this."

Craver takes a step forward. He is about ten feet away from the woman now. Yoder can't remember her name but he has a memory of her and Craver standing outside the office, sneaking cigarettes to the side, behind the wall hiding the dumpster. He was always a little jealous.

She was pretty, he was good-looking, both of them seemed to hate everything about the office, to be properly embarrassed to be spending their time in this way.

Craver's hands are shaking. There are tears streaming down his face.

Craver turns to Garner, who is leaning against the wall, hands behind his back. "I was in on it," he says. "I played. I'm pretty sure I fucking played, you asshole, and now they won't even let me look at the email."

Garner opens his mouth but no words come out. He raises his hands as if he is being mugged. Craver is pointing the gun right at him.

"Come on," the young woman says. "You know that's not true."

A cell phone goes off, the ringtone the chord exchange from AC/DC's "Back in Black." Craver wheels and fires, a series of pop pop pop pops, like fireworks, a finale, and the room is pandemonium. Pappas clutches his chest and falls. Everybody is running, screaming. Yoder feels the whoosh again and he is standing behind Russell. He is watching his old friend hyperventilating, crying, his hand shaking so hard the pistol twitches like a dog scratching at a flea. He has gained weight. His hair is thinning. He does not look good.

Craver wheels around and pop pop pops and a woman Yoder vaguely recognizes goes down. She makes a sickly gasp. Two guys Yoder doesn't recognize fall to the ground. One of them cries out in pain. People are lurching toward the exits. Screaming. Craver shouts for everybody to stop. He waves the gun around. He is crying and shouting "I won I won I should have won I should have won I have done nothing wrong."

Sarah walks toward him with her hands up. She is wearing a yellow dress, a little more than business casual, a little less than dressy. "Put the gun down, Scott," Sarah says. Her calm voice cuts through the shouts and cries. Craver pauses. People stream out of the door, behind the stage, some of them are still curled up in balls behind the bar, in the corners.

"I can't," Craver says. "Don't you see? It's over now. I finally did it. I finally made it."

Russell turns and looks in his direction. At first Yoder assumes he is looking for an exit, but his eyes narrow. They focus. "Arthur?" he whispers. "It can't be."

Yoder feels his body swell with warmth. Even as people cry, as Pappas bleeds and his body goes still, as Craver weeps silently and waves the gun around while the rest of the room remains trapped, he has been seen.

He puts a hand on Russell's shoulder, gently turns him toward the center of the room, where Craver raises the gun toward Sarah and the young woman, standing in the center of the room, both of them speaking with their forced calm voices. Yoder puts his hand on the back of Russell's arm. He raises the gun, eases the shaking. He pulls the trigger.

CHASTAIN

IT IS A HUNCH BUT sure enough there is his car in the parking lot. Even tonight, he parked in the same place—three rows back, over toward the right of the building. He is one of the side stairs people, the people who do not want to be bothered with small talk and office gossip, who maybe tend to come in late and leave early, slipping out before a supervisor or even Sarah might catch them.

She fobs in and takes the elevator. It is no longer strange, walking the deserted hallways, or certainly not as strange as it would have been just one year ago. There is no light in his cubicle so she takes another guess and walks the stairway that leads to the roof.

She opens the door and is not surprised to find Russell sitting a safe distance away from the edge. She kicks at the gravel, rubs at the goosebumps on her arms. The lights from campus glow in the distance. Beyond that the rise of Valley Mountain like a smudge in the night. She steps over tattered police tape and moves onto the roof.

"Thought I might find you here," Chastain says.

"You're a good person," he says, surprising her with the emotion welling up in his voice.

"You too," she says. He pats the ground and she sits.

"You okay? I know you were friends, somehow," he says. "With him."

She pauses. "It's beautiful up here. We should have been coming here the whole time, right? How many times I walked by that staircase and never even thought about the roof until…"

The night is crisp and the lights on campus look like a postcard. She remembers that part in *Station Eleven* when the lights come on. It is all a miracle, everything, all of this life a series of small miracles.

He looks out at the lights, the mountain. "I had that same thought awhile back," he says. "About the roof. How nice it is once you're up here."

"Thank you," she says. "For…you know."

"I guess I'm lucky the police understood what happened."

"We were friends," she says. "Me and Craver. Sometimes more than that. I think he wanted it to be more. I know he did." She flashes on a memory, the night of the lottery, his drunken proposal that they drive to San Francisco together, start over. He must have really meant it. She feels her cheeks flushing.

"You're a good person," he says again, as if he knows what she has been thinking. "What you and Sarah have been doing here, protecting everybody, trying to make us feel normal, even if it maybe didn't quite work all the time…"

"Chad Fucking Stephenson," she says, and they both laugh.

"It's okay," he says. "You know? It's all okay."

"It is," she says. "Is that Valley Mountain?" Somehow she has lived in this town for years and managed to never even hike the Valley.

"Beautiful up there, isn't it?" he says.

"You know, I've never done it? The hike. All this time living here and I just never got around to it, I guess."

"It's lovely," he says. "I'll take you there. You'd like my wife. She's the hiker. She's the good one."

"I'd like that," she says, and she is a little surprised to find that she means it. She and Russell have become friends. Craver is dead. Yoder is dead. Some of the rest of those idiots hit the lottery. So there is that.

"It just didn't mean anything," he says.

"It did, though," she says. "It all meant something."

"But not what they thought it did. Not what we thought it did." She leans back. "You don't have any cigarettes, do you?" she says.

He laughs. "Maybe in my glove compartment, to be honest."

"Maybe in his glove compartment," she says. It did mean something. Not the charts and the numbers, the pushed-back deadlines and ad buys and key performance indicators. Not any one thing. But all of it together, all of them working together, the way Sarah looked out for each and every one of them—thank you for being here today—it all did mean something. It all does mean something.

They sit. The gravel rubs at her palms. She remembers that Yoder had taken off his shoes, placed them there next to his wallet and cell phone.

"It does mean something," Chastain says. "But not that. Not what most people think."

He reaches over and puts a hand on hers for just a moment. He squeezes.

"Hey," she says. "Thank you for being here today." She squeezes back with both hands and then pulls back.

"We have all the time in the world, don't we?" he says. "All kinds of time."

She stands and stretches. "I'm going to go home," she says. "I guess I'll see you on Monday?"

He stands, takes her hand as he wobbles. "I'm going to stay a few more minutes," he says. "See you Monday."

Thank You Thank You Thank You

What an honor and a joy to be in a position to thank all the wonderful people who supported me and the writing, editing, and production of this book.

Thanks to Jimmy Patterson and Rose Solari from Alan Squire Publishing for believing in this book—the first people other than me to do so—and helping it make its way through a pandemic and out into the world. Thanks to Hannah Grieco for such insightful editing and for calling me on my bullshit and just generally making this book so much stronger. Thanks to Nita Congress for making the interior of this book look so wonderful, and to Randy Stanard for making such a beautiful cover.

Thanks to Monica Prince (Friendship and Susquehanna!) and Andrew Gifford of the mighty Santa Fe Writers Project.

Thanks to my Barrelhouse family, who always help me remember that this writing deal can be fun and supportive and to always keep it weird: Becky Barnard, Christina Beasley, Dan Brady, Tara Campbell, Killian Czuba, Erin Fitzgerald, Chris Gonzalez, Mike Ingram, Tom McAllister, Susan Muaddi-Darraj, Matt Perez, and Sheila Squillante.

Thanks to the Monday Night Pandemic Paranoid Thriller Movie Club, who literally helped me stay sane during lockdown and the pandemic: Becky Barnard (who deserves two mentions and is hopefully blushing and trying to change the subject somewhere right now), Aaron Burch, and Caleb Curtiss. Into it!

Thanks to Matt Bell, Angie Kim, and Leslie Pietrzyk for taking the time out of their own writing projects and lives to read this book and say some very nice things about it.

The poem quoted by Gibbons—the heart of the ship, the heart of the ship, you are working in the heart of the ship—is "Yellowshirt

Elegy" by Meghan Phillips, originally published in *Barrelhouse*. The short story referenced by Lawson about the girl pulling veins out of her arms is "Prestidigitation" by Aaron Burch, also originally published in *Barrelhouse*.

This is a book about work. Throughout my writing life I've never not had a full-time desk-style job and this is as close as I'm likely to get to those two worlds colliding. First of all, thanks to Dave McClelland for running the lottery group in Penn State World Campus Marketing. Every one of those emails was like an alarm that said "finish that book!" I've been lucky to have worked with and for some great people in my now-kind-of-long career. Thanks to Keith Johnson, Diana Blais, Mark Rovner, and Shelby Thayer for putting up with me at various points in my life and also for showing me that how you treat people means so much more than deadlines or spreadsheets or KPIs ever could.

Thanks to my family for, well, everything: Don Housley, Grace Housley, Debbie Cooper, Joe Cooper, Nick Cooper, Pete Cooper, Kate Curran, Mark Liddington, Lisa Liddington, Nina Liddington, Rhea Liddington, Skip Wieder, and Linda Wieder.

As always thanks the most to my very wonderful partner Lori Wieder and my son Benny. Your love and patience and good humor are everything to me.

A little about us...

Alan Squire Publishing is an independent literary press, founded in 2010. We publish books of fiction, nonfiction, and poetry that are beautifully written and beautifully made, with the avid reader and book-lover in mind. We are committed to bringing to the public books of great merit that deserve a wide readership, in boutique editions that will last the reader's lifetime and beyond.

In 2014, we founded our Legacy Series. Modeled after the "readers" popular in academia in the mid-twentieth century, our series allows readers to trace the arc of a significant writer's literary development in a single, representative volume. All of our Legacy authors are fluent in more than one genre, have built their careers with and through independent presses, and are consistent and influential champions of other writers' work.

We love book clubs, independent bookstores, literary bloggers, and all other means of getting our books into the right hands. Please visit alansquirepublishing.com for further information.

Alan Squire Publishing: A Small Press With Big Ideas

Previous Titles

Red Riviera: A Daria Vinci Investigation, David Downie (novel)

Woman Drinking Absinthe, Katherine E. Young (poetry)

Melanie's Song, Joanna Biggar (novel)

Navigating the Divide: Selected Poetry & Prose, Linda Watanabe McFerrin (Legacy Series)

Scattered Clouds: New & Selected Poems, Reuben Jackson

Girl Like Us, Elizabeth Hazen (poetry)

Other Voices, Other Lives: A Grace Cavalieri Collection (Legacy Series)

The Last Girl, Rose Solari (poetry)

Roughnecks, James J. Patterson (novel)

The Richard Peabody Reader (Legacy Series)

Chaos Theories, Elizabeth Hazen (poetry)

A Secret Woman, Rose Solari (novel)

Billy Christmas, Mark A. Pritchard (novel)

Bermuda Shorts, James J. Patterson (essays/short fiction)

That Paris Year, Joanna Biggar (novel)